VOICES

INTREPID WOMEN SERIES, BOOK 4
A MEYERS SECURITY STORY

BY: KATHRYN JANE

VOICES

Intrepid Women Series, Book 4

A Meyers Security Story

By: Kathryn Jane

Cover by The Killion Group

Layout by Formatting Fairies

Electronic ISBN: 978-0-9920195-7-0

Print ISBN: 978-0-9920195-8-7

Intrepid Women Series

Book 1: Do Not Tell Me No
Book 2: Touch Me
Book 3: Daring to Love
Book 4: Voices

VOICES

She's desperate to stop a killer....

Rachel Meyers has been on the run long enough—hiding from more than just death. But now the murders happening around her are forcing her to take a stand and the only person she can trust to help is the man she ran away from. Her husband.

He's desperate to have his wife back....

Quinn Meyers has spent two years searching for Rachel. Now she's back, scared and asking for help. But Quinn wants answers. Helping her is a given, he won't say no, but he also won't let her go again. Not without a fight.

Desperate love...

Quinn's body still aches for Rachel, even though he's guarded his heart since the day she left. Her continued secrecy is tearing apart any hope of saving their marriage. But more than love is at stake if Quinn and Rachel can't find the killer.

For the horses who've been there through the love and the laughter.

There was no word for that sound. Yet her soul recognized the reverberation of air and energy being hurled from deep inside the human body—the macabre cadence of death's dance.

CHAPTER 1

Adrenaline rocketed through Rachel's system, driving her out of the stall with feet pounding the hard-packed dirt. Every step a promise for the fallen man.

Bellowed warnings of "*LOOSE HORSE!*" mixed with shouts for an ambulance and the echoes of other boots.

She dug for speed—had to get to him first.

Silent.

Still. A crumpled heap of humanity.

Rachel dropped to her knees. *Must be quick, before anyone gets too close.*

Positioned at the top of his head, she placed a hand on either side, hooked her fingertips under the jawbone to open his airway. Her thumbs eased his eyelids down as she blew a soft breath across his face. *You will not die here.*

Maintaining the classic position—as though merely stabilizing his cervical spine—she concentrated, used every scrap of energy she had. Drove power down her arms, deftly sending it through her fingertips to his barely quivering heart. *You will not die here.*

And he didn't.

With a gut-deep moan of pain, his chest rose, and not a moment too soon.

She didn't move when the first aid attendants arrived, puffing and blowing from the long run.

"Taking over," said the woman who knelt beside her, and they carefully switched positions while keeping the man's head and neck immobile. Rachel backed away, melted into the gathering crowd.

Bits and pieces of onlooker comments registered as she slipped away. And one answer to the question of what happened, stood out.

"Spooky popped him from the nearside. Kidney shot."

Apparently the man had been on the left side of the horse, the safest place to be, but had still been kicked. And the power of a direct blow to the lower back from a beast the size of Spooky could certainly be enough to stop a heart. No point wondering if other forces had been at work.

And, chances were, they'd have gotten him back with a defibrillator if she hadn't been there.

The tunnel vision started. No good deed went unpunished, she thought, as the residual effects of intervening swamped her. Weakened by the energy drain, and shaking from the adrenaline dump, each step became an effort as she worked her way back toward the stall she'd been mucking.

Her breath caught when she spotted a city ambulance and a police car pulling up at the end of the barn.

Crap. She slipped in alongside the racehorse she'd left tied to the wall.

"Sorry, pal." She wrapped her arms around his neck, buried her face against the soft hide, and tried to settle.

"Rachel?" Don, one of the sweetest, kindest trainers she'd ever worked for, stood outside the stall frowning at her. "You okay, girl?"

She shook her head, and promptly slithered down the horse's front leg into the straw.

She woke up to the sharp smell of rubbing alcohol. She pushed the damp towel away from her face and met her boss's concerned look.

"You okay, kiddo?"

She grimaced. "Yeah. Delayed reaction, I guess."

His smile was sympathetic. "No biggie. Why don't you rest here a minute? I'll finish that stall while you get steady. Won't be able to do much else for a bit anyhow. At least not 'til they ship that guy off and the shedrow gets clear. Then the cops will harass everyone with questions."

Her flesh went cold. "He died?"

"No, no. Relax."

Her heart banged against her ribs. "Then why the police?"

"Somebody called 911 instead of on-site medical and they got all excited, saying the guy had been attacked by a known killer. Idiot. So the cops got sent, along with the paramedic wagon." He shrugged. "Might be a good thing in the long run. Everybody knows that horse is like a loaded weapon. Maybe they'll finally nail the guy who made him that way."

She raised her eyebrows and he grimaced. "Guy's got a rep for, well…" He went to the door, looked out, and then pushed it shut.

"He abuses horses?"

"Seems like."

She swung her legs over the side of the cot with care. "Why hasn't he been reported?"

Don filled two cups with coffee, dropped a couple of sugar cubes and a spoon in hers, then handed it to her. "Somebody did once and nothing ever came of it. Nothing good anyways. Kid lost his job, ended up disappearing—probably left town, moved on to another track. So don't get any ideas about talking to the cops. Let somebody else do it."

No worries there. The last thing she needed was to show up on law enforcement radar. She shrugged for emphasis. "They'd never listen to me anyway. I'm just a barn rat, and female to boot. She started to get up. "I'd better get back to work."

"You sit tight for a few more minutes. Make sure you're steady." He had an odd expression on his face as he left.

Something was off. She glanced around the tiny room. Plain leather racing bridles with shiny bits hung in a row on the far wall, while the training tack was draped over the hook near the door, waiting to be cleaned.

She dragged the tub of dry laundry toward her, and with automatic motions, rolled bandages, then folded and stacked rub-rags. The flesh at the back of her neck suddenly chilled as though a breeze had slipped into the room. Her gaze tracked to the rag on the cot where she'd woken up. She picked up the torn square of white bath towel and stared at the dark brown smudge of her pasty face makeup.

Sonofabitch. Even if he hadn't seen, hadn't realized her coloring was fake, he'd picked her up from the floor of the stall and carried her, hadn't he? Must have noticed she wasn't nearly as heavy as she looked. Would he keep his observations to himself? Most likely, but combined with the other stuff…

No choice.

Grabbing her backpack from under the chair in the corner, she took a quick look around, checked for anything that shouldn't be left behind, gulped down one last mouthful of coffee and reached for the door knob. Time to go. Quickly, while everyone was distracted.

She ducked through the barn's side exit and into the early morning drizzle. Hidden between the huge metal manure bins, she tugged the bottoms of her jeans out of her gumboots to smooth them down and cover the tops. Then she put her pack on backwards unzipped the main compartment and dug out a thin green raincoat. She dragged it on and yanked the hood up to partially hide her face before making her way through the barn area gates.

Rachel followed her well-rehearsed escape plan to the letter. Within thirty minutes she was in a shopping mall washroom, toeing out of the size-twelve boots to reveal beige, cotton slip-ons. She shed the raincoat and backpack, popped the snaps of the enormous plaid work-shirt, slid out of it and the faded jeans. It felt damned good to be down a couple of layers to the khaki cargos and matching shirt.

Next to go was the ball cap with the attached curly black ponytail. When she undid the elastic, her own dark brown hair cascaded to cover the darker dyed underside. She slung a canvas messenger bag over her shoulder, and leaving her outerwear and backpack hanging in the stall, stepped out to look in the mirror.

The streaky makeup had to go. Using a cloth soaked in a special solution, she went to work on first her face, and then her hands, to remove the dark and expose her pale skin. She switched the dark gray contacts for green, and with a sigh, tied her hair back up and donned a blond wig.

Fifteen minutes later, she left the mall with a shopping bag full of new things.

Three buses, a train and a cab ride later, she was in the airport washroom doing another identity change. This time she dragged off the double layer of spandex that held the foam padding in place. In the blink of an eye, she changed from a size sixteen to a size eight. She pulled on one of the new outfits, hot pink capris with a matching jacket over a white tank, slipped into white flip-flops and wiggled her toes, happy to be free of the bulky disguise for a while.

With the padded suit and all stuffed into the big bag, she swung out of the washroom and into the concourse with a smile on her face. She checked the departures board, saw a commuter flight to Portland leaving in about fifteen minutes. It would do. On that short flight, she'd think about her next move.

CHAPTER 2

Two weeks later

Quinn dumped coffee cups and soda cans into the sink, crammed leftover donuts into the fridge, then cranked up the air conditioner to clear the smell of sweat and fear from the room. Six more clients had come through his office today. Men shaken to the ground by setbacks triggered by July 4th fireworks. Heroes. Very human heroes still struggling with the aftereffects of war. One after another, they'd left. A little stronger, and back in control.

Shaking off the lingering connections and the weight of their burdens, he wondered about those he hadn't heard from this week. Had post-traumatic stress disorder created havoc for them? Their families and others? PTSD's tentacles reached much further than the individual with the diagnosis.

He sat at the wide desk in the business half of his office to finish the day's notes and wrap up his week. It had been long and brutal. For the first three days, he'd advised, encouraged, and reassured those worried about what would come with nightfall on Wednesday. From the cracks of simple firecrackers to the big booms of elaborate fireworks displays. Sounds that could trigger anything from debilitating flashbacks and horrible nightmares to isolation behavior and suicidal thoughts.

He'd put heart and soul into preparing them with tools and strategies designed specifically for each man's unique circumstances.

Then, Thursday and today, he'd dealt with the fallout. Helped them get their lives back in order, file the setbacks, and move forward. He glanced across at the pool table, thankful so many were able to spill their guts with a cue in their hands—one of the things he'd been right about when he'd set up his practice. A game or two worked just as well as a walk and talk, and much better than the old-fashioned therapist's couch. At least for those he dealt with.

Quinn was finishing up his notes when his brother came through the open doorway. A simple raised finger had Trent wandering silently to the window to wait. It only took a minute.

Closing the file, and leaning back in his big leather chair, Quinn asked, "What's up?"

"Your phone's off."

"Busy day." He sighed. "Still cleaning up after the fireworks."

Trent's mouth twisted into a pained expression. "Crap. Gotta be hard on your people. Everyone okay?"

"So far. Some setbacks. A few family members a bit shaken by flashbacks they'd thought were over. Doesn't seem to matter how often they're warned about recurrences, they're never expecting their loved ones to react the way they did in the beginning.

"Then, of course, the guys feel like shit for scaring the wife or kids, and the circle continues." He scrubbed at his face. "But a couple fared well and couldn't wait to tell me about it."

"Gotta feel good."

"Yeah. The moments I live for. When a man stands there with a shit-eating grin on his face and tells me he watched the fireworks with his kids and never once felt a need to dive under a parked car." He tipped his chin. "What's up?"

Trent smiled. "I was at the hangar when I started getting messages because your phone was off. Figured I'd hop over and touch base."

Quinn thumbed the beeper on his belt and it made a soft sound. "Battery's not dead, so if there was an emergency, my service would have called. Must mean Mother wanted me for something."

"She wasn't the only one," he said as he scrolled through his Blackberry. "Angie's text was the first, in all caps, 'DO NOT BRING QUINN HOME.'"

Dad. Quinn put a hand to muscles gone tense at the back of his neck.

"The next was from security. 'Contact base immediately for important message re: Quinn.'"

He sucked in a breath. Rachel.

"Mother's message, was of course an order. 'Bring Quinn home, now.'" He grinned. "And Dhillon's, in all caps like his mother's, but followed by many exclamation points, 'SHE'S HOME!!!!'"

"Rachel." Without another thought, Quinn snapped the laptop shut, slid it into a case, and circled the desk. Fire and ice flashed alternately through his system. Joy and dread. Love and…

Trent headed out the door and poked the elevator button. "I called Security. She showed up at Family Gate and tried to use an old password."

Two years, three months, and twenty-two days ago, his wife had run away. Was she back for good or just passing through again? He'd bloody well find out before she made her next move.

Minutes later, climbing into the helicopter on the roof of the building, Quinn sent a text to Security: DON'T LET HER OFF THE PROPERTY.

And one to his mother: ON MY WAY.

While Trent fired up the bird, Quinn scrolled through the calls he'd missed. A text from his sister, Angie: WANT ME TO LOSE HER OR TIE HER TO A TREE?

Grinning, he replied: BE NICE.

***

Things never went as Rachel expected.

After entering what she expected to be the wrong numbers on the gate's keypad, she'd stayed seated in the rental car—certain the camera wouldn't get a clear shot of her face—and worked through the calming rituals, practicing square breathing. *Breathe in, hold, breathe out, hold.*

The property was vast. It would take at least twenty minutes for a security car to drive over. Her anticipatory tension had just started to ease when spotting a telltale spec low in the sky had her heart banging against her ribs and her flesh going hot as though the AC had shut down.

Once the swirling dust and grit settled, a large man climbed out of the ominous looking helo. Sunglasses and a cowboy hat pulled low made it hard to tell if he was someone she'd known from before, so she stayed put, with both hands on the steering wheel. Just in case.

He peered through the window, spoke into the radio clipped to his collar, then opened her door, and a blast of Texas heat washed over her.

"Ms. Rachel, welcome home."

When she took his outstretched hand, he pulled her from the car and into a hug.

Her throat closed and she squeezed her eyes shut to prevent tears from escaping. The welcome, unlike what she'd been expecting from the head of ranch Security, felt so good.

Until she'd handed over her car keys, climbed aboard the aircraft, and glanced at the pilot. Angie, Quinn's sister, was staring at her with undisguised fury and disbelief.

Well hell, this ought to be fun, Rachel thought as she fastened the safety harness. She was officially in the hands of one of the most intense families in existence. The miles square ranch was filled with sisters, brothers, cousins and employees of Meyers Industries, an umbrella corporation containing both a ranching business and a high-tech security company with both government and private contracts worldwide.

About halfway to the family's headquarters, Angie landed them on the paved road and flicked off a bunch of switches. Silence barely settled before she pinned Rachel with a fierce look and a snarled question. "Why the hell have you come back?"

No point dancing around. "I need help."

"Why would my family help you?"

Rachel maintained unflinching eye contact. "Maybe because I saved your kid's life?"

Angie turned away, then back. "Why did you disappear that day?"

"Not going there. I don't have to explain myself to you." Yet she wanted to do just that. She clamped her jaw against the urge and said, "I need help and I'm willing to pay Meyers Security by the hour if that's what it's going to take."

"You fuck with my brother's head again and all the king's horses won't be enough help for you."

Maybe she *was* making a mistake coming here, but she didn't see any other options. She fought the clench of an imaginary fist around her heart, bit back the words she wanted to say, and instead said through gritted teeth, "I won't explain myself to you."

Angie's nostrils flared. "Quinn loved you and you turned your back on him. Don't expect me to *ever* forget that."

CHAPTER 3

Rachel perched on a white brocade wingback chair, spine straight, feet firmly planted on the floor. She kept the expression on her face pleasant in spite of refusing to answer her mother-in-law's questions.

Quinn deserved first crack at her. It would be his call how much his family was told about the reasons she'd left and had now returned.

Pacing between the window and her massive antique desk, Julia looked as though she was trying to work out a new strategy.

"Will you be staying?" she finally asked.

Ah, change of tactics. The woman was no rookie at managing and manipulating people. "Depends on what Quinn wants."

"Let me reword the question. If my son wants you to stay—asks you to stay—will you?"

"Yes." But would he ask? Could he after all this time? Or would he toss her out like last week's leftovers? There might be someone else in his life by now. And didn't that thought burn a hole in her gut. Just because she'd been faithful didn't mean he had. Lifting the weighty crystal tumbler, she sipped and found the lemonade horribly in need of sugar.

"You love him." It was a quiet statement. "Even if he doesn't ask, please don't leave without telling him how you feel." She smoothed elegant hands down jeans the color of dark chocolate. "The men in this family may be quick and fearless when it comes to physical risks and challenges, but they're cautious with their hearts."

Rachel shook her head. "Quinn wasn't."

"He will be now."

And that's on me. "I'm sorry for what I put him through. Put you and the rest of the family through. But I believed my actions were—" she searched for the right word—"necessary."

A door slammed somewhere in the sprawling house and every muscle in her body tensed. Booted feet on polished hardwood echoed down the hallway as her heart crept up her throat.

The footsteps slowed, then stopped.

Quinn stood in the doorway for a moment, fighting the need to go to her, touch her, suck in her scent like a dying man gulping his last breath. He reached deep. Got a grip. Shifted his gaze to his mother.

"She's still here. I'm impressed."

"Quinn." Julia's tone was sharp.

Jaw tight, he struggled for manners. "Mother, good afternoon. Would you mind leaving us alone?"

"I'd prefer you and Rachel go to your own home to speak."

But he didn't want her back in their house. Not until he knew.

"The walk will do you both good."

"Don't handle me, Mother."

She was well-versed in diffusing volatile situations, because of his father. But Quinn wasn't broken inside like the man whose rages and paranoia were only a shadow in their lives now.

Without another word he spun and marched out the door.

Rachel rubbed her knuckles over the ache in her heart. She never should have come back. Should have known better.

"Rachel." The sharp edge of Julia's voice cut through the haze of self-pity. "Go with your husband and do the work. This won't be easy for either of you, but perhaps time and distance has given you both the clarity you were previously lacking."

Ouch.

Rachel did as she was told. Followed him into the burning sunlight, but made no effort to keep up to the grueling pace he set.

Gradually dropping back and losing sight of his stiff shoulders and clenched fists, she worked on her own backbone. She'd left for a good reason. And returned likewise. Now she'd deal with the consequences.

Rounding the last bend and seeing the house brought tears to her eyes. Home. The only safe one she'd ever had. Where she hadn't had to worry about what she'd encounter when she stepped inside.

Until now.

The back door stood open like an invitation, but to what, she wasn't sure. God hates a coward, she thought. She stepped inside, and before her eyes could adjust to the dim interior, she bumped into a solid wall of man.

She lifted her chin and stared into the eyes of the first real friend she'd ever had—well, aside from Grace, but that was different.

He didn't step back. Didn't flinch. Stared her down with an intensity most people would back away from.

She didn't move. Spoke instead. "I'm sorry."

"For what exactly?"

"For hurting you and your family." Aching to put her hands on him, she stuffed them into her back pockets.

"You fucking bolted, Rachel."

"I had reasons," she snapped back.

He spun and stormed into the kitchen. Opened the fridge, barely looked in, shut it again with force. Drew a long hard breath, exhaled slowly. "If they were such good fucking reasons why the hell didn't you tell me?"

"I couldn't."

"Why?"

"Because I was afraid you'd talk me out of it."

"Go fucking figure. Tell me now. Make me understand why you *thought* leaving me was the right thing to do."

She edged past him to her favorite chair in the den. A leather monstrosity. Curling her legs up under her, she felt the stretch of time that lay between then and now. She'd loved starting her day right there with a cup of tea or coffee and a slice of raisin toast, her system still humming from sex in the shower, or wherever.

Now, feeling brittle, she stared at her bony hands.

"Where's your ring?"

She pulled a chain from under her shirt. Her wedding ring hung alongside the Saint Christopher's medal he'd given her only months after they'd met.

"Well, at least you didn't throw it off a bridge somewhere."

"What about yours?" she asked.

"Threw it off a bridge."

Did that mean they were over? Beyond fixing? Fear grew teeth and snapped at her.

"Explain to me why you walked out on what I thought was a pretty damned good life."

Was that hurt and maybe even hope she saw in his eyes? Julia had told her to do the work. She gritted her teeth. It was time she told him everything.

"After the second time Death happened here, when Carlos collapsed in the barn, I began to fear that I was the cause."

"And you kept that to yourself."

With a shrug she said, "When I tried to put it into words, it sounded silly." She rubbed her palm on her knee. "I tried not to think about it too much. Convinced myself I was making a mountain out of a mere coincidence. Until the day Dhillon's heart stopped."

She closed her eyes for a moment before continuing. "On the helicopter ride to the hospital, once his heart was beating normally again, I knew what I needed to do. Death would stop stalking the people I cared about if I wasn't here. If I left, it would go with me. My…" She shook her head. "*Your* family would be okay. I could stop worrying and—"

"Seriously?"

She jumped up, paced to the window, stared blindly into the yard. Arms wrapped around her aching middle, she went on, "Do you have any idea what it's like? When people I love drop dead in front of me and *I have to fight*? Have to go to battle with a force I don't understand? Blindly pouring energy into a dead person and begging them to live?"

She forced herself to look at him. "Your sister's child *died*, Quinn. Dhillon's heart stopped. And there I was. Alone. His only chance at survival. I didn't dare take my hands off him to call her or anyone until his heart began to beat again and it seemed to take forever."

Quinn gritted his teeth and battled his instincts. Fought the desire to take her in his arms, wipe the tears from her face. He didn't dare weaken. Not now, not yet. "When you left the hospital, you went right past my bloody office. Why the hell didn't you come to me? Call me at least. Why run away instead?" He wanted to reach for her, shake sense into her, curse her for the sheer stupidity of her actions. Instead he looked away.

"I *did* call you. But your phone was off because you were with a client." She lifted her hands, palms up, then let them drop to her side. "I took that as a sign. I had to leave because Death was stalking your family." Her shoulders slumped. "It follows me still, Quinn. Its voices taunt me."

She believed what she was saying. He reeled in his temper. "Death can't taunt you, Rachel. It's not an entity. It's something that happens at the end of a life."

Rachel didn't know how to make him understand. Fear gnawed at her, made her want to curl into herself, close her eyes, and escape. But she had to face reality. Had to put it into words. Now.

She turned away from his sharp gaze, leaned her forehead against the cool glass of the big window and squeezed her eyes shut. Struggled to find the words.

When she heard him move, hope blossomed. *Please, please touch me. Hold me, and help me get through this.*

When nothing but silence wrapped around her, she plowed on, needing to get it over with.

"I hear voices, Quinn, just like my mother did. Voices like the ones that put her in the nut-house and me in foster care. The same ones that told her to drain the blood from her body because it was time for her to go." The lump in her throat stopped the rest of the words.

As she opened her eyes and swiped at the tears to clear her vision, shock ran through her. Quinn was at the far end of the yard. Closing the gate behind him. He'd left. Hadn't heard a word she'd said.

Or had he?

CHAPTER 4

Standing toe-to-toe with his brother Trent, Quinn's voice echoed in the hangar. "What the hell do you mean, no?"

"Sorry, bro, I'm not allowed to take you off the property for twenty-four hours." He took a quick step back.

"Says who?" he snarled.

"Trent, leave us alone, please." The voice of authority came from behind him.

As Quinn spun toward his mother, Trent ducked past the Citation and disappeared.

"Mother. I need transportation back to the office. My vehicle is there, as well as work I walked away from."

"You had no more clients booked today. I checked."

"There's paperwork."

She raised an eyebrow. "Give me a little credit. There is nothing you can't do from here. Running away from Rachel and the conflict inside of you is a pointless exercise."

"I'm not a child. You don't get to tell me what to do anymore." Shit, he sounded like a twelve-year-old. "All due respect, Mother, but butt out." He wheeled and marched toward the exit.

Three steps from a clean getaway, Julia's voice stopped him. "You love each other."

He stared blankly at his hand on the doorknob. Grimaced. "Sometimes, that's not enough," he muttered as he wrenched open the door and left.

Ten minutes later, astride a big rangy quarter horse, he disappeared into the woods. The ranch covered seventy thousand square miles of land. Somewhere out there, he'd find an answer.

***

Julia's frustration mixed with disappointment and left her wandering the hangar where the family's aircraft were maintained and repaired. So straightforward with machinery. Unlike people. She wanted Quinn back with his wife, but she wasn't quite sure how to fix what was broken.

"I'm always amazed by how well you know us." Trent rounded the tail of a plane.

"I'm your mother. It's my job."

"We're adults with lives away from here now. Big chunks you know nothing about," he said as they headed outside. He held open the door of a dark red SUV and she settled into the passenger seat.

"You're still the boys I raised—who have more in common with your father than most of you care to admit."

"Do you miss him?" Trent asked as he drove the two miles to the house they'd grown up in.

"Of course." *But there are also days like today when I'm glad he's not here, getting in Quinn's face, issuing orders.* Julia nearly laughed out loud. True enough, she'd done exactly that, but in a much more subtle and open-ended way. Her husband had never understood the word *subtle*. "What about you?"

"Sure. But…"

When the silence stretched on, she gave up waiting for him to continue. "But what?"

He heaved a sigh "Back there, with Quinn? There'd have been bruises."

Truer words. Yet. She clamped her jaw. No point arguing.

"Dad would have started it by getting in Quinn's face, challenging him. Then neither of them would have been able to back down." He shook his head. "Weird, really. Quinn's the family peacemaker, always the one in control. Able to handle everyone in crisis. But Dad managed to push his buttons. Seemed to love making Quinn snap."

It hadn't always been that way. But Quinn was ten when Trent was born, so by the time he was storing memories… "Your father is a good man." She rubbed her thumb across the inside of her wedding band. "I'm not excusing his behavior. But he's had a lot to overcome."

***

Quinn was gone. She'd tried to explain, but he'd bolted. Rachel stared at the small piece of white paper stuck on the fridge, reading words she'd never forget.

Quinn. I have to leave. Everyone will be better off. I'm sorry. I'll love you forever. Rachel.

She remembered feeling like her heart was being ripped from her chest. Shaking so hard she could barely write on the scrap of paper she'd borrowed from the nurses' station.

He'd stuck it between a grocery list and the pretty ivory heart she'd put there years ago. The one with the words they'd said to each other on their wedding day. *Love, trust and respect bind us together… forever.* And *Love, Trust, and Respect* was engraved on their rings.

Well, I blew that all to pieces, didn't I?

They'd been apart now longer than they'd been married, so the questions hanging in the air like the scent of a skunk were fairly straightforward. Could she ever make him understand why she'd taken off? Would he ever forgive her? And would he help her now?

Refusing to dwell on the uncertainties, she slipped into old routines. Put together a couple of sandwiches, stacked them on a plate with pickles and cherry tomatoes, covered it all with plastic wrap, and left it front-and-center in the fridge for when Quinn returned.

After tidying the kitchen, she swept the mudroom, dusted, vacuumed, and did a load of laundry, whipping the entire lower floor into shape before finally facing what she'd been avoiding. Their bedroom.

She found the closets where she'd kept her clothes empty, the dresser drawers as well. When had he given up on her? How long had it taken? Had he burned everything in a fit of rage?

No, Quinn was too controlled for that. More likely, he'd boxed it for charity. Had he gone through it himself, or had Angie stepped in to help?

And why in heaven's name should the details matter? She had left him.

And he apparently didn't want her back.

***

Rachel was wide awake, lying on a couch near the kitchen when the security light came on at two o'clock in the morning.

Every muscle tensed, waiting for the back door to open, but nothing happened. She listened intently. Not a sound. She had to assume a passing animal had set off the sensor.

She settled back, pulled the blanket up to her chin, and inhaled the clinging scent of Quinn.

Security lights again flooded the back yard. And this time, she scurried to the window and spotted him before they blinked off.

He sat on the bench she'd insisted they needed in a shady spot at the far end of the back yard. He was bent forward, elbows on his knees, hands hanging limp. He seemed to be staring at the house.

She didn't allow herself to think or hesitate. Slipped out the door and walked toward him, slow and steady. Without a word, she settled on the bench, almost close enough for their legs to touch, but not quite.

Time slipped by. It could have been minutes or hours, there was nothing to mark it by. Several times she opened her mouth to say something, but didn't.

It was when she tried to suppress a second shiver that he finally moved. Slid an arm across her shoulders and pulled her against him.

She whispered, "Oh, God, Quinn, I'm so sorry I did such a stupid thing."

"C'mere." He pulled her into his lap and wrapped her up tight. His chin rested on top of her head, and her soul sighed. She was home.

***

She woke to the scent of him surrounding her. And a warmth that went beyond skin deep. When the heat of his breath and the touch of his mouth grazed her forehead, a small contented sound slipped from her throat and he went still. That's when she opened her eyes to the reality of where and when.

They were stretched out on the couch in the den. Fully dressed, with a light blanket pulled over them, she'd snuggled in against his chest.

Tipping back to look at his face, she was met by a look that only served to confuse her. One that belied all the softness, warmth, and acceptance she'd felt emanating from him physically. He was definitely still mad at her. Which was reasonable. She'd have to earn his forgiveness.

She extricated herself and sat on the edge of the couch to gather her wits before making a beeline to the bathroom. Once there, she resisted the impulse to stare at herself in the mirror, asking questions she couldn't answer and wallowing in self-pity because the man she'd always loved might not want her back.

The betrayal and rejection she felt in her heart had no basis in reality. She'd left *him*. Had she expected he'd been pining for her for two years and would fall at her feet when she came back? Of course not. But was it wrong to hope he'd forgive her?

She washed, and brushed her teeth using one of the packaged toothbrushes she knew to find in the lidded basket beside the sink. That made her heart clench. It had been her idea to always have a stash of supplies for visitors, what she called her "just in case" basket. And when she'd spotted one shaped and painted to resemble a slice of watermelon, she'd known it would be the perfect container.

She didn't linger, wasn't the type to put off the inevitable when it was so close at hand. Back in the kitchen she started the coffee, heard the shower running upstairs, and decided to make breakfast.

She gathered eggs, tomatoes, hot peppers, and ham from the fridge, sliced, diced, whipped, and prepped the ingredients for an omelet, then set to work at the stove. That must have been when he slipped by her. The movement she'd caught out of the corner of her eye was him driving away.

Gutted. She was empty where the warm had been building—the hug-herself-and-savor kind of warm. But the feeling was gone so fast and so completely, she couldn't even pull back the memory.

She shut off the stove, dumped the contents of the pan into the trash, pulled the bread out of the toaster, and put it back in the bag. Slow and steady, one move at a time, the kitchen went back to the way she'd found it. Except for the coffee. She poured herself a cup, then left the pot on the warmer.

Curling up in the corner of the couch, she sipped and stared out the window at the empty bench in the back corner of the yard and considered Plan B.

***

Quinn's head came up when his office door opened.

Trent stood there with a grin on his face. "I thought you were grounded."

Quinn smiled back. "Yeah, that's how it felt."

"Guess she figured it was worth a shot to get you and Rachel back together." Trent's cocky words were at odds with the way he hovered near the door.

"Don't bother fishing. I'm not talking." Quinn made a point of swinging his gaze to the computer screen.

"Wrong answer, bro." Trent leaned against the doorjamb. "You should talk about it."

"What, you're doing counseling now?"

"Just saying that maybe you need to get something off your chest."

"Nope. Just you and Julia off my back. Close the door on your way out."

Trent tipped his head toward the pool table. "Want a game?"

Quinn shook his head. "No. I have work."

Once he was alone, he leaned back in his chair, swiveled around, and propped his feet on the windowsill. He'd stayed awake all night with Rachel asleep in his arms. Tried to make sense of where they were at now and what would happen next.

She claimed she'd been driven by fear for him and his family. Doubted his ability to fix what was wrong. Didn't trust him to...

Bottom line, lack of trust. Instead of coming to him when she thought her back was against a wall, she'd taken off. Run away like she'd done all her life. And he still found that damned hard to swallow.

Could they get past it? Was this a second chance for a life with the woman who'd crawled inside his soul the day they'd met? Or was he asking for another swift kick in the nuts?

Assessing the odds and making decisions were his forte. Yet, here he sat like a fucking lovesick teenager with a zit on his chin—wondering if he should ask the pretty girl for a date.

CHAPTER 5

Rachel studied the back of Quinn's head. She couldn't see much more of him as he was facing the window, his feet up on the wide ledge. It wasn't like him to stare off into space. Dammit, she wasn't going to feel sorry for him.

When she slammed the door, his feet hit the floor and he spun around to stare as she marched across the room and planted herself in front of his desk, hands on hips, jaw set. "Why did you leave this morning?"

His gaze moved from her heaving chest to her mouth, then back down.

"Quinn." She stomped her foot like an angry child and wondered if a smack up alongside the head would get his attention. The smoky look in his eyes and the half-smile on his mouth left her in no doubt of where his mind had gone. And although that should have annoyed her, it made her a little warmer inside. What had Julia said? *Use whatever tools you have, to get the job done.*

She smiled inside at the quick mental image. Seduction was so not her.

But then her eyes met his.

Well hell.

She stepped around the desk and he reached for her hand, tugged until their mouths met, melded in a raw blend of need and greed. They both took, neither gave. But it was right. They changed angles, teeth clacked and scraped while tongues fought for supremacy, and their hands worked buttons and snaps.

When the sound of the phone finally penetrated, they came up breathing hard. Rachel braced her hands on his chest. His hot, naked chest. That's when it occurred to her that she was straddling his lap. Her shirt also gaped open, as did her pants. And his belt.

The phone stopped ringing.

Their gazes locked. He lifted her hand, nibbled on the tips of her fingers, and she was sinking fast. Her voice when she tried to use it felt rusty.

"Stop."

"Why?"

"We're in your office. The door's not locked. Anyone could walk in."

"And catch me with *my wife*?"

She tried to slide off his lap, but he wouldn't let her go. Instead, he rolled them a little closer to the desk, picked up the phone and punched a few buttons.

"Rachel is here and we need to have a very long talk. Please see that we aren't disturbed."

When the person on the other end said something, he smiled. "Thanks." He hung up.

"Turns out that was Trent calling a minute ago to say he was on his way out. He'll lock up." He leaned forward and touched her throat with his lips, brushed light kisses down to the space between her breasts.

Rachel fought for control. "Stop. Please stop."

He leaned back and studied her face. "Why?"

"Because we have to fix things first. Sex will make us think everything is all right, but it won't be."

His brows dipped in a frown. "So you'd rather talk?"

"Yes. But no. Well. I think we *should* talk first."

His lips quirked. "Okay, tell me what you want to talk about."

"Us." His fingertips started on her forehead, skimmed her jaw line, throat, and collarbone on a path of fire. "We need to clear the air." She gulped as his journey stalled at the edge of her bra.

"Okay." His gaze met hers, then dropped to her mouth as she moistened her lips.

She cleared her throat and cut to the chase. "Can you forgive me for running away?"

"This time." His hands were on the move again, quick to unfasten the front clasp.

"Have you forgiven me?"

"Almost."

She sucked in a breath as he concentrated his attention on her left breast. "Quinn? I can't think when you're doing that."

"Good." He leaned forward and put his mouth on her, his tongue teasing as his fingers had.

"Are we okay?" she whispered.

He lifted his head, their eyes met and he said quietly, "I love you. Now shut up." And ensured she would by covering her mouth with his.

She was happy to take the order, follow his lead and allow herself to simply feel wanted, cherished, loved. But she wasn't a passive participant.

***

Quinn wanted more. He watched Rachel sleep and admitted to himself that he wanted much, much, more than sex. Not that he wasn't ready to jump her bones all over again, but his vision of the rest of his life had grown stagnant without her.

He would have to find a way to hold on to her this time, keep her from running away. But she wasn't the kind of woman he *could* hold, and that was probably a good portion of the draw. He went back and forth in his head, debating the topic, until she opened her eyes and smiled at him.

"How long was I asleep?"

"Long enough for me to decide to keep you handcuffed to my bed for the next week or two." His fingers brushed her lips on the way to sinking into her hair and urging her toward him. He devoured her mouth, took control. Took. Yet somehow, in minutes, he found himself on his back being ridden by a woman with an exultant grin on her face. How the hell had that happened?

"About those handcuffs."

***

Quinn stayed silent on the drive to the Meyers' downtown apartment. No way he was broaching the subject of why she'd come home until he was sure they wouldn't be interrupted.

He'd informed his family they weren't to be disturbed, promising he'd disappear to a hotel in another state if anyone bothered them.

He needed time with her and not just for sex. He had to get to the bottom of whatever the hell had gone wrong with their marriage because he wanted his wife back.

He took his attention off the traffic for just an instant, and their gazes met. Electricity zinged between them. Conversation, he reminded himself, was what they needed most. But clothing would be optional.

***

When they arrived at the penthouse, Quinn locked the elevator in place and dropped the key in his pocket. Standard procedure, but good to know she wouldn't be able to take off on him, he thought, as he watched her wander through the kitchen archway to stand with her back to him, hands in pockets, staring out at the vast landscape.

He tamped down the need to spin her around and demand she talk to him, but he couldn't deal with her yet. Meyers Security procedures had to be followed first. Besides that, he needed to get a grip.

Accessing one of the safes, he withdrew and activated the hardware to tap into the data-stream scrolled back to the last time a Meyers employee had been in the apartment. Head office monitored the equipment twenty-four/seven, but protocol required a visual confirmation and review upon arriving at the residence.

He couldn't help but smile at the series of spikes registered when they'd come in. The sensors picked up everything from body heat and voices to pheromones. Nanotechnology was freaking amazing.

For that reason, to preserve their privacy, he input his code and shut down the sensors before rejoining Rachel.

He headed for the fridge, and she tensed visibly as he passed her.

"You want anything?" he asked while twisting the cap off a bottle of water.

"Water's fine, thanks."

He took a swallow before passing it to her, then had to turn away as she put her mouth where his had been. Reminded of their habit of sharing a bottle of water after making love, his heart thudded. He cleared his throat. "It's time we talked about why you ran away."

"I'd just as soon not get into it right now."

He tried not to watch when she took another drink.

"Tough. I need some answers."

She thumped the plastic bottle on the table. "And I need help with something much more important."

He refused to be side-tracked. "Why did you come back?"

Her hands fisted. "I need you to listen to me."

"What about what *I* need, Rachel?"

"Look. There's something evil going on. Something I can't fix by myself."

Head. Hard surface. He gave in. "Fine. Tell me about it."

She wandered to the window. "Somebody's tampering with racehorses."

"Seriously?" Hell, he was an animal lover, even an advocate of sorts. But somebody else's horses couldn't be more important right this minute than fixing what was wrong between them.

Her nostrils flared. "I've witnessed a rash of accidents. Horses and people are dying, and I'm connected to it somehow."

He leaned his butt against the counter and crossed his arms. "And?"

She stared at him for a moment before continuing. "I've been working as a groom at racetracks around the country and I've seen some unusual accidents. On four separate occasions, at four different locations, not only were horses injured or killed, but human hearts stopped as well."

"And you were on the grounds of each track at the time of the accidents."

She nodded. "Yes, but I've only been able to intervene twice."

"What happened—"

"One guy was too far away from me. The horse flipped over on him in the saddling paddock and I was in the backstretch. The other was a broken neck so—"

"There was nothing you could do to change the outcome. The ones you could—*did*—help, what were the injuries?"

"Both appeared to have massive body trauma, but I don't know the final diagnosis because whenever I had to use my power—"

"You ran away."

Rachel's mouth had gone dry and the water bottle was empty, so she grabbed another one out of the fridge, and passed it to Quinn. He twisted off the top and handed it back to her.

She savored the cold as it slid down her throat.

"You ran away each time because you were afraid you'd be noticed. Recognized. That I'd find you."

Not much she could say to that.

"Yet here you are."

The hurt in his eyes had her stepping toward him, touching his arm. "It was always because I loved you too much. Didn't want to bring you more pain." Her chin crumpled as she fought to get the words out. "I'd rather spend my life missing you than hurting you, Quinn."

"Plan backfired. You ripped my guts out when you left. Not a damned thing helpful about that."

She slipped her arms around him and rested her cheek over his heart. "I'm sorry I was so stupid. Very, very sorry for what I put you through."

He turned her face up so she was looking at him, and his voice was gruff. "You know how I feel about that word."

"Okay, I'm not stupid, but—"

"You made a bad decision. A monumentally bad decision, with—"

"The best of intentions."

Amazing, thought Rachel. One moment it felt as though they'd been apart forever, and then all the distance faded away and they were finishing each other's sentences. It was an odd, but not uncomfortable, sensation of almost.

"We need to work through your thoughts and feelings building up to when you made the decision to leave."

The way he watched her emphasized the invisible but gaping distance between them. She'd put it there, she understood that. But she desperately needed their closeness back without the lingering sense that he was trying to read her mood. Anticipate her thoughts and actions.

She wouldn't be treated like one of his clients. If she wanted to talk to a shrink, she would. Yes, she'd married a psychologist. But that part of his persona had never encroached on their relationship before, and she didn't want it there now—like a stranger stepping between them.

She sighed. "When you act like Dr. Meyers, I feel like a kid again, in the office at the hospital where my mom was. Those doctors made me feel small and insignificant. Powerless."

Her arrow found its mark and she winced when the color drained from his face.

CHAPTER 6

Quinn tried to deflect the insult by reminding himself that she was at least talking. Expressing what she needed, or didn't. That was new.

"I'm sorry if I've hurt you." Brilliant blue eyes locked onto his. "But I grew up with a perception of the shrink-slash-man-in-power thing that I haven't been able to shake off. The roots are wrapped around my soul, Quinn." Her attempt at a smile fell flat. "Cliché, I know, but really, it's about me, not you.

He sighed. "Okay, I'll try to keep my ego and vocation out of this. Go ahead and tell me about what brought you home."

She walked away and the distance between them widened in every way.

"When I left here, I made my way to the northeast."

As far away from me as she could get.

"I knew my funds wouldn't last forever, so I decided to go back to working with horses. I got a job as a groom at a training center. But there were only a few people working there, and I was noticeably new, so once I got the feel of the job, I left and headed for one of the big tracks." She shrugged. "I figured, in an eighty-head barn with about thirty employees, nobody would notice me."

She picked up the water bottle, put it back down. "I rubbed four horses. Cheap claimers, until somebody quit and the barn foreman gave me a couple of good horses to look after." She turned to lean against the window frame.

How, he wondered, had she managed to work at the track and not use her ID? How did she get a security pass?

"Peco was entered in a stake race, so I stayed over in the barn for a few nights before the race, slept on a cot in front of his stall. You know, to make sure nobody tried to drug him or anything. I woke up about midnight because of the voices. It was like being outside a house where a party was going on. All the sound was mushed together.

"I walked around the barn and saw nothing out of order. Talked to the night watchman stationed outside, and he said it had been—" she finger-quoted, "—quiet all night."

"It wasn't the first time I'd heard voices and I thought, great, the nut doesn't fall far from the tree." Meeting his steady gaze she said, "One more confirmation, I'd inherited my mother's freakishness."

"You're not a freak and neither was your mother."

"Well anyway, I didn't get much sleep after that. The voices kept up their mumbling until the barn got into full swing around five in the morning. Or at least, I didn't notice them once I was busy. Forgot about them until Peco broke his leg in the race. Had to be euthanized on the track.

"I packed up my stuff and hooked a ride on a van full of horses headed southwest to Pennsylvania. I figured if I kept moving, the evil following me wouldn't get to do too much damage. I'd work for a month, then move to another track. Things were okay for nearly a year. No voices. But then it all went sideways."

She walked to an armchair and plunked into it.

"The next time I heard them, a horse snapped both front legs, the rider was thrown through the air, and the horse landed on him. There was nothing I could do to change the outcome." She tipped her head back against the chair. "Then it got uglier. Seemed like endless accidents.

"One horse bolted right through the outside fence and broke his neck when he hit the ditch on the other side. Then another one flipped over behind the gate and landed on his jockey. Shattered the guy's pelvis."

"Those aren't such unusual accidents. Horses, especially racehorses, can be unpredictable."

"But each time, the voices came first."

An odd tingling sensation had him rubbing at the back of his neck.

"I still couldn't make out the words, but each time I heard them, something nasty would happen the next day."

"Coincidence?" He didn't believe in coincidence.

"I'd hoped so the first couple of times, but then it got to be too perfect. I kept a journal, and the proof was there. Each and every time they preceded a horrible accident. And it got worse."

"In what way?"

"I started doing research and discovered that bizarre-type occurrences were taking place at dozens of tracks."

"Where you weren't directly involved."

"Correct. I probably wouldn't have noticed anything at all if it weren't for the voices making me pay attention to what was going on around me. Because I kept moving on, I began to see the vast extent of what was happening, and recorded everything in my journal. Between the racetrack grapevine and the Internet,

I was able to keep tabs on most of the tracks in North America. My book is back at your place, and trust me, you need to see it."

"You've obviously drawn some conclusions, so give me the gist of what you think," he said as he settled into a chair across from her.

"Someone is abusing horses, controlling them, making them behave in an irrational manner. It could be by remote control, or a programmed implant. The only tracks not yet hit are the ones that do necropsies on any horse that dies on their grounds."

If he hadn't done extensive reading on the possible applications of nanotechnology and remotes, he'd have thought her ideas ludicrous. "How do you tie in the voices?"

"Now you'll think I'm crazy for sure." She wrapped her arms around her middle. "I'm involved. Connected to what's happening."

Quinn studied the serious face of the woman he wished he understood. "Who do you think is behind the voices, Rachel?" Hearing the psychologist in his voice, he mentally crossed his fingers and held his breath.

She got up and headed again for a window, staring out silently for a moment before she spoke in barely more than a whisper, "I hope it's either horses or ghosts."

"Interesting possibilities."

"There's more."

"Tell me."

She turned her back to the window. "I'm afraid I'm the one doing it." Her gaze lifted, fixed on his, and he watched tears slide down her face. "I'm afraid it's me, Quinn. I'm causing the horrors myself. I need you to stop me."

His gut twisted. This couldn't be happening.

"I'm afraid I may be worse than my mother. I may have multiple personality disorder. How else could I know what was going to happen? How else can I know who will be hurt unless one of me is causing the accidents?"

"Have you ever tried to prevent an incident?"

She nodded. "Every time. But it makes no difference. I can't stop it, but sometimes I can fix it."

"You mean by healing them with your hands."

She nodded again. "Like the last one, when a man was kicked and his heart stopped. Once he was breathing again, I vanished. Got the hell out of Dodge before someone started asking questions. No one else knew he'd died, so I was okay that way, but I was afraid someone would notice it wasn't the first time I'd been around for one of these accidents."

He stayed silent, not daring to interrupt in spite of the dozens of questions he wanted to ask.

"Somebody's bound to add things up eventually and wonder if I'm the one bringing on the life-threatening occurrences. Kind of like a firebug, or a Munchhausen mother, you know?"

Finally an opening. "What's changed, Rachel? Why come back now? You've stayed under the radar this long, why not keep running?"

She plunked back into the chair. "Because when I think about it, I don't see any reason behind the events. And if I can't see a reason, why would I—how could I—?" She threw up her hands. "Someone else has to be behind all of this. Someone with an agenda." She shook her head. "It's all so damned fuzzy and frustrating."

He studied her face. "Close your eyes for a minute. I want to try something."

She frowned. "Like what?"

"Do you trust me?"

"I guess I must if I've come to you for help."

"Do you trust me?"

"More than anyone else, I suppose."

The *suppose* stung, but whatever. "All I'm going to do is ask you some questions. But I'd like you to close your eyes because it will help you find the answers."

She was skeptical, but gave in, leaned her head against the chair's back, and closed her eyes.

"Think back to the day you took off. When you left Dhillon and Angie at the hospital. Where did you go first?"

"To the Grand Hotel. I needed to get to somewhere I could stop and think."

"So you had no—"

"Plan? No. When I couldn't reach you by phone, I walked to the hotel to get a room and the desk clerk gave me a funny look because I had no luggage. I told her my husband had gone straight to his meeting and our bags were in his car—the lie came without thought. Then she was all smiles. When I got to the room, I got panicky, thinking I'd be too easy to find because I'd used my credit card. That's when my brain finally began working."

"What did you do next?"

"I pulled all the cash I could out of the account, rented a car, put on a ton of miles, abandoned the car, and carried on from there using only cash. Then I found work at a horse farm, and from there, I got onto the grounds at the local track.

"It wasn't hard to get work and stay hidden on the grounds. There's a group of backstretchers who look out for the illegals and runaways. Through them, I got phony ID, then I traveled from track to track on horse vans."

"If you had to pick one, would you say the voices are male, or female?"

"Both."

"Can you conjure them up in your head and just listen for a minute? See if you can pick out even one word."

He watched the frown form, then evaporate. Her eyelashes fluttered, her jaw clenched, and her chest rose with an exaggerated inhale.

"Stop," he said. "Exhale very slowly through your mouth." He waited. "Okay, now, tell me what you heard."

"I can't hear an individual voice. But it makes me think of pictures."

His own frown deepened. "Describe what you see."

"I see horses. All standing with their heads over their stall doors. Stomping their feet. Shaking their heads. Teeth snapping together. Voices are louder. Why don't I know the words? Are the horses talking to me? Trying to warn me?"

Her hands fisted, the pulse in her throat was rapid, her eyelids shot up to expose widened pupils and he noted a sheen of dampness on her skin. He'd get nothing solid from her until he could run down her adrenalin.

Rachel recognized the calculating look and a chill went clear to her bones. She'd seen him study case files that way. He was assessing her. Hell, she was sounding like a fruit loop so why wouldn't he? Talking horses? Oh god, where the heck had that come from? And why now? She needed to get a grip.

"Look, no matter what the voices sound like, or who's behind them…" *whether the whole thing's a product of my imagination or not,* "apparently, it's on me to fix what's wrong. And I have no idea how to go about it. I need you and Meyers Security."

"But I thought you were staying away from us because you were afraid you were putting us in danger?"

"Well, yes, but—"

"But now everything's changed because some horses have talked to you and need help?"

She blew out a breath. "Sounds crazy and insensitive when you put it like that. But it's more."

"More crazy and insensitive?"

"Oh stop it." She heaved herself out of the chair and stalked to the window again. "I told you before we got married I was a bad bet. It's still true and I think you'd agree with me now." She turned to face him. "But aside from running away once, I've always been honest—"

"Somehow, running away and staying hidden for more than two years seems like more than a single infraction."

She threw up her hands. "Guilty. I can't undo any of it." There was little point in saying anything more.

"Let's leave it alone for now. Concentrate on the details of what you've seen and heard so we can lay it all out for the Meyers team at the meeting tomorrow." He pulled out his laptop and opened a document, started to record her story.

Hours later, Quinn wandered the living area while his wife slept alone.

He'd managed to rationalize his way past the frustration of her self-appointed mission. He had two choices. Suck it up and go along or… or what? Would she bolt again? He sighed. Probably.

He'd move heaven and earth to uncover whatever was going on with the horse and human deaths, but there would have to be compromise. She'd have no option but to stick around.

He'd need more than a promise this time around.

Could he get her to agree to counseling? Or maybe combine the best of all possibilities and get her to work with ETCETERA? One department could help her identify and deal with the voices, while another focused on her healing powers.

They'd want her at headquarters, the underground metropolis hundreds of miles away.

He'd go with her. Alternative methods of communication were well established with his clients. His responsibilities with Meyers Security had made that a necessity from the time he'd opened his practice. Plus, he had a backup counselor for those who required a face-to-face meeting.

Would she be willing to go?

He scrubbed his hands over his face. Needed sleep. Couldn't afford to be fuzzy-headed tomorrow.

With a shrug, he wandered to the bedroom. Leaned on the doorjamb and listened to her even breathing. Couldn't help himself.

He slid under the covers, draped an arm around her middle, and drifted into oblivion.

CHAPTER 7

Quinn's mother stared hard at the pewter-framed photograph.

Grace, was her niece. The daughter of Isaac, a half-brother Julia had never met. He'd been murdered before she'd had any knowledge of the dozen or so people she was related to—all the progeny of a world-famous Argentinian polo player. A man better at spreading his seed than tending it. A man whose DNA was the reason behind the extra abilities she and his other offspring had been gifted with.

Meeting Grace a few years ago and learning of their vast extended family had been amazing enough, but the lifelong sensation of being watched, suddenly made sense. Grace had been a silent observer in her life for years, unaware of their relationship until recently, when the mysteries of the half-siblings, the mysteries of Francesco's children, surfaced.

The phone on the ornate desk rang with a gentle, unobtrusive tone.

"Hello?" Julia was careful to sound curious even though she knew who would be on the line.

"How are you?" asked Grace.

"I'm well. Lonely without James, of course." Understanding why her husband had to be away didn't make the longing any less.

"Why don't you come and hang with me for a few days? Change of scenery and all that."

Julia carefully fixed a picture of Rachel in her mind. "The kids will all be around this weekend. Why don't you come here instead?"

Grace's chuckle was soft. "Sounds like fun."

***

The funny burring sound of the car's tires on the cobblestones in front of the main house gave Quinn a sense of homecoming. Family. He and his brothers had spent an entire teenaged summer placing the hundreds of interlocking bricks. He wondered if his parents knew about the smart-assed comments they'd painted on the undersides.

The house itself was a study of odd angles. What began as a three room rancher had expanded over the years. First, they'd needed room for all the children, then with increasing wealth, came other requirements. Business offices and a boardroom, space for entertaining corporate guests, accommodations for international visitors, pool, patios, decks, and an entire wing for indoor sports.

"She finally got the white roses to bloom."

"What?"

"Your mother once told me she'd planted white roses when the last of her children left the armed forces. But they refused to bloom. She was worried, thought it meant someone was going to reenlist."

The front door swung open, and Julia waved for them to hurry inside.

"What's the rush?" he asked.

"There's a call for you."

"Who is it?"

"I don't know," she said as she took Rachel by the arm. "You can come with me, dear, while he tends to business."

Rachel stiffened. "I'll stay with Quinn, thanks." She pulled out of Julia's grasp and grabbed hold of his shirt. "I'm with you," she muttered.

"We'll be right back," he said drawing her along with him.

"Fine. I'll be in my studio." Julia flicked him a cool look and marched away.

"You okay?" he asked as they moved toward the business rooms.

"She spooked me."

"Manipulation is her middle name, but she'd never do anything to harm you."

There was a slight hesitation before she responded. "In my head, I know that. But something was off, and I've been surrounded by *off* for so long that it gave me a bit of a chill, you know?"

"I do." He draped an arm across her shoulders and stifled a grin when she slipped her hand into his back pocket as they wove through the maze of hallways.

Not the least bit surprised to pick up the phone and find no one on the line, he said, "I think Julia concocted the phone call idea so she could talk to you alone. Find out how our reunion was going."

Ten minutes later, after verifying there had been no incoming call, Quinn and Rachel joined his mother and discovered she wasn't alone.

"Grace," Rachel whispered, rushing across the room and into the other woman's arms.

"I wanted to give them a bit of time alone," Julia said pointedly, as though explaining the phone call she'd fabricated.

"You shouldn't have lied to her, Mother. She's been through an awful lot and learned to trust her instincts above all else."

"So be it." Julia shrugged. "They're together now, and I think we should give them some privacy."

He didn't want to let Rachel out of his sight. Didn't trust her. But he needed to loosen his grip. "Fine."

Catching the movement out of the corner of her eye, Rachel stepped away from Grace. "Wait. I'd rather not have to repeat my story over and over again. Why don't I wait until the meeting and do it once for everyone?"

"That works. What time will the others be here?" he asked his mother.

"Within the hour."

"We should get set up then." But he didn't move. Appeared to be waiting for her.

Julia gave him a bit of a push toward the door. "I'll help you. It will give these two a chance to catch up."

"I'll come back for you," he said to Rachel.

"I can find my way. I promise I won't disappear." She wasn't sure which held more pent- up frustration, his nod or his grimace.

When the door closed behind them, she sighed. "Who knew life could get this damned complicated?"

"You mean your feelings, don't you?"

She met Grace's serious look. "Yes."

"Talk to me, Rachel. How long have you been hearing voices?"

She'd nearly forgotten there were few secrets when Grace was around. She'd dig out the damnedest details, in spite of a person believing their thoughts were protected. She sighed. "For years. I kept it buried because I thought I was like my mom. She was terrified when she heard them. I didn't want to be crippled by fear the way she was.

"I used to visit her in the hospital. The drugs made her face go slack and her hair hung limp and dull, but the worst was the look in her eyes. Like she was trapped inside her body. Like my nightmares, when something is chasing me and I can't run, can't scream. That's how she looked sometimes."

"Not all meds do that."

"The stuff they said she had to take when she was at home made her mouth taste horrible and gave her the runs. So she'd stop taking it and then the voices would start, and she'd take tranqs to get past the terror.

"I don't want to live that cycle. I may hate that she took her own life, but I understand why she did. Why she thought there was no other way."

Grace grabbed both her hands and squeezed. "It isn't like that anymore. The medications have been refined. A person can live a perfectly normal and enjoyable life in spite of schizophrenia. I don't want to ever hear you say that suicide is an acceptable way out. How do you know her life after death is any better?"

Rachel opened her mouth, but the response was cut off as Grace shook her.

"Do you hear me? If you *ever* have thoughts about ending your life, you call me, day or night. Please. Promise me that." Her jaw was clenched and her gaze sharp on Rachel's.

"I promise," she said without hesitation. "But you don't have to worry. I'd never do that to Quinn. To you. When my mother committed suicide, I lived the horror. The sense of failure. The rejection of my love. I'd never subject someone else to that. Not ever."

"Good." Grace loosened her grip. "Now we can join the others."

***

Raised voices had Rachel hesitating outside the boardroom.

"How can you trust her, Quinn? She ran out on us. On you. What's stopping her from doing it again?"

"Back off, Angie."

"Fine, but know this. I, for one, don't trust her."

"Your prerogative, baby sister, but for the record? Be nice. Anyone who makes Rachel feel anything less than welcome will answer to me."

As she turned to walk away, Grace caught her arm. Held her in place while Angie went on.

"I'm keeping Dhillon away from her for a while. He was too broken when she took off. I'm not putting him through another situation like—"

"Again, your prerogative. But harsh. She did save his life."

Her voice lost its edge. "But he was in her care when his heart stopped."

"That's exactly why I left, Angie," said Rachel as she stepped through the doorway. "I was worried for your family. Afraid

I was the reason all the bad was happening. Has there been another incident since I left?"

"No."

She shuddered. "I'll stay as far from everyone as Quinn will allow, but apparently, I'm being held prisoner."

"Oh hell, this sounds too familiar," said a tall woman standing beside Quinn's brother. She stepped forward and held out her hand. "I'm Cass, Gage's wife. I've heard a lot about you."

Rachel managed a smile. "Not all good, I'm sure."

"Enough," growled Quinn. "Let's get started. And please keep in mind that we're meeting as Meyers Security, not as family. So we'll stick to business."

Gage gave his brother an "up yours" look and hugged Rachel. "But we are family. And we missed you. Welcome back, kiddo."

With a lump in her throat, she could only nod.

Family was everything to this group. They all had homes on the ranch, jobs within the businesses, and a loyalty that would stand up to any challenge.

Quinn, and possibly, Cass, were the only ones in the room who weren't retired military. Gage had been Special Forces, Trent a PJ, Angie and Julia both Air Force. The empty chair at the end of the table belonged to James, the family patriarch and he'd been Special Forces as well.

Julia had always spoken of him as though she believed he'd sit in that chair again one day. And the rest of the family tiptoed around the subject. Rachel had never been privy to the details.

Once everyone settled around the huge conference table, Quinn told them what Rachel had witnessed at racetracks around the country. Explained how she'd kept a record of events and drawn a conclusion about horses being tampered with.

Rachel's gut twisted each time a question was asked, and relaxed when her answer came easily. After a while, when the discussion moved to various crime groups and the possible motives behind such an operation, she allowed herself to disconnect.

Her attention wandered as she watched Julia slip out of the room. In spite of putting an itch between her shoulder blades, the woman was supportive. Unlike her youngest daughter.

Angie's words, or more specifically, the attitude behind them, grated.

Yes, Rachel thought, she'd run out on Quinn, but for crying out loud, it had been with the best of intentions. To listen to her sister-in-law, one would think Rachel had plotted to bring down the entire family.

***

An hour later, Rachel turned at a sound and nearly came undone. Chance, the greyhound she'd rescued a month before she'd left was standing in the doorway with Dhillon. Both stared at her as she shoved back her chair and strode toward them.

With the gangly boy in her arms, and the dog crushed between them, the lump in her throat threatened to escape as sobs. She swallowed hard and squeezed her eyelids too late to stop the tears drenching those she held against her heart. The waves of distrust emanating from Angie didn't matter to her. Love was more important. Boy and canine had been together the day Dhillon's heart stopped. Chance's frantic barking had brought her running, and thank God, she'd been able to cheat Death.

Julia's voice seeped in. "I've brought snacks. Angie, give me a hand with this, would you?" she said as she pushed a cart to the back of the room where the coffee maker was set up. The tray bore a lot more food than what one would expect of a snack. But then, Julia knew the men she'd raised.

Rachel loosened her grip on the kid and stood to ruffle his hair. Hair that was black now—a side-effect of the healing energy in her hands.

Dhillon focused on her while he hung onto the dog, and seemed to not even notice the rest of the people in the room. "I watched when you put your hands on my head and I saw the lightning flashes. The others stopped yelling then."

"What others?" she asked.

"The people. I don't know where they came from, but they were there when I woke up and saw myself on the ground. That's when Chance was freaking out, like he was trying to keep them from coming near me."

"Were they trying to come closer?" she asked, and he nodded. "What else do you remember?"

"They weren't making any sense. It was like bunches of words and nobody was listening to anyone else. But then when you came running out of the house, their voices got really, like, quiet, and then they were pointing at you and watching what you were doing."

"What happened next?"

"When the lightning stuff happened, they started backing away, toward the fence, and then I couldn't see anything. I woke up in the hospital and you weren't there. Neither was Chance, or the people. Just the doctor and my mom."

"Can you describe any of the people? The crowd that day?"

"There were lots of old ones, like with gray hair, but there were others all kinds of ages, too. Some were wearing funny clothes."

"Like what?"

"Big dresses like on TV, in the western movies, and there was a man in one of those kilts, and he was playing bagpipes like the guy in the parade last year. And mostly, all the others kind of blended together."

"Thanks, Dhillon. Is there anything else you remember from that day?"

"Nope, just the voices that sounded so weird."

"Did you help load the food cart?"

"Yep."

"Are there any of Cook's famous cranberry oatmeal cookies on it?"

A grin spread across his face and he reached into his pocket to pull out a napkin-wrapped package containing two cookies. "I snagged a couple because I knew they'd go fast."

Angie's voice carried across the room. "You should have a sandwich before you eat more cookies, Dhillon."

He looked at Rachel and sighed. "Radar. She knows I ate two in the kitchen. I better go get a sandwich before she brings me one with salad in it."

Boy and dog made for the far side of the room, and Rachel leaned against the wall. He'd heard the voices and had seen people. Were they ghosts? Angels? Or just a wild imagination? After all, he also claimed lightning had come from her hands, and she knew that hadn't happened.

Had it?

She wasn't surprised he'd watched what was happening to him. In the past, others had told her similar stories of being above, looking down, but this was the first mention of the crowd, the voices, and of course the lightning. Dare she hope?

"Rachel," said Quinn.

She straightened and faced him. Most of the group had their backs to her as they gathered around the food. Her mother-in-law watched from the back of the room.

"You should get something to eat."

"I'm not hungry, thanks," she said, hovering near the door. She didn't know where she would go if she left now, but she needed to feel like she could, in fact, leave. But, of course, she couldn't. She needed to see this through. They'd yet to comment on her story except for speculation as to who might be involved.

She rubbed her wrist. Now they needed to figure out a way to stop the killing. She had an idea, but didn't think Quinn would go for it.

CHAPTER 8

Studying the woman, Quinn saw the girl. He'd bet a million that she desperately wanted to flee. Running was what she did when things got hard. Back in the beginning of their marriage, he'd tried to get her to work through the crap from her past, but she'd resisted then, and he assumed she'd do the same now. What would it take to get her to open up and do the work, so she could put the past away for good?

Julia stood beside her as sentry. With a sigh, he went to where the food was laid out, and Gage's wife, Cassandra, passed him a sandwich. As he took his first bite she asked, "Can I be useful somehow, Quinn?"

He frowned. Why did women do that? He sloughed off the thought and finished chewing before he answered. "I'm sure she could use a friend. One without any baggage regarding her disappearance," he said with a glance toward Angie.

Cassandra smiled. "My first-hand experience with being cornered by this family can't hurt either."

"Ouch. You weren't cornered so much as surrounded for your protection."

"Ah, yes, but let us not forget that I didn't have any idea why I was being held captive."

He grinned. "Yeah, but you still pulled off a brilliant escape. Ran my poor brother ragged for days." He sobered. "We were all very lucky you weren't killed when the mission tanked. What made you decide to forgive Gage and marry him instead of having him beheaded or something?"

Cass shot a look across the room and her face flushed when her husband's gaze met hers. "Same thing that brought your wife home. And I don't mean some random deaths at racetracks. I'll go talk to her," she said. She stopped first for a quick word with Gage, before strolling over to Rachel, who stiffened at first, but appeared to relax as Cass talked.

His mother filled the space Cass had vacated and passed him a napkin. "Mayo," she said and Quinn automatically wiped his mouth. "You need to ease up. You're watching her like she's headed for an open gate and you're going to have to outrun her."

"She's already looking for a way out."

"I think she'll stick. Especially with Grace being here. But in any case, you need to use some horse sense around her. If you want to keep her, make staying her idea. Earn her trust. Be calm. Be predictable. And most of all, bend in the direction she wants to go. She will need to leave here. Put on your listening ears and go with her."

Gage had stood silently beside them for a minute. Now he added, "She'll be more comfortable after she's talked to Cass for a while. Bonded a bit with someone who doesn't have the history the rest of us do."

"She wants to bolt. The only thing keeping her here is what brought her home. Help from the security company." *Not me. She didn't come back because of me.* That part was hard to swallow. Yet, he still wanted her every time he looked at her. What kind of an idiot was he? A big one. Fucking pussy-whipped.

The last bite of sandwich became a dry, tasteless lump. He popped the top off a soda and guzzled. Frigid bubbles seared a path down his throat.

Julia wrapped a single cookie in a napkin and took it to Dhillon. "To the kitchen now. Take your dog and help Cook tend the smoker."

"And try to keep the sauce off your shirt, pal," added Angie with a mock frown.

When the kid rolled his eyes, Quinn found himself smiling… and wasn't that a welcome change in his day.

With a sideways glance at his mother, he stifled a belch under his hand. "Everyone ready to get back to work?"

Gage took control of the meeting and strategies were discussed.

The tension riding Quinn's shoulders shot up his neck when Rachel said, "It would be quicker and easier to send me in so I can draw them out."

"You'd be a sitting duck," blurted Quinn.

Her chin lifted. "I was always in disguise. Forty pounds heavier, with dark skin and gray contacts." She smiled at Grace. "I wore canvas skids inside gumboots to alter my walk as well. Besides, Meyers Security will have my back."

"She's right, Quinn," said Angie.

"Bullshit. The racing community is too freaking tight. We drop in a couple of people to protect her, and the entire backstretch will know."

"Not if we go in together." She had everyone's attention now. "We ship into a track with a horse for a race. A big race so we go as a team. Money outfits ship with a trainer, an exercise rider, a groom, a hotwalker and even a pony horse as a companion."

Gage was nodding. "That could work."

Rachel continued. "And we could start at a track where there are lots of ship-ins for stake races, so new faces are expected and accepted without question. Problem is, we need a horse."

"Far too complicated once you put a horse and a race in the mix," said Julia. "What about going in as buyers instead?"

"Excellent idea," said Grace.

***

Thankful for the reprieve, Rachel opted to go for a ride instead of walking back to Quinn's house to wait out the three hours before the big family dinner. She wanted to be alone with him, yet didn't. At least on horseback, there was little chance he'd get her naked, and that's what she was avoiding.

She needed to fix what was wrong first. She'd chosen to ride a gelding she didn't know. One purchased while she'd been away. She wanted no reminders of rides they'd taken back when she'd been stupid in love.

Riding single file through the pines, she turned in the saddle to ask, "How's the practice going?"

He grinned. "Pretty good. But I haven't been taking new patients for a while because of a new project I'm working on. The research has taken some time, but I'm ready to make a move now."

The trail widened, so she slowed her horse's pace to ride alongside him. "What kind of project?"

"There are a few outfits around the country using new models for treating soldiers fresh from the battlefield. Five-to-ten-day programs for them to decompress, learn how to deal with everyday life. They include counselling, meditation, team-building exercises, and they incorporate a ton of outdoor activities from white-water rafting to rock climbing, hiking, sailing, riding, and paddle boarding. You name it, some program is offering it. Then there's the other type of activities like art and music and gardening. Men can learn how to set up community gardens and co-ops. It's endless really.

"I've already taken on partners. We'll offer what I'm calling an *inside program*, as well. Individual counselling, family counselling, mentorships. Then there's massage therapy, physiotherapy, and even reiki. It'll be a work in progress for a few years, but by the time we're done, it will be a full-service facility. I've even got a dentist and an attorney wanting on board."

And there he was. The intense, passionate man she loved. The man everyone else thought was laid-back and easygoing. The man driven to help others. To make their lives better in some small way.

"Will Veteran's Affairs work with you?"

"I'm in contact and I expect they'll only participate in what's proven scientifically. They tend to frown on treatments that don't have a ton of empirical data. And that's fair." He grinned. "I've also got some researchers interested in doing studies from day one. So we'll have our proof in a few years."

He went on to share details, ideas, facts, and figures. He stayed animated and engaged, talking about separate programs for emergency workers, as they had different issues than the military participants. His voice held her captive, and she was enthralled by the way he grabbed his subject, owned it.

But too soon they'd completed the loop they'd set out on and the paddocks came into view. As did Grace.

When they drew nearer, Rachel noticed an unusual tenseness in the woman's posture.

"Something's up," said Quinn, as he'd clearly noticed the same.

Rachel tamped down worry. No point. Not yet anyway.

Grace strolled toward them and Rachel wasted no time. "What's wrong?"

"Nothing," she replied with a smile. "But I've got us an opportunity to go to ETCETERA immediately. If we leave within the hour, Kelton and his team will be able to work with you for half a day. Long enough to work through the possibilities, and then put into place whatever options are chosen."

"But…" With her heart bumping hard in her chest, Rachel scrambled to find a way to slow things down. "Why the rush? Couldn't we go tomorrow?"

"They have a full slate tomorrow. If not now, we'll have to wait a week. Up to you, of course."

A young man came toward them with a couple of lead ropes.

"Just in case, Julia arranged for the horses to be taken care of. You can get off here and Ricardo will look after them."

Rachel glanced at Quinn and saw no answers there. This was her decision. And hadn't she come back here with the sole purpose of stopping the murderers?

She swung down from the saddle, loosened off the girth, and patted the gelding's neck before handing over the reins. "Then we'd best get on with it. Thank you, Ricardo."

Quinn followed suit.

In less than an hour, they'd had a short briefing in the Meyers office, gathered a change of clothes, and were driving toward the landing strip.

Thinking about what was to come—allowing the entities of ETCETERA into her mind—Rachel's stomach ached as though she'd eaten a cup of raw onions… chased by a tumbler of tequila.

CHAPTER 9

"Mildred?"

That's not my name.

"I know you're awake." Lips tickled the edge of her ear, then he nibbled down the side of her neck. "Talk to me, honey."

She kept her eyes closed, savored his mouth, his hands as they caressed her skin. She was about to go up in flames when a voice inside her head shouted, *Stop!*

Her eyes popped open and she pulled out of unresisting arms. Sat up quickly on the edge of the bed and the room spun—a sensation similar to being underwater, unsure of which way was up.

Where am I? Ohmygod, Who *am I?* A vaguely familiar and ominous presence stirred in her chest, making her heart hiccup between beats and her skin chill. She took a deep breath, looked around the room. A cabin? She opened her senses, strained for sounds from outside.

Silence.

Eerie, empty silence.

She spotted her neatly folded clothing on an old wooden chair near the foot of the bed. Looking down at her nakedness, what she saw looked familiar, yet she had no idea who she was, where she was, or who she was with.

She glanced over her shoulder at the gorgeous stranger propped up on one elbow. He studied her with a somewhat amused expression. Sleep-tousled mahogany brown hair made her fingers itch to run through it, and he had the kind of face she could imagine somewhere exotic. On a ski slope in Switzerland, on a beach in Brazil, on television, billboards, in magazines. His was not a face any normal woman would expect to find in her bed. Except in her dreams.

And the body, well, that nearly made her sigh out loud. Muscular, tanned, sexy. The soft dusting of hair on his chest angled downward enticingly to where the sheet was pulled over what she'd felt tucked against her backside only moments ago.

She sucked in a shaky breath and met his gaze square on, and went for over-the-top bold. "Okay, I give. You're gorgeous and I want you. Now. Inside me. But first one question."

The corners of his mouth twitched. "And that would be?"

She hesitated for only the briefest of moments. "Who. Are. You?"

His smile was beguiling.

Beguiling? Really? What the heck did that mean?

He reached for her hand. Toyed with the thin gold band on her ring finger. She tore her gaze from the intimacy of the movement, but was quickly consumed by the dark blue eyes, and she barely heard his response as his mouth settled over hers.

"Your husband."

Two hours later, sitting in a booth at Martha's Diner, Rachel studied him while he read the ancient menu.

He glanced up. "You already know what you want?"

She nodded. Toast and coffee were like a religion to her. No matter what state, country or continent, she could always get toast and coffee for breakfast. How did she know that, and not her name?

He ordered a manly plateful of eggs, bacon and potatoes.

They ate in silence. And when the bill came, she watched him pull out his wallet, waited just long enough, then with the speed of a striking cobra, plucked it from his hand. She rifled through the cards for a minute, then handed it back to him with a smile.

"So, Quinn, what's my name, and what's our next move?"

***

Quinn drove in silence for nearly two hours after her questions had been answered as best as he was able. She hadn't liked hearing that she'd been the one to ask for the memory wipe. That she was essentially working blind on this mission.

She'd wanted detailed explanations, but he'd been unable to tell her more than what had been established by ETCETERA at the time of programming. A microscopic chemical implant at the back of her neck would be activated by any effort to retrieve specific blocked memories. Those she had hidden from herself, under the direction of Dr. Kelton, while she was under hypnosis. Prior to the procedure, he'd sat in on the meeting with Grace and Kelton, and that was when the decisions had been made about what memories needed to be suppressed in order to keep her safe while they toured racetracks, trying to identify the people involved in the murders.

Now, not only was she visually different, but if anyone was watching for recognition responses, she would also be safe.

The procedure had been developed to prevent an undercover agent's involuntary reactions—those of the autonomic nervous system—from exposing them. Nothing worse than starting to sweat when the enemy, or whatever target came into a room, and being forced to waste energy regulating one's own heart rate and being conscious of every breath.

Now, there would be no familiar faces. No memories would get in the way. Anything she picked up on would be current and immediate.

Once parked in the shadow of the Hartley Downs grandstand, he touched Rachel's arm.

"Hey, where are you?"

She blinked, and looked around. "Hmmm?"

"Care to go to the races or would you rather sit here?"

She reached for the door handle. "We'll bake to death if we stay in here."

With his hand on her lower back, he steered her toward the gate for licensees only. He held out passes to show the guard, got a nod, and they went through. She shot him a curious look as he led her toward the saddling paddock. He smiled, took her hand in his, and said, "We're meeting someone here in a couple of minutes. As soon as this race is on the track."

The call for "Riders up!" went out and she watched the dance of colorful silks as each jockey was legged up onto his mount. The horses pranced alongside their grooms until handed over to the lead ponies. She somehow knew the announcer would introduce each horse, its trainer, owner, and jockey as they paraded past the grandstand, then the warm-up would begin. Most would gallop alongside the pony-horse for up to a half-mile before being jogged and then walked for a few minutes before the gate was put in place and the horses called forward to load.

Quinn kept his eye on Rachel as she watched the horses with a quiet smile on her face. Part of their purpose here was to test her memory block. See if she had any recollection of being here before.

"Quinn?"

He greeted his old friend, Gordon, with the expected back-slapping handshake. "Hey, bro, good to see you."

"What brings you to Hartley?"

"You."

His brows went up and he scanned the area. "I'm supposed to meet a bloodstock agent here, exactly where you're standing. You saying he's not coming?"

"He was shopping for me," said Quinn. "But I got free at the last minute and decided to surprise you."

"Well, that you did. How the heck are you? Gawd, it's been years."

"A dozen or so, anyways. Belated congrats on your Breeder's Cup wins and condolences on the Triple Crown. Sucks to get so close and miss by a nose. What was that, three years ago?"

"Four." His gaze had settled on Rachel.

"I'd like you to meet my wife. Honey, this is Gordon Riley." Rachel had been adamant about not answering to Mildred, said it felt too awkward. So he'd agreed to avoid it as much as possible. She held out her hand, smiling. "Mr. Riley, it's a pleasure to meet such a famous trainer."

He laughed. "Famous? Ha, it's fleeting in this business. If I don't come up with a cup winner this year or a triple-crown contender by spring, nobody will even remember my name."

She smiled. "Only as good as your last good horse? I've heard that saying before."

"And it's true. I have two *good* horses this year, but they're both due for retirement after the Breeders Cup in the fall. Next year, I'll be back to a barn full of claimers."

Quinn laughed then. "Yeah, but a barn full of high claimers, hundred-granders. The kind you could take to a lesser track and clean up with."

"True enough, but still claimers at home."

Home, Rachel thought. Why did that word feel like it had an echo? She studied the other man now. "Where is home?" And why did she care?

"Well, my base tracks are in New York and Florida. We keep about twenty head at each, but then there's also a dozen in California and half that in Toronto."

"You don't race in Kentucky?"

"We ship in to run at Churchill and Keenland, but most of my clients are on the east coast."

"It must be very hard to be in so many places. You must spend all your time traveling." Noticing he wore no wedding band, she added, "No time for a home life I suppose." Again, why did she care?

He grinned. "Successful business comes with perks to make the job easier. We have a farm in Lexington where my wife oversees the young horses and the lay-ups—the ones on vacation. And I have amazingly talented assistant trainers running my operations at each racetrack. I manage the horses and their careers, plan their campaigns, constantly work on plans B, C, and so on. When life happens, I'm prepared to fly by the seat of my pants, both literally and figuratively."

Quinn took the opening. "You don't spend much time in Kentucky?"

"I get home a couple of times a month on dark days—non-racing days," he explained. "And Rachel, my wife, travels with me as often as she can."

Quinn had tensed suddenly, but when she looked up in question, he simply smiled and went on, "You said you didn't have much time to meet today so I should get to the point. I heard you had a couple of nice colts for sale."

"Decent colts. What kind of ability are you looking for?"

"Same as everybody else. I'd love to see my silks on the track on the first Saturday in May."

He shook his head. "Not that kind of quality. If they were, I'd be keeping them. I have some contacts though. Do you remember…"

Rachel lost interest in their conversation and drifted away, drawn to the horses warming up for the race. As they approached the starting gate positioned right in front of the grandstand, they were nearly close enough to touch. The sweet smell of sweat filled the air, veins stood out, and energy throbbed.

Her attention was captured by a pretty bay with big expressive eyes and a finely sculpted jaw. A lone filly in a field of boys.

Rachel laughed at one of the colts who'd noticed the female among them. His nostrils were wide and flickering, trying to catch her scent. Good chance he'd been swabbed with a strong smelling ointment before the race, but his eyes hadn't been tricked.

The rider on the amorous colt said something to the girl on his lead pony. With a quick look at the filly, she nodded, then steered her charge to the opposite side of the track, and the distraction proved useful as the colt glanced toward the starting gate and put his game face on.

Warm breath fanned Rachel's ear and sent a shiver down her back. "He hasn't forgotten the filly, just put the thought on a back burner for now," murmured Quinn. He slipped his hands around her waist, pulled her back against him, and rested his chin on the top of her head. They watched the loading process together.

The assistant starters each led a horse into the gate and climbed up alongside. With a hand on the bridle, heads were held in position while groundsmen scrambled to close the tailgates.

Rachel held her breath when the number four horse started to rear. Shouts came from inside the gate.

"No, boss!"

"No, no!"

Number three shied sideways from the noise and action.

"No, boss."

Horses were fidgeting, and riders were glancing around while the starter, the man on the stand out in front of the gate, waited patiently for everyone to settle. His gaze swung back and forth across the front of the gate as though checking for all faces to be pointed forward, all feet on the ground.

With a horrendous metallic crashing noise—like cars colliding—and the clanging of a loud bell, the doors opened, and horses exploded from the gate in one huge wave, power and color charging toward the clubhouse turn.

Establishing position, switching leads, and settling into stride went from exciting to terrifying in the blink of an eye. Rachel spun, buried her face in Quinn's chest and simply held on, unsure what she was afraid of.

His hands ran up and down her back, gentle, soothing. Lips pressed against her temple as he whispered, "It's okay, baby. Let's get out of here."

They made their escape. Bright colors bled together. Shouting and cheering blended with the announcer's voice, and everything blurred. Legs leaden, lungs screaming for more air, she dug deep as Quinn half-dragged her through the parking lot.

When they got to the car and Quinn folded her into the seat, her muscles went limp. Her eyes didn't see and she heard nothing but distorted memories. Echoes of horror. First, the staccato crack like a gunshot. Then her voice, the scream. The word that was *Noooooo,* went on and on and on as though forever, when the horse's head suddenly dropped, his legs flailing for balance, his center of gravity shifting backward. The broken front leg swung wildly. Then the horrible sound created by thousands of people gasping in shock when he fell. Nausea rose in her throat.

She groped for the handle, flung open the door, leaned out, and retched until she was certain her stomach lining must lay on the pavement.

She drooped sideways in the seat and leaned there, spent, moaning, as cold sweat slid between her breasts. Tears dripped off her face. And thank God, the vividness of the memory faded.

Quinn appeared in front of her with a bottle of water. He tugged off his T-shirt, slopped water on it, and wiped her face, her chest, and the back of her neck with the soft cotton.

She raised her eyes to his and saw the concern. "I'm okay."

"No, you're not." He handed her the rest of the water. "Try a drink of that, or rinse and spit, whatever helps." He stood over her.

"Better back up so I don't puke on your shoes."

He smiled, backed away. "Anything else I can do?"

CHAPTER 10

She rubbed a hand around the back of her neck. "Grab me the pink striped thing out of my duffel."

He rifled through their luggage, brought her the cosmetic bag, and she pawed around until she found the tiny bottle of mouthwash.

She rinsed, spit, and wondered about her lack of embarrassment around him, then shrugged it off as meaning he wasn't lying about them being married. Feeling marginally better, she relaxed in her seat and looked over at him.

"Let's get the hell out of Dodge."

He smiled. "Sure you're okay?"

"Yup."

The highway was busy with weekend travelers. Although she noticed they were headed north, she didn't ask why. Didn't care really. At this rate, they'd be at the Canadian border by suppertime.

After nearly an hour of comfortable silence she said, "You knew it was coming. You expected me to fall apart back there."

He nodded. "We were supposed to be gone before the horses left the gate."

"Then why were we still there?"

"I got caught up."

She studied his profile. "Bullshit."

His lack of reply had her frowning.

"How long have we been married?"

Something bleak crossed his face for the most fleeting moment, before being replaced by a devilish grin. "Long enough for me to know you intimately."

She rolled her eyes. "Yeah, I got that. Tell me how many weeks, months, years."

He sighed. "I can't."

"Won't."

"Orders. I can't."

"Orders. Hmm. I obviously trust you, but the manipulation, putting me here, putting me there, that part's starting to create tingles at the back of my neck. So I need some answers."

"Ah but, darlin'—"

"Don't *darlin'* me. I'm serious."

"I need to make a phone call first."

He took the exit for a state park, and when he finally stopped, they were alongside the ocean. She opened the window and inhaled fresh, crisp air while Quinn hit speed dial and waited for someone to answer.

"Quinn here. She has questions. Needs to talk to you," he said and clicked off.

"Who was that?"

"It was a machine. Relay system to get Dr. Kelton to call us back." He held up the old- fashioned flip phone. "Secure line."

"Am I supposed to know this doctor?"

Quinn wasn't happy with the way things were working out. Had hated setting her up for that fall back at the track. He chewed the inside of his cheek while he watched the numbers change on the digital clock. Fuck it. "You are the reason we're on this mission. You were a witness to events and you brought your concerns home." How to word this? "There was a meeting with a security group, as well as Grace, and some strategies were discussed."

"Grace is my friend."

"She is, yes. She's the one who suggested you work with Kelton. You made all the decisions. Pretty much wrote the script and the rest of us went along."

"Why block my memory?"

"Your previous exposure to some of the people we could encounter could have put a wrinkle in things. Grace and I both tried to talk you out of working this one, but you refused to back away, so Kelton devised a way to make it work."

"What about my appearance? Won't I be recognizable?"

"No. You were always in deep cover. Trust me, no one will recognize you."

She stared out at the ocean for a minute or two. "Who exactly is Dr. Kelton?"

"He's head of psi at ETC."

"What is sigh and where is ee tee sea?"

"That's psi as in psychology, psychiatry and the like. ETC is the short version of ETCETERA, a clandestine agency Grace is affiliated with. The mission we're on is a collaborative affair involving ETC, Meyers, FBI, and IRIA.

When her eyebrows went up he added, "Meyers ' ' security company, and IRIA stands for International R Investigations Agency. They're based in Britain and inves questionable practices involving horseracing worldwide. "

"Am I working for any of these organizations?"

He grinned. "Nope."

"Good. At least I haven't lost my mind completely."

When the phone on the dash vibrated, he pushed the speaker button, and Rachel quickly dispensed with the pleasantries. Got right to the purpose of the call.

"Tell me what you've done to my mind."

"We used a process similar to the one Grace was involuntarily exposed to some years ago. It was very effective, though faulty in its early stages of development. You *chose* the procedure. First, a chemical was introduced to your system, then you underwent very specific and controlled hypnosis. If you try to access suppressed memories, the chemical does something similar to short-circuiting the system and memory retrieval will be thwarted.

"Grace experienced debilitating headaches, but the medication and procedures have been fine-tuned over the last few years so you'll have no such symptoms."

"How can it be that I remember Grace, and you, now that I've heard your voice, yet not my own husband?"

"That was intentional. Grace and I are your anchors. We can be reached anytime, day or night to pick you up and reverse the procedure. There's also a way to interrupt the memory-disconnect in case of an emergency."

"Great. How do I do it?"

"If you're in trouble, and I mean that. This isn't to be used to get you by a difficult moment. It's to save your life."

"I understand."

"All you have to do is either think, or say Grace's name, over and over again. It will take at least twenty seconds of this to temporarily put you in reach of all your memories."

"It will also bring her running won't it? She'll pick me up telepathically."

"Exactly. A twofold rescue net."

"How long will this hypnosis last?"

"You've been implanted with a single chemical dose which will wear off in approximately thirty days."

"Approximately doesn't sound very scientific."

"Body chemistry is an unknown factor in the equation. Test subjects netted results ranging from twenty-five to thirty-five days. And no, there didn't seem to be any trends. Nothing that would point to men versus women, or body mass, or even metabolism."

"What about an antidote. Is there something I can take?"

"Nothing. The only way to stop the process is through hearing a specific string of words."

"Okay." She took a deep breath. "So. About the mission. Can you give me a rundown so I know what to expect?"

"Negative. All you need to know is that your husband is considering buying a racehorse. He's traveling to different racetracks to make contact with sellers and agents. You don't know anything about racehorses besides the fact that you think they're gorgeous."

When she didn't reply he asked, "Anything else, Mildred?"

She shuddered. "Who the hell picked out that name?"

"You did."

She rolled her eyes. "I guess I was looking for something totally not me."

"Those were your exact words at the time."

"Figures. Okay. Thanks."

"Call anytime."

She clicked the phone off. "Okay, cowboy, where to next?"

"I think we'll find somewhere to spend the night and wait to hear from our connections in the morning. Then it's either north to Vancouver, or east to any number of tracks."

He drove along the beach road, past lovely private cottages and a few grander homes, finally pulling in at a place with two rows of quaint cabins painted cheery colors.

While he went into the office where a vacancy sign hung, she laid her head back against the seat and closed her eyes, exhausted from the emotional rollercoaster. She allowed her mind to drift back to the conversation with Kelton.

Grace. What better rescue word could they have come up with? Grace had been her savior more than once. There was the time—

She shook her head. Blinked and tried to retrieve her thought. Nothing. She had no idea what she'd been thinking about. She shrugged and focused on a tiny pink cottage. Judging by the number of towels and the variety of bathing suits flapping on the line tied across the porch, there was a family staying there. She couldn't imagine how they all squeezed inside.

The one next to it was orange and there was a bicycle built for two leaning near where a young couple sat on the porch, snuggled together as though honeymooners, not noticing the outside world at all.

Quinn emerged from the office with a woman wearing a dress in a dozen shades of red, orange, yellow, and pink. Her flip-flops sported big floppy flowers the same scarlet as her lipstick. Her smile was wide when she stopped beside the car. "Welcome to the Sunset, Mildred, I'm Evelyn. If there's anything you need, just whistle."

"I'll do that, thanks, Evelyn. Can you recommend a good restaurant close by?"

She nodded. "Hang a right out of here, and you'll find three about a mile down the road. All good. We know how to do food around here." She lifted a hand in a wave. "Enjoy."

As she walked away, Quinn studied Rachel's face. "You're hungry?"

"Ravenous."

"Then get back in the car and we'll go for food first."

"I could use a good wash first."

"How about we get some takeout and come back here?"

"Why not leave me here and go for the food while I take a shower?"

"Not gonna happen. Not leaving you alone." He opened her door for her.

She shrugged and got in.

After passing a candy store and several bike rental kiosks, they spotted a pizza joint, and within thirty minutes, they were back at the cabin with a large pepperoni, extra cheese, and a large kitchen sink, hold the anchovies.

Rachel packed in the food, beer, and sodas, while Quinn brought their bags.

The delicious smell made her stomach rumble, and she promptly forgot the shower she'd wanted. She sunk her teeth into a slice of extra cheese, scooping up strings with a moan as she dropped into a chair.

A grin spread across Quinn's face. "You really were hungry."

"Um-hm." She swallowed and took another bite. Her eyes closed and another happy sound came from her throat

"Well, at least you've recovered." He popped the top cola, then his beer. "You want a glass?"

She shook her head no, reached for the can, and chugged down several swallows to chase the pizza. "Ah, now that feels better."

When his phone rang her contented smile faded.

It was the call Quinn was expecting. "Hello, Gordon."

"Hey, Quinn. Sorry I didn't get back to you after the race. With the incident and all, I got tied up."

"Incident? Sorry, we took off before the race was over, my wife wasn't feeling well. What happened?"

"Colt spooked and went through the inside fence after the race. Rider had to be airlifted to the trauma center."

"I'm sorry to hear that. Is the boy okay?" Quinn held his breath. If the jockey was dead, Rachel would blame herself for not being there to save him.

"He's out of surgery and can feel his fingers and his toes, so that's a good thing."

"A very good thing."

"Anyway, I got to thinking. I should set you up with, Rick. He's a friend of mine and a top-rung bloodstock agent."

"Sounds good. Give him my number."

"Will do. In the meantime, there's a monster filly you might be interested in. She's pretty special and the owner's kept her Oaks and Derby eligible."

"I'd rather a colt with potential for the breeding shed."

"Oh well, it was worth a shot," he responded. "By the way, how much are you planning to spend?"

"Depends. What will it take?"

"If you want the first Saturday in May, *with* paper, you'll have to part with close to a million. I could get you the filly for about half that."

"I'd thought by coming to Hartley I could find something with potential, but for a lot less money than say Churchill, or Belmont. I'd heard a person could buy anything on the grounds of the smaller tracks for a hundred grand or so."

"True enough, but you'll be getting talent without the kind of bloodlines you're looking for. Unless of course there's a major conformation flaw."

"I'm not overly concerned with what the experts might call a flaw, as long as the horse can run. Tell you what. Let your agent friend know what I'm looking for, and see if he can find me a handful to look at."

"How far are you willing to travel?"

"Depends on what he finds."

"Okay, but bottom line, you want a Derby horse."

"And let him know I'm not averse to a package deal. Six horses max as long as there's a couple that could go the distance next May."

"Six horses?"

"My trainer has room for six. I wouldn't mind a nice mixed group to hit the stake circuit with."

"Will he be coming with you to check out the horses?"

"No. She won't. I always do my own buying. Look, I've gotta go. Thanks for helping me out, and tell Rick to call me as soon as he has anything."

"Will do. Great talking to you again, bro, and see ya around."

"Back atcha."

Quinn clicked off and grinned. "That ought to get the wheels turning."

Rachel nodded. "Care to wager how soon?"

"Any agent worth his salt will have horses for us to look at by tomorrow morning."

She shook her head. "Nope. He'll call you tomorrow to set things up for the following day. That way he'll be able to park you in the grandstand to watch at least a half dozen horses either gallop or breeze. It'll take a day to set it up with trainers, exercise riders, pony riders, and maybe even a jockey or two."

She blinked. "And why are those details all within my reach, but my own name escapes me?"

"Like I told you, specific details are being blocked."

Rachel's stomach began to churn. "Oh no, not again." She pushed the pizza box closed. Is this going to happen every time?"

He frowned. "Not that I know of, but we'd better call Kelton and find out if this is a side effect he wasn't aware of."

He pulled the dedicated cell phone from his pocket and hit speed dial then set it on the table between them.

"Kelton."

"Hey. Mildred's had a second bout of nausea, and without the major triggers."

"Let me talk to her."

Rachel leaned forward. "I'm here."

"Tell me your symptoms."

"Pretty basic stomach roll. But no puking."

"What were you thinking about?"

"The annoyance of not knowing my own name."

"Stop thinking about it. The nausea is there for a reason. It's to prevent you from continuing to search for an answer we've blocked for your own safety. So leave it alone."

"Fine."

"What you're doing, the sacrifice you've made, is huge, Mildred. Go with the flow for now and the reward will be far greater than any discomfort you're experiencing."

"Thanks."

Rachel left Quinn to finish the call, and went to the window. She slid it open and immediately felt the breeze, moist and gentle, as it pushed her hair back from her face. The ocean was so close she could see whitecaps on the waves and practically taste the briny air.

When he came to stand behind her, she leaned back, and his arms came around her middle. With his chin brushing the top of her head, his warmth rocketed through her like a comfortable cloak.

"How about a walk on the beach?" he murmured.

"Later." She wanted to soak in this momentary peaceful sensation. Everything would change as soon as the phone rang again. But in the meantime… "Could you just hold me for a while?"

His arms tightened and she felt his sigh. "All bloody day if that's what you need. All bloody day."

CHAPTER 11

Thirty-six hours later, they sat in an empty grandstand watching horses train.

Quinn was edgy, likely due to a long night of feigning sleep when he wanted to be making love with his frustrating wife. Before her memories had been blocked, they'd agreed it would be best if they didn't muddy the waters by having sex while they were virtually strangers. But the first night didn't count. It was surmised that their intimacy would set things up, establish their relationship for the duration.

He crumpled his empty coffee cup and tossed it into a nearby trash bin.

"Two points." Rachel was smiling at him.

"The next horse coming for us is lightly raced but shows potential."

"Are you actually shopping?"

"Yes."

"Oh. I thought this was just part of the ruse, the mission."

"Two birds."

"Well, then I guess I'd better pay more attention."

More guilt for his bottomless well. Yes, he was shopping, but mostly, he was watching her for reactions. Involuntary reactions to point the team in the direction of a murderer. They didn't know quite what to expect.

Kelton suspected she was being led to places where evil of some kind was about to happen. However, there were other theories. The plan so far was to put her at tracks where there hadn't yet been an incident, in hope that it would be one of the next ones hit.

For now, she watched horses in training while he studied her. Last night he'd put in a call to his brother, Gage. Had him ship a special bracelet for Rachel. One that would monitor her heart rate, blood pressure, and respirations. All of which would be transmitted to Quinn's phone so he could see any changes as they happened. Whether or not he explained its purpose to Rachel was a decision he still hadn't made.

Luckily, the horses they watched had potential. So they'd take the next step and go to the barn area where they could see them up close.

They met Rick at the backstretch pass gate. He'd already done the paperwork to get them into the barn area, so they pinned on their temporary badges and proceeded to where the leading trainer was stabled. Three grooms were grazing horses on the boulevard alongside the wash rack where two others dipped big, fat sponges into pails of soapy water to bathe their charges.

Rachel's grip on Quinn's hand tightened and he studied her face. She'd gone dead-white. "Mildred?"

"Keep their attention off me," she said. "I can do this."

A reaction the first time was not what he'd expected and it forced him to rapidly regroup. While the others were out of earshot he muttered, "Talk to me."

"There was a faint murmuring sound, not unlike the buzzing of bees in my head. It ended quickly, but made me feel funny. Probably something from a person or a horse going by. If it happens again, I'll give you a signal, and you can look around. See if anything jumps out at you."

Her color was coming back, which was handy, as the agent was approaching with two other men. "Okay."

Quinn took some time viewing the horses the trainer had brought out of their stalls for him and asking questions while Rachel remained silent at his side for the duration.

When they'd spent enough time, Rick escorted them back to their vehicle.

"How about breakfast? There's a good spot close by."

"Thanks, but we have plans."

"You'll call? Let me know if you want to make an offer?"

"I'll touch base tomorrow."

As they merged onto the interstate, Rachel shot a look over her shoulder. "You realize, of course, he's still behind us."

"And he'll be going past any minute." He smiled and waved at the man when exactly that happened.

"Smart ass," she muttered.

"What else is going on?"

She huffed out a breath. "My reactions. That's what all this is about, isn't it? You're using me like a bloodhound to sniff something out."

"Sort of. But remember, you set all of this in motion. You wanted to be bait but we convinced you to modify the plan. For the record, I was against the whole project. But you couldn't be discouraged. I only stuck with it because I refused to let you do it alone."

She sat up straighter, and when he glanced over, he noted the wide eyes and open mouth. Credit to him, he didn't flinch.

"*Let*? As in allow? You refused to *let* me do something?"

"Not what I meant." And he wished he'd been more careful with his wording. He knew better than to push that button.

"I may be missing some brain cells or have a synapse or two out of commission, but I can't imagine asking anyone for permission. Ever."

"Well, yes, your personality is still very much intact, and no, you don't ask my permission for anything, nor do I want you to. But in the case of this mission, I had major objections. You're putting your life in danger, and other people are being exposed to a complex and volatile situation."

"I obviously ignored the warnings, so I presume this must be very important to me." She tipped her head and studied his face. "Tell me. If I wasn't your wife, if another woman, one not connected to you, had the same goal, would you have gone along with it?"

"Yes, which is why you're not chained to a wall in the basement. I knew I was being unreasonable and emotional. That doesn't sit well with me, as it wouldn't for most men. So we're here. And I'm determined to keep you safe."

"You don't think I can look after myself?"

"Bloody hell, can we just leave all this shit behind and get done what needs doing right now?"

She smiled. Was definitely enjoying his discomfort. "Okay," she said. "You turned down breakfast but I'm starving. Could we stop somewhere?"

"Is twenty minutes too long to wait?"

"Nope, I'll survive. Where are we going?"

"Let it be a surprise."

And it was.

She was impressed with the view from the top of the hill. "Well, at least I can see why they call it the Emerald City. Talk about green."

"In a thousand variations," he muttered.

"So, you're an artist."

The corner of his mouth quirked. "Nice guess, but no."

"Men don't notice variations of color."

"They do if they've ever been a teenager working in a paint store. One of my duties was to put the paint chips back in the right slots. I was plunking them in, one at a time, when an older lady decked out in diamonds and furs dropped that line on me. She wanted the perfect green to match her collection of ferns. Two of my workmates hid in the next aisle listening to her go on and on. They tortured me for days."

"I have a hard time imagining you as an intimidated teenager."

"My mother beat respect for our elders into us at a young age." And then there were his father's lessons. "So that day? I respectfully went through every freaking paint chip, trying to find the right one for the old girl."

"Your mother's tough?"

"You have no idea." He rubbed a hand over his face. "Actually you do."

"Did I get along with her okay?"

His half laugh amused her. "She was always on your side."

"There was a need to choose sides? That doesn't sound good. Did we fight a lot?" She held up a hand. "Not fight. I'd never fight, but I bet we had some rollicking disagreements."

"Got it in one."

"Yeah, even with the pieces missing."

There were few people in the restaurant, so service was brisk, and in a short time, she was pushing her empty plate aside. "Good thing I knew how much I'd enjoy a Spanish omelet."

"I confess to knowing your preferences and the reputation of this place."

"How long have we—"

"Kelton said not to go there. But if someone asks, we only met a year ago."

"Right. I remember what you told me. We met at a grocery store. You were trying to decide what flowers to buy for your mother."

"And you came to the rescue, telling me to go with the sunflowers instead of the carnations. I happen to like carnations."

"But the way you described your mother, I was pretty sure she wasn't a carnation type of woman."

"Exactly. We dated for six weeks, then flew to Mexico and got married."

"What other background should I know?"

"You rode horses when you were a kid. That'll cover your comfort level around equines. And you've been a kindergarten teacher for five years."

"Where did I get my degree?"

"McLain College in Northern Alberta."

She frowned. "Canada?"

"You know another Alberta?"

With a roll of her eyes she said, "I'm questioning the wisdom of making me from another country."

"Makes it less likely that someone will claim to know you. And you can go online and learn the basics. Enough to get you by."

"Sure, but so far, I've had no access to the Internet."

"You can study later." He pointed at her empty plate. "You want anything more?"

When she said no, he drained his glass of water. "Good, then let's get out of here."

***

They were back at the track shortly after sunrise the next morning. Quinn had requested another viewing of three of the horses they'd seen the day before. This time, he insisted on watching as they were prepped for their morning exercise. He explained that temperament and attitude were important factors to him.

What he didn't voice was the concern of whether legs were being iced before training, or required any other special treatment. He was pleased to see this trainer's regimen included proper stretching and warm-up, as well as nothing on their legs but protective bandages. And the staff was treated equally well.

He'd been in barns much different than this. Outfits where staff was treated with little regard for their own needs. This trainer had a well-stocked coffee room and community fridge where everyone partook of the doughnuts, sandwiches, and fresh fruit. With one man being the groom of two of the horses they were there to watch, the order of viewing was such that the other horse was seen in between, so the groom could easily prepare one after the other had been bathed and put in the hands of a hot-walker for cooling out.

Rachel stood near the entranceway and simply observed, gazing out at the vast number of horses and people passing on their way to and from the track. At first, she'd been almost holding her breath, waiting for the zing of energy or wash of fear, but nothing happened. So she began to relax and enjoy the bright colors, the smell of horses and hay and sawdust. The muted thudding of hooves on hard-packed dirt. Snorting and blowing of horses. Men and women laughing.

The clinking and jingling of metal on metal had her searching for the source and smiling as she spotted a horse chewing at his ring-bit.

Along with knowing the type of bit and recognizing the sound, the rest of the sights, sounds and smells were very, very familiar. She knew this place, or one like it. This time the wave of nausea was relatively tame, but enough to tell her she needed to change the channel in her head.

She swung around to see where Quinn was, but the contrasting darkness inside the barn had her blinking, trying to focus.

Then, the murmuring began and her flesh went cold.

She tried to call out, but could make no sound. Braced against the wall, she fought panic, widened her nostrils and sucked in a long deep breath. Held it for a count of ten and exhaled through her mouth. Her fingertips tingled. Focus, she told herself. Find the source.

She leaned against the wall and, without moving her head, searched for a visual. Something the least bit wrong or out of place. Anything to account for the feelings swirling around inside of her.

The murmuring stopped as abruptly as it began. Relief threatened to overwhelm her and take her out at the knees, but she stayed upright, kept searching for the source. Something—no—some*one* was responsible, dammit. And it was important—she only wished she knew why.

"Rachel?" Quinn startled her. "You okay?"

"I heard something."

"Like yesterday?"

Frowning, she thought about it. "No. But there's a connection."

"To what?"

"Me. Us. Just a feeling. I've never had premonitions before but maybe…" She shrugged. "I tried to take in everything going on around me. See if I could put it together with what happened yesterday. But all I'm coming up with is an image of men's boots—worn thin on the inside by stirrups."

"That's good. More than we had yesterday. The brown gelding's ready to gallop now. Are you okay to walk to the track?"

"I think so. Not as wobbly as I was a few minutes ago. But stay close, okay? Just in case."

He hooked an arm around her shoulders and kissed the top of her head. "I've gotcha, baby."

His warmth seeped into her, pushing out the chill and easing the tightness in her chest, but there was still a niggling at the edge of her mind. A message she couldn't bring into focus.

Walking to the track was uneventful, although the drone of the sales agent's voice was beginning to annoy her as he repeated the same lines over and over again. Wishing she could tell him to shut the fuck up, she bit her lip instead and tuned him out, once again taking in the sights, sounds, and scent of her surroundings.

It was organized chaos. Groups of horses decked out in fuzzy nosebands and martingales, with legs wrapped in every color of the rainbow. Foam dripped from the chewing of bits. Brassy chains rattled through metal rings. And woven throughout was the earthy smell of sweat overlaid by iodine and fruity shampoo.

Nausea hit like a bucket of ice water. She stumbled and Quinn's arm tightened, righted her.

"Thanks," died on her lips when she saw the concern on his face. She must look as bad as she felt. "Sorry," she muttered. "Memories again."

He pointed to the little stack of bleacher seats. "Can you make it there?"

"Sure." She hoped she sounded more confident than she felt as she concentrated on moving one foot, then the next. Quinn said something to the others, then sat with her.

"Am I creating a scene?"

He smiled. "No one even noticed you trip. Only I knew you were struggling to stay upright."

The big gelding they were there to watch trotted the wrong way around the track in the company of a pony-horse, then turned around and began to gallop. As he approached the quarter pole, the pony-rider released him, and the jockey leaned low over the beast's neck as he picked up speed and flew down the lane.

Little more than a speck on the far side of the white rail, he appeared to be moving smoothly, increasing speed with every stride as he came toward them. Once past the wire, the jockey stood in his stirrups, and the horse slowed down as he rounded the clubhouse turn where they sat.

He wasn't even blowing hard as he exited the track, once again in the company and control of the pony-horse and rider. But that was as expected. Had he been winded by such a short work, there'd be immediate concern. Instead, he was revved up, bucking and kicking at imaginary foes or playmates.

Rachel felt better, too. Not as ready as the gelding to dance yet, but recovered sufficiently to walk back to the barn and wait while the next horse was readied for them.

In all, it took an hour to view the three workouts, then they observed the recovery and cooling-out process as well. There were no repeats of Rachel's nausea nor was there any murmuring.

Before they left, Quinn made an offer on one of the brown geldings, subject to the approval of his veterinarian. The agent could barely contain his excitement, and fawned over Quinn to the point of making Rachel want to gag.

Once back in their car, she said, "How can you stand dealing with him? Aren't there other agents?"

He smiled. "He has the connections we need."

"But you're actually going to buy that horse, aren't you? The gelding. You liked him. And that kiss-ass will get a commission."

"The horse won't vet out so it won't be an issue."

"Why? What's wrong with him?"

"It's ever so slight yet, but I could hear something off in his breathing. My vet will scope him, and likely find he has a flapper problem."

She frowned. "I didn't notice."

"It was minute. But I suspect you'd have been able to hear it if he'd worked farther, maybe a half mile instead of a quarter."

"What a shame. He seemed to have ability."

"Absolutely. And after this case is settled and out of the way, if Doc Olsen thinks surgery could fix his air problem, I may go back and make them a lower offer."

"Why didn't you like the filly?"

"She was too easygoing for me."

"You like feisty girls."

He grinned. "Like you."

She rolled her eyes. "I've finally found the words to describe the dark feeling I had at the barn."

"And?"

"Impending doom."

Chapter 12

Quinn had no doubt what she'd felt was real. Which was exactly why they'd relocated to a safe house on Whidbey Island while Meyers and ETCETERA teams stayed on site at the track. At least until the event she hadn't quite predicted took place. It was unfortunate she hadn't picked up anything specific, but that couldn't be helped.

For now they'd wait.

It took only twenty-four hours. A filly flipped over in the saddling paddock, got away from her handler, and ran through the fence into the crowd of race-goers, trampling several. One man sustained a head injury and died on the way to the hospital.

Quinn made sure Rachel saw or heard nothing of this news. Meyers ran an investigation of their own without the knowledge of local law enforcement. They hacked into the security department of the track and accessed surveillance tapes from all areas, both public access and the barns where only licensed personnel or approved guests could enter. So far, they had few leads.

Quinn and Rachel moved on, this time, to a track in the Midwest. One chosen by the Meyers team.

They went through the same process. Contacting prospective sellers through an agent, viewing horses from the grandstand, then going to the barns the next day. Quinn bought a three-year-old gelding. A sprinter of fine bloodlines. Bred for distance but unable to get more than a mile. The horse would be shipped to a trainer he knew in Oklahoma. A woman renowned for her ability to stretch a horse out.

And there were no voices. No premonition-like moments, so they moved on to the east then south. Striking out at four tracks in a row prompted a reevaluation by the agencies, and groups involved.

A meeting was arranged. But Rachel wouldn't be attending.

***

It was odd, thought Quinn, to have so many outsiders in the Meyers conference room. Two from the FBI, one from IRIA, one ETC rep, Grace, and two people from her team. Added to the usual family players, they filled the room to capacity. Not a single empty chair. Yet, there *was* an empty space, because Rachel wasn't there.

When Gage tapped a spoon against his coffee cup, silence ensued and all attention swung to him. The meeting began with reports from each area, all regarding the one incident Rachel's voices had preceded.

FBI agent Foley was well used to dealing with ETCETERA teams, so psychic phenomena didn't have him raising his eyebrows. But he did have one area where believability was a concern. "I don't understand how a horse can be programmed to run over a particular person in a crowd."

"You think the dead man having ties to the Minnows was a coincidence?" asked Quinn.

"No. It was too convenient to be ignored. But in the ranks of organized crime groups, the Minnows don't come off as the sharpest team in the water. So them using something so scientifically advanced strikes me as over their heads."

Gage added his opinion to the mix. "Their internal turf war has been going on for years." He smiled at his wife. "Cassandra was a target for a long time because they were out to find her brother—the only witness to the execution of their leader. Why wouldn't they simply pay for a hit on this guy? It would make way more sense to me."

"Paid hit," said Foley, "is exactly what the Bureau suspects, as we've taken the records kept by Rachel, plugged all the information into our computer programs—dates, locations, identities etcetera—and there is not a single commonality to be found, aside from the involvement of horses.

"We've also researched records from all the tracks and not come up with a single person common to even two incidents."

"It could be a hit team," said Grace. "But that seems a bit extreme as the pool of tracks to use is not all that big, and eventually, the incidents will come to the attention of the authorities. They couldn't have any idea someone with Rachel's abilities would recognize the accidents for what they were and blow a whistle."

The IRIA representative, a middle-aged woman dressed in black slacks and a mannish jacket, leaned back in her chair, elbows resting on the arms, fingers steepled in front of her. "Actually, if you think about racetracks worldwide, there is a substantial pool of venues. However, from the data I pulled before this meeting, I see no issues elsewhere. Not a single racetrack death in the last four years. Records further back are being reviewed by my office as we speak."

Gage tapped the table in front of him. "What about other horse-centered events? If a tool such as we suspect *has* been developed, there are endless applications. One would wonder, as well, if it could be taken a step further and used on humans. Say, have a police officer fire on his partner or into a crowd. Ugly, ugly connotations here, folks."

"The team at ETCETERA," said Grace, "has been looking into those possibilities, and there's some good news. The tool, for lack of a better word, appears to be based on reflexive reactions, which makes it better suited to use on animals. Not saying what you suggest couldn't happen, but from what we know so far, it's a pretty big jump from here to there."

"Good. That will help us stay on task," said Foley. "However, we, too, have a department studying the possibility of human application."

"All considered," said Grace, "the sooner we identify the players, the sooner this worry can be put away."

"Exactly." And the sooner he could have Rachel back where she belonged.

"Then let's take a look at what our team found this week," said Angie.

Gage pushed a few buttons on a keyboard and the big wall screens lit up with a succession of still photos.

Angie used a laser pointer. "From the last incident Rachel predicted, these are stills extracted from the paddock's video stream. In the first frame, you can see the filly rearing. Her center of gravity is too far back for her to recover. On the second, she's gone over backwards and hit the ground. That's when the handler lets go of the lead shank. Then she's up and immediately bolts for the gate. All perfectly normal. She's headed back the way she came. She's frightened and retreating to the safety of her barn on the backstretch." She nodded at Gage and four new photos came up.

"When you watch this as a continuous video, you don't even notice, but on the frame-by-frame you can see her ears suddenly go from flat back to straight forward."

"Something catches her attention."

"But," said Angie, "she's panicked. In full flight mode, so this is abnormal."

"Also," Gage added, "whatever she's noticed is not directly in her path. Her head is tipped ever so slightly to the right of the gate. She angles that way for three full strides, then her ears go flat again, and she shifts slightly left, then plows into the victim."

Angie grinned. "My kid went over the footage for about three hours last night before he found it. Run the super slow-mo, Gage, with the security footage alongside."

Gage pushed the appropriate buttons and the screen changed. "These are synched to exactly the same time." On the left screen, the filly, one frame before her change in ear position and direction of travel. On the right, the man who was run over and ultimately died of his injuries.

Angie put the red dot on a man behind the victim. "This guy has his hand shoved into his pocket, and he appears to make some kind of motion with that hand at exactly the same instant the fleeing horse changes directions. Both times. And more damning, he didn't act either surprised or frightened as he stepped out of the way of the charging equine at the last second."

Gage scanned the group at the table. "We've run him through all our recognition programs and we're coming up empty."

"What about Rachel?" asked Foley. "Does she recognize him?"

Grace answered, "No, she doesn't."

Quinn's eyebrows went up. Did that mean Rachel's memory had been restored?

CHAPTER 13

Rachel stood at the window, peering out through the wooden strips of old-fashioned blinds. For the first day or two, she'd savored being free of Quinn's watchfulness. Enjoyed the lack of pressure. But now, she itched to fling open a door or window. Was it just air she needed? Or was it the need to run that dogged her?

Logan—her bodyguard and Grace's husband—wouldn't allow her to bolt. She studied the man who'd been with her since she and Quinn parted company two weeks ago. The first week she'd been kept busy with several procedures at ETC headquarters.

Kelton asked her to stay there until the assignment continued, but she'd have lost her mind for sure. The facility was too high-tech, too… well, too everything. A small city buried underground with only the illusion of windows and daylight. And even though the residential suites didn't have the same crazy surveillance as the offices, labs, and medical facilities, the unpleasant prickling at the back of her neck confirmed she was still being watched.

Granted, there were electronic eyes here too, but there was also air, sunshine, trees, even flowers in the window boxes to give her a happy buzz. But nothing like the tingle under her skin, the familiar feeling of Quinn's hand settled low on her back as he walked alongside her.

She missed him. And it was a hell of a lot more than sex. Which they'd apparently decided to take off the table while she didn't have any memory of their relationship. Didn't know him. Yet her body and soul recognized him, ached for him. She needed—

Logan's voice jerked her back to reality. "You okay over there?"

"Just frustrated." No pun intended.

"Pretty big sighs. Anything I can help with?"

She nearly snickered. Going for distraction she asked, "Can you still hear my thoughts?"

"Nope. The blocking techniques we went over are working very well for you."

"Tell me what it's really like, being telepathic. Does it become more of a curse than a gift?"

"Like anything else it has its moments." He smiled. "It was part of my introduction to Grace, so that was good. But at the beginning of a relationship, sharing thoughts, can put new meaning on awkward."

"I've heard voices before, but not the way you do. It's more random, less recognizable as specific words. Lots of mumbling. My mother was schizophrenic." And why the hell had she told him that?

He closed his laptop and reached for the mug of what must now be cold coffee. "Have you inherited her illness?"

"I don't know." She rubbed the inside of her wrist as she wandered to the other window.

"Why haven't you been evaluated?"

She shook her head. "I watched her suffer for years before she killed herself."

"The pharmaceuticals have vastly improved, and side-effects are much more manageable than they were even five years ago."

"But it could still interfere…" She held out her hands, palms up, and stared at them.

"With your life-giving power."

"Exactly. Will it still be there if the drugs alter something inside my head?"

"Have you talked to Kelton about this?"

"God, no." She suppressed a shudder. "First they'd have to do testing to see what it is I'm doing, to figure out how it works. Then there would have to be experiments, and how can they do that without killing something for me to revive? Sure, they'd start small, like on mice, but what happens if I fail? Why should even a mouse have to die?" She couldn't stay still. Had to keep moving so the thoughts crawling around inside her didn't have a chance to take root.

"And what happens when I succeed? Do they move me up to cats and dogs and then humans?" Stopping, spinning back to face him, she said, "I can't do it. Can't face the possible consequences."

"Rachel, sit down for a minute." His tone was both soothing and compelling.

She flung herself into an armchair. "Giving up control has always been hard for me, but now? It's terrifying to think what could happen."

"And yet you opted to go through the ETC procedures for this mission's success."

"Ah, yes. But with a very specific contract in my hands. I have not, and will not, give them permission to even speak to me unless either you, Grace, or Quinn is there to advocate for me.

"Grace had a really hard time with ETCETERA. Even though her sister married Dr. Kelton, Grace only agreed to sign on as a consultant, not a full-fledged member of the organization." His smile was a bit wry. "My wife and the doctor butt heads on a regular basis. As a matter of fact, he wanted you in an ETC safe house, but she insisted on using one of ours instead."

"I assumed this was a Meyers property," she said scanning the room. "I remember Paradise and Grace's other inns, but I didn't know she had simple places like this."

"We felt a need to expand to a collection of smaller, easier to access residences. There's at least one in every major city, plus many in outlying areas."

"So do you have a company name or something?"

He smiled. "Nothing official. No alphabets, no name plates. We call ourselves independent facilitators, and have contracts with many agencies. Much of what we do is simply making connections with or between the right people."

"But you work with Meyers and ETC a lot."

"Your mother-in-law is Grace's aunt, so we're part of a family network."

"And you said Kelton is married to Grace's sister."

"Yes, hence the ETC unbreakable link."

"That brings us back to Kelton. I've seen the contract I signed. But I still wonder why I would let him do this memory-adjusting hypnosis thing on me when my gut says I don't trust him?"

"The way I understand it, you were motivated to let him help with this one project, driven by the desperation to fix something specific. There's nothing wrong with that."

She tipped her head to one side. No wonder Grace had fallen for the guy. It was more than looks, and boy-howdy, he had those. More than the aura of kindness and a great sense of humor. He was reasonable. Not a very sexy word, but it suited him.

Grace, the most skeptical and distrusting woman she knew, had given herself to this man. Trusted him completely. She sighed. Was her own bond with Quinn that strong? That extraordinary?

No. Her gut told her their relationship was off. The details escaped her, but there was a chink in what should be the solid entity of their marriage. A question in the way he studied her when he thought she wasn't paying attention. A microscopic gap between them when he touched her. As though he had to reach through something to get to where she was.

The beep of Logan's phone brought her back to the here and now.

"Hello." He listened intently for a minute before responding with a, "Copy that," then stuffed the phone back into his pocket.

"Time for a change of scenery. Grab your stuff."

She scooted up the stairs and into the room where her packed case sat by the door. What she'd learned in foster care held with the current way she was living. Never unpack. That way there was no danger of leaving something important behind when you were suddenly moved to a different house. They'd never been homes. Even the good ones. Because she'd had a home and didn't want a new one. What she'd always needed was her mother's condition to stabilize so she'd be released from the hospital and then Rachel would look after her. Until she didn't want anyone near her again. And the world would tilt on its axis one more time.

She shook off the morbid thoughts, brushed her teeth and washed her face—because who knew when she'd get to do that again—then made her way back downstairs.

Logan led the way to a closet and swung the rack of coats to one side to reveal an open doorway. He motioned for Rachel to step through into the dimly lit stairwell leading to a long narrow hallway.

After walking for about ten minutes, Logan used a key fob to let them into a furnished basement. From there, they made their way up to a garage, where he helped her through the driver's door and into the back of a panel van before jumping into the driver's seat. As he started the engine, the garage door rolled up, and in a matter of minutes, they were on a highway.

Rachel pulled her jacket tighter. "Freaking cold for September." She couldn't see out of the van so had no idea where they were. "I hope we're headed for a warmer climate this time?"

Logan met her gaze in the rear-view mirror. "Anywhere in particular you'd like to go?"

"Hmmm. Wouldn't mind watching palm trees blow in the breeze."

"Hold that thought," said Logan.

Rachel had come to recognize the ever so slight softening of his expression, something in his eyes when he spoke with Grace telepathically. And while she couldn't clearly see his face right now, his mouth hinted at a smile for a few minutes before he met her gaze in the mirror again.

"Southern California or Florida? Your choice."

The skin at the back of her neck tightened. She put a hand to her mouth and swallowed hard. Her heart thumped. "This is important."

"Don't overthink it. Go with your gut."

"Humid. Florida. That's where I want to go."

"Then that's where we'll go.

***

Grace finished her telepathic conversation with Logan, consulted her notes, then said to the group in the Meyers meeting room, "I'd like to make a suggestion based on a hunch. Because really, we have nothing else to go on."

Foley studied her like a bug under glass. "A hunch?"

"The bloodstock agent has found horses for Quinn to look at throughout the country, four of which are at a brand new facility in Florida. I propose we start there."

She was aware of Foley's track record working with ETCETERA, and had no qualms about him dealing with psychic phenomenon. However, there were others in the room who might not be so receptive. She shrugged. "Got a better idea?"

The corner of his mouth quirked. "No." He glanced around the table. "Everyone good with this? Any concerns?"

"None," said Quinn. "I'll contact my agent. When do we want to go in?"

"We'll need at least two days to get into position, four would be better. Does Thursday work?" said Foley.

Grace nodded. "I'll have Rachel moved."

Once the room cleared of all the official types, Grace said to Quinn, "She's already on her way. They'll be in the air shortly, and safely tucked away by early evening."

"Care to explain your hunch?"

"Rachel always ended up at the tracks where incidents happened. And it occurred to Logan that she was being sent, or set up to be where she was needed. So he played with the idea, asking her where she wanted to go next, and she chose this location. I'm betting Logan hit it right on the money, so we need to be prepared."

"The sooner this is over, the better. I want my wife and her memories back."

"Ah, one thing. I think we need to stay this time. Be there for the accident. Let it play out."

"That puts her—"

"In a position to do what she does."

He shook his head. "I hate her having to go through that."

"But you want your wife back."

Running a hand around the back of his neck and digging fingertips into the knotted muscles, he grimaced. "Yeah, but we have to step up security around her. I won't let her be vulnerable to the Minnows or whoever's behind the bizarre murders."

"She won't be, Quinn. Logan and I will have her back, and Caroline and Sergei will be there as well. Not to mention all the other agencies involved."

"She'll recognize Caroline and Sergei from her Paradise days. Those memories are still intact."

"Actually, she's never met Sergei, only spoken with him on the phone. We'll make sure she doesn't cross paths with Caroline."

Grace knew exactly where she wanted to position her friend.

CHAPTER 14

Backlit by the pale light of dawn and enveloped in steam, horses stood quietly in wash-racks while grooms bathed away the sweat and dirt of their morning gallop. Crisp air ripe with the scents of shampoo, fresh wood shavings, and bitter coffee enveloped Rachel as she puzzled over the comfort of familiar surroundings she had no long-term memory of. Quinn squeezed her hand as though understanding and she frowned. She'd spent time last night learning to manipulate her mind blocks so Grace could hear her thoughts. According to both Grace and Logan, she wouldn't be vulnerable because the channel was a very specific connection. Others could not gain access.

Quinn must be picking up her feelings and nothing more. Not that she'd mind having a telepathic connection with her husband, as it was likely the only way she'd ever be able to figure him out. Last night, when she'd hoped to have some quality time with him, he'd left her with Grace while he and Logan had gone to another room to work on surveillance strategies.

She'd crawled into bed alone and woken up the same way this morning—although the mangled pillow beside hers suggested he'd been there at some point. She sighed. The conflict of zigzagging emotions was starting to wear her down.

Sharp voices jerked her back to her surroundings. Two men in a heated discussion in the next barn held all of her attention, and she focused on the few words she could make out.

"You fucking spun me," yelled one.

"I didn't know he was going in there!"

"Tough luck got him. You gave me the call first."

"We ride his whole barn, for Christ sake. You know I can't pull off one horse."

There were more heated words said too low to hear, then one man stormed away, while the other pitched an empty bucket at a wall. The clatter had horses spooking and skidding all around, and more yelling followed from several directions.

The bloodstock agent walking alongside Quinn explained that the jockey's agent had promised his rider would take the mount in a particular race, but he'd changed his mind and left the trainer needing to find a new jockey.

"Does that kind of thing happen often?" asked Quinn.

"Often enough. There will be other agents scurrying in like rats trying to get the call now because the horse is live."

Rachel asked, "What does that mean in layman's terms?"

"A live horse is one with a good chance to win. And every jockey has an agent to take care of his business by securing good horses for him to ride. When a *live* horse comes open, the other agents all want a chance to get their boy on it. Or as we say, to pick up the mount."

"So what happened back there?" Was this a set-up to put someone in harm's way? Or to protect them due to inside knowledge of a set-up?

"Probably the agent had promised the trainer that his jockey would ride a horse, then another trainer offered that jockey a better horse, so the agent went back and spun the first trainer, which means he hung a story on him and turned down the mount."

"Okay, I get it now. Thanks for the explanation. I didn't realize so much went on behind the scenes besides getting horses fit enough for racing."

He grinned. "Anybody can get a horse fit. It's the game of getting a horse into the right race, against the right company, with the right jockey. That's what makes or breaks a career. And all it takes is one bad step to end it all."

She shivered at an odd wash of cold air and looked over her shoulder. *Grace, a man just walked past me, fiftyish, white, five-ten, blue ball cap, blue vest, black T-shirt, and clean jeans. Hands in his pockets like he's hiding something.*

Quinn was studying her. "You feeling okay?"

"A little queasy. Probably from skipping breakfast."

"Cook shack's right there," said the agent with a wave of his hand. "Why don't we grab something before we check out the horses?"

The rich scents of coffee and cinnamon assailed them as they entered. Old restaurant-style tables and chairs of mismatched color and design were lined up in rows, and at the center of every table sat a bottle of hot sauce.

They were the only people in the place besides the gray-haired guy behind the counter. He kept his head down as he buttered the dozen or so slices of bread on the counter. "Coffee's a buck a cup, you can make your own change." He glanced over his shoulder and his gaze slowed when he spotted Rachel. "Tea's the same. You people want food?"

"Soup crackers would work for me," said Rachel. "And a bottle of water would be great."

He grunted, wiped his hands on his apron, and fetched what she'd asked for while the two men helped themselves to coffee.

They sat at a reasonably clean table, and Quinn ran through some questions about the horses they'd be seeing. He made notes on the pages he'd been given on each one, while keeping an eye on Rachel, no doubt watching for her color to come back to normal.

An hour later, as they watched a lovely chestnut mare being cooled out after working three-quarters of a mile, Rachel began to hear murmuring voices. She spun, searching for the source, but there was no one anywhere near them. The whole side of the barn was virtually deserted. She bumped Quinn with her arm and kept her voice low. "Do you hear something?"

Slowly, he turned his head from side-to-side as though tracking for sound. "Nothing. What do you hear?"

"Voices, lots of them down very low. Like being outside the closed door of a cafeteria or something. And my fingers are starting to tingle."

"Tell Grace."

She nodded. "I'd forgotten." *Grace! I'm hearing voices, down low, and I can't make out what they're saying.* "I think we should leave here before I keel over or something."

"We have to take off now," he said to the groom pouring ice water on the horse's bandages. "You can tell the trainer I'll be in touch." The girl held out a hand with her thumb up, and carried on.

Oh, God, thought Rachel, I need to get out of here. Now. "Faster," she said, tugging on Quinn's hand.

His grip tightened. "Just walk if you can, or you'll draw attention. I'm not leaving your side. You'll be fine. Are the voices changing at all?"

"Still down low and I can't make out the words."

"Male or female?"

"Can't tell. But it feels important."

"I don't know if I'm supposed to tell you this, but you usually hear voices before an incident, so this probably means something's going to happen here."

She stopped dead in her tracks. "Then I need to stay. I can stop Death from taking someone. I can reverse it if I'm right there when it happens."

"If it's no more than murmuring, it's an advance warning you're getting. Whatever's going to take place won't happen for a day or two, so we've got time to work it out. We'll do everything we can to prevent a death, but we need to get a handle on your reactions. Tell Grace we're leaving. We'll meet them back at the house."

Once again, she called out telepathically, and hoped Grace in fact heard her internal voice. She'd done well when they'd practiced, but this time she didn't have the feedback to tell her if it worked or not.

***

Sprawled on two sofas with three large pizzas on the table between them, they brainstormed. Rachel had a pencil and a big pad of paper to write down every thought and idea. Where they were going was unknown territory, so who knew what would or wouldn't work.

As always, Kelton's timing was impeccable. His call came as they'd closed the boxes and refilled their glasses of soda.

Once Grace had given him a summary of the situation, she put the call on speaker, and he opened the floor with, "What are your ideas so far?"

Quinn replied, "Rachel and I should go back for a second look at the horses. It will put us in all the same places we went today and there could be something more from the voices."

"Agreed."

Grace spoke next. "I'd like to go in as well. I can use a cover of my own, or go as an outsider to give Quinn my opinion on the stock he's interested in."

Kelton's hesitation was obvious. "It would be better if you weren't connected to the others. I'd rather see both you and Logan going in independently."

Logan smiled. "I like that." Grace punched his arm. "Ouch. Can I help it if I love watching you work?"

"You just don't want me working alone. And you know damned well I can look after myself."

"Absolutely. But it's more fun when we play together."

Rachel was grinning at the other couple as they sparred. But Quinn wore an odd look, one she had no time to interpret.

"Dr. Kelton," she said. "Wouldn't it make sense to remove my memory block, so I could be more useful by possibly recognizing someone? Also then the nausea wouldn't take me out when least expected?"

"But—" Quinn's protest was interrupted by Kelton's response.

"Good question, Rachel. I'm sorry you're experiencing the nausea—"

"Got to be better than the blinding migraines I had," said Grace.

"As I was about to say," Kelton said, then paused. "If you can manage with the side effects for at least one more day, it will make you much more effective than if I remove the block. Trust me on this. The interference of what's there in your mind will create another type of complication you would be best without."

Rachel noticed the other three seemed to relax then which reminded her that they all knew what she didn't about herself. She rolled her shoulders and shook off the nagging worry. It didn't matter right now. She'd face whatever it was when the time came.

Kelton continued with, "Tomorrow evening, we'll revisit this question."

"Fine," she replied. Quinn laid a hand on the back of her neck and she leaned into it. She liked his touch. It centered her.

"Will you update the FBI or shall I take care of that end?"

"Meyers will be keeping everyone advised."

"I'll let you continue your meeting then."

A clicking sound came through the speaker, and Grace leaned forward to flick it off. "The man never ever says goodbye. Simply hangs up."

"You've worked with him for quite a while, haven't you?" Rachel asked.

Grace grimaced. "That's one way to put it. Our previously strained relationship has morphed into a guarded one. I was terribly distrustful of ETCETERA for a very long time, but they did save my life a couple of years ago, so I cut Kelton some slack for that."

"Hey. I thought I was the one who saved you?" said Logan.

"Well yes, you got me to the ETCETERA medical team and they did their bit. Then of course, your figurative slap upside my head when I had a bit of a slip along the way gave you bonus points, so yeah, you can have the credit." She leaned into him and he planted a kiss on her forehead.

"Damn sure I get the credit," he said. "After the hell you put me through."

Grace grinned. "You see what it's like? They never let you forget if you make a little tiny mistake. Or maybe it was more like seven or eight mistakes and maybe they weren't so small. But he loves me anyway and that still freaking amazes me."

"I hope getting my memory back tomorrow will give me some of that." She glanced over her shoulder at Quinn and was surprised by the furrow on his brow and the line of his mouth. Trepidation crept under her skin. "But then, maybe we didn't have such a good relationship. Maybe that's why Kelton wants to keep me in the dark."

"Don't borrow trouble, Rachel. Our marriage has nothing to do with Kelton. He's protecting you from being conflicted by the situation you're about to be immersed in. It's all about appearing new to an incident. Not having a preconceived notion about what is going to unfold."

She shuddered, and rubbed her wrist. "Sounds even more ominous now."

Logan reached across and touched her hand. "Trust us, kiddo. We're all in this together and we're looking out for you. You have to try to take things as they come."

She nodded. "I will. I do trust you. All of you. But this gap in my memory makes me a little crazy sometimes."

"Amen," said Grace. "I've walked in those shoes, my friend. How about we get back to the planning now? Once we've got that figured out, we could all take a little down time."

"Shouldn't I practice projecting my thoughts some more?"

"No need. We both heard you loud and clear today. You did good."

She felt the smile come, and noticed the pressure she'd felt in her chest earlier was completely gone. "Quinn had to remind me to call out to you once."

"Maybe tomorrow we'll get you to give us an update every ten minutes, so you'll be opening the channel more naturally and won't even have to think about it."

"That sounds like a good plan."

"Speaking of… Have you figured out a cover for tomorrow?"

Logan's smile was cocky. "I think we should go in as private investigators searching for someone."

"Who?" prodded his wife.

"We'll make someone up." He seemed lost in thought for a moment. "A man. We've been given information he might be hiding out as a groom at the track. He's also been known to work as an exercise rider so we'll have cause to go through barns and to hang out to watch the horses going on and off the track."

"Great idea," said Quinn. "I'll put in a call to Gage and have Meyers mock up a fuzzy photo and stats for you to use."

"Perfect," said Grace.

"So what exactly are *we* looking for?" asked Rachel.

"Anything that sets off your spidey senses. What you experienced today is similar to the preamble that's come with previous life-threatening incidents. Our mission is to find the person or persons behind what we're calling murders." He hesitated. "These deaths have so far been ruled accidental, but we think there's more to them. Unfortunately, we haven't been able to prove anything after the fact, so now we're trying to anticipate an occurrence and nail the perpetrators in the act."

"Well." Rachel nodded. "That explains it all right. Although I don't understand why I've been kept in the dark up until now."

"You may have been exposed to these people when you were undercover, which could have triggered a visceral reaction. If your memory hadn't been blocked, there was a fear that you'd give yourself away with something as simple as an elevated blood pressure. The perp could have technology on him to pick up your responses."

"What about the reactions I'm having?"

"No worries there. The nausea wouldn't register aside from the one incident in Hartley. What you think you're feeling is actually manifested in your mind and, therefore, your blood pressure, heart rate, and respiration are unaffected."

"That makes sense to me."

Quinn's smile grew. "It should. The whole project was your idea."

"Oh, well. Then I suppose it's a good thing I still like it. And I like tomorrow's plan, too. But I need to take some time to mull it over. I think I'll head up to my room. I'll see you all in the morning." She smiled at Grace and Logan. "Or I may bump into you in the night as I'm sure to be wandering while my mind chews. I don't sleep worth a damn these days, and I won't take anything like I did last night. Knocked me cold. G'night, all."

She listened for the door opening again after she'd left the room, half-expecting Quinn to follow her. Relief and disappointment warred within when he didn't. The room she'd been assigned was on the second floor, next to Quinn's room. Without hesitation, she went to their adjoining door and opened it wide. No point making him wonder if he'd be welcome.

She didn't want to sleep alone. She was beginning to feel more connected to him with every hour they spent together, and she was ready to share more than space with him. He was her husband for heaven's sake. And her body recognized him. Wanted him. She'd also wager she'd get some decent sleep, too.

But until he came upstairs, she had some thinking to get done. Needed to work out the finer points of what the four of them had been discussing.

Apparently, she'd had ideas about who the perpetrators were. What she hadn't asked, was the specifics of the murders. She'd have to quiz Quinn later.

In the meantime, she was going to mine those reactions she'd been having for every detail of her surroundings at the time, particularly the people and horses present. She switched her jeans and sweater for a long sleep-shirt, and encased in the warm duvet, she snuggled in for a long ponder.

When she woke up, at first there was the classic, *where am I?* Fear barely had time to take root before it was chased away by the presence of Quinn. His warm body pressed against her back, and his arm draped around her middle, holding her in place. She brought the masculine hand to her mouth, but his breathing never changed, so she let him sleep, closed her own eyes, and drifted off as though she'd never been awake.

Quinn lay perfectly still. Rachel was wrapped up in the duvet, so he couldn't feel her skin, but when she'd found his hand and kissed him, all thought had headed south. His body wanted her—hell his heart and head did, too. But the timing was all wrong. If he made love with her now, every time she looked at him tomorrow, his guts would squeeze the blood out of his brain and send it elsewhere. He couldn't afford that kind of distraction.

So instead, he kept his lower body away from her, didn't allow his hand to caress her breast, and counted backwards from a thousand. At eight-hundred and thirty, he changed tactics and thought about tomorrow's op. Ran possible complications around in his head, planned for every possible contingency.

There'd be no room for error.

CHAPTER 15

Before the morning sky began to lighten, they were up and on their way to the track in separate cars. Grace and Logan would take a roundabout route that had them approaching from the north as though coming from downtown. They'd go directly to the racing commission office and clear their investigation through the proper channels—Meyers Security had produced a whole packet of documentation regarding the man they were allegedly looking for.

Quinn and Rachel drove directly to the track, parked in the horsemen's lot, and were signed in through Security by the bloodstock agent they'd been with the day before.

Energy poured from every barn as training hours were well underway. Outside lights made eerie shadows as grooms hosed legs and stuffed bandages into wash buckets. Wheelbarrows were heaped with everything from bales of hay and stacks of feed tubs, to steaming manure. Pony-horses tied outside ate a quick breakfast while being brushed off and readied for the morning's work. Conversations were in muted tones, as though in reverence to the stillness of predawn.

Rachel inhaled deeply, enjoying the raw mix of horsey scents overlaid with industrial-strength coffee. Familiar and comfortable, even though she couldn't pull up a memory to go with it. She remembered her duty then. *Grace? Checking in. The barns are in full swing, getting ready for morning training. We just passed Barn-A, headed for C.*

They slowed at the sound of running footsteps. A young man, barely into his teens sprinted past them, yanking on a jacket as he ran. Late for work, she thought.

A pony-horse nickered softly when they approached the stocky fellow tied to the rail and already saddled, with his bridle hung over the saddle horn. Rachel stopped for a moment to rub his face while the agent went into the barn to inform the trainer of their arrival.

Within minutes, they were invited to watch the big three-year-old Quinn was considering buying. Today would be a walk-day, so his groom was replacing the stable bandages with thick, foam-lined walking boots to prevent injury if the horse's legs were bumped or banged.

The handsome gelding stood quietly while brushes were run over his coat and a comb through his mane and tail. But when the brush went to the underside of his belly, he kicked out as if to warn the groom he was too close to a private area. The boy laughed and said, "An idle threat. He'd never really hurt me, he's too kind-hearted."

"Others would purposely hurt someone?"

"Hell, yeah. I rub a chestnut filly who's a total bitch. She'd as soon plant a foot on your forehead as look at you. And only a two-year-old, so it's not like she's had a hard life and gone sour. Not like that gray bastard." He used his thumb to point toward the next stall.

The kid was chatty, so Rachel kept priming him. "He's bad?"

"Oh man, to catch the bastard you have to swing the lead shank toward him and when he lunges out and grabs it in his teeth, you snake your hand up under his jaw and grab the halter. Ain't nobody Dweezle hasn't bit at least once."

"Why would anyone keep a horse like that around if he's dangerous?"

"Fucker used to be able to run a hole in the wind. And once you've got hold of him, he's got manners."

"Was he always like this?"

"Dweezle's old. I mean like ten or something and been in a dozen different barns 'cause he's a claimer now. Gotta figure that can make a horse owly."

"Interesting. Do they ever just go bad, like somebody flipped a switch? You know, the way some people do?"

He nodded. "Once in a while, but ya always gotta figure somebody got to them."

"What do you mean?"

"Hung a beating on them, or worked 'em over with a stock prod or something."

"Isn't that illegal?"

"You bet, but ya never know what might go on when a horse is away from the track and the track police and stuff aren't around."

"Billy!"

"He poked his head out of the stall. "Yeah, boss?"

"If that horse is ready to walk, let's get him on the tow ring."

"K," he responded and grinned at Rachel. "He sounds tough, but he's a good boss. I gotta get this horse out now."

Rachel and Quinn backed away to give him room, and they watched boy and horse amble away and hang a left at the end of the barn.

The trainer pointed behind them. "He'll come around that way if you want to watch his approach. He'll make laps around the barn here for about forty-five minutes, then he'll go to the pen for a roll."

"We'll watch him for a while, then come back later, if that's all right with you," said Quinn.

"Whatever you like. I'll be at the track until the break at eight when they shut down for maintenance."

"We'll talk to you then. I'm almost certain I want to make an offer on the gelding."

"Sounds good." He slipped the bridle onto the pony, checked the girth, then climbed aboard as Quinn and Rachel left.

"I wish we could have asked him more."

"We'll go back."

"Our next stop's Barn D?"

"Yep. We'll stick to the plan as long as possible."

Grace? We're headed to Barn D now.

She was getting more comfortable about sending her thoughts out without hearing any kind of response. And like she'd been told, it would get to be a reflex after a while. What she couldn't imagine, was what it would be like on the receiving end. To have a voice come from out of nowhere when you least expect it.

Different, she realized, than the ones she heard.

At their next stop, Quinn and Rachel were settled on a bench on the outside of the shedrow so they'd be out of the way. This barn had an interior tow ring. Horses and handlers circled the inside of the barn, right in front of the stalls so space was tight. They were told horses often kicked out playfully, so people always stayed away from the outside wall as it was a danger zone.

It didn't take long to see why they'd been seated outside. A bouncy bay lifted her rear end and pounded the wooden wall with her back feet. The sound was as loud as a gunshot and Quinn's heart rate jumped for a few seconds.

Rachel snickered. "Gun-shy?"

He shook his head. "How the hell come it didn't startle you?"

Her smile widened. "Saw it coming." She tipped her head toward the walking horses. "She was on the prod, barely able to contain herself. It was only a matter of time until she took a poke at something."

He'd been looking the other way and missed the cues.

"Brace yourself, here she comes again."

Sure enough, the bay was the next around the corner, but the hot-walker had rearranged the chain on her halter so he had better control now and she didn't kick the wall on this pass.

Next out of the barn was a bay colt Quinn had looked at the morning before. But there was something off about him now. No brightness in his eyes today. No swagger in his step. And thick bandages covered his legs.

"Is there something wrong with him?" asked Quinn.

The groom nodded. "He must've taken a bad step yesterday. He's not right behind, so the vet's going over him later. I guess you don't want to buy him now."

"Well," said Quinn. "That all depends on what his problem is, and how far down his price comes." He reached out to run a hand along the sleek neck, and with ears suddenly going flat, the bay swung and snapped with lightning speed, barely missing Quinn's fingertips.

The handler jerked the shank, pulling the colt away as Quinn jumped back.

"Sorry, man, he's never done anything like that before." He kept a tight hold, backing the horse around so his hind end was safely pointed toward the barn. "It must be because he's in pain."

"Poor thing." The back of Rachel's neck tingled while she studied the agitated equine.

CHAPTER 16

They headed for the racetrack kitchen to meet the agent and were amazed at the transformation. With the track shut down for maintenance, dozens of workers had swarmed to the small building and business was brisk. But only a few people were seated. The others were departing with doughnuts, sandwiches, and coffee in hand, eating as they walked. Some obviously had orders for their barns as they carried trays of coffees and bags of food.

Quinn muttered under his breath, "Guess we stick out like sore thumbs dressed like this."

They weren't in fancy clothes, but amid a crowd of people who'd already spent several hours tending horses, their cleanliness stood out.

But the workers paid them little mind. There was the odd perusal and a friendly smile or two, but these people were pretty caught up in their own routine and not overly interested in a couple of strangers.

Until Grace and Logan walked up. They hung out near the door, and showed the paper they carried to everyone leaving the place. Word spread up the line, and there were lots of surreptitious glances and much quiet discussion among the crowd.

Rachel and Quinn sat at a table beside the window to enjoy their breakfast sandwiches and watch the show. Most notable were the expressions of relief when folks looked at the picture and shook their heads. It made Quinn think they'd anticipated a need to lie.

Rachel touched his hand. "Look who," she whispered. The groom she'd spoken with earlier was in the lineup. She smiled when he spotted her and waved before saying something to the guy behind him, who then checked her out.

"They think you're hot," said Quinn. "Should I be jealous?"

She snickered. "They're kinda cute, but I'm not into boys." When they got their orders she waved them over. "You got a minute?"

He checked his watch. "Not really. I have to help wash off a horse going out first after."

"Oh well. We should get moving too," she said as she rose and Quinn followed suit. "How's our horse doing?"

"He's all tucked in. I had time to run his bandages before I put him away, so he's finished for now. Probably napping. So you're gonna buy him?"

"We'll make an offer and see what happens," said Quinn.

"That's too bad. He's a class act and a cool horse to rub. I'll miss him."

"Will the trainer give you another in his place?"

"Sure. There's always something coming in off the farm."

She lowered her voice. "You mentioned the farm not being a good place maybe."

"Not all of them."

"Oh. One of the horses we're looking at needs to be turned out for a while. Is there a good place around here? I'd hate him to end up somewhere he'd be abused."

With a furtive look from side-to-side he said, "I've heard bad things about Hot Shot Acres. I gotta go now or I'm gonna get shit."

"Sorry we held you up. If you get in trouble, tell your boss we wanted to talk to you about the gelding we're going to make an offer on and I'm sure he'll understand. Thanks for your time." She grinned when he saluted, stuffed the rest of his sandwich in his mouth, and took off at a trot.

"Well, that was useful."

"Good work."

"The kid likes me."

"No shit."

She elbowed him and he grabbed her hand, lifted it to his mouth and bit her thumb.

"Hey."

"Have you been updating Grace?"

"About every twenty minutes or so."

"Let them know we've got some information." He spotted the trainer he wanted to talk to among the crowd milling around the track entrance. He was mounted on a stable pony, with a lead line on a horse with a jockey aboard. "Let's watch a few of these before we go back to the barn."

"Right after the break, the track is at its best and that's when horses are sent out to work. To work means the horse is going very fast, as in racing speed, and being timed by the official clockers," said Rachel. She frowned. "And why did that tidbit of information shoot out of my mouth?"

"A memory byte, I guess."

Her frown deepened. "Should that be happening?"

"I don't know. Maybe be careful, just in case. And we'll call Kelton later."

She shook her head and drew the dedicated cell from her pocket. "I can't take that chance." She pushed the button and waited.

"Kelton."

She told him what had happened and his response was quick. "I don't think it's a problem. Specific information wasn't blocked unless it was directly related to your previous experience. From the wording and the way you said it, I suspect this was something you'd read. Still, let Grace know. She may have some insight."

"So I don't need to worry every time I open my mouth."

"Absolutely."

"Thanks."

"No worries," he said and disconnected.

She smiled. "No need to watch my every word."

Quinn draped an arm around her shoulders. "That's great." He guided her to the small bank of bleacher seats where they chose the highest bench for a good view. There was no one else there. The rest of the observers, most with stop watches in hand, were stationed on a narrow strip of platform built alongside the outside rail. Everyone seemed very serious as they focused on specific horses beginning their works.

"The striped poles along the inside are distance markers." She pointed at them one at a time. "Quarter pole, Three-eighths pole, Half-mile pole. The miles are broken down into furlongs which are an eighth of a mile, so a quarter mile is two eights, or two furlongs." She grinned. "I do believe I must have studied this. I wonder what else I learned."

Quinn shook his head. "Heaven only knows."

The murmuring seeped in so insidiously that Rachel glanced over her shoulder, expecting to see people behind them. But there was no one there, and a wave of apprehension settled on her like a heavy cloak. She reached for Quinn's hand, gripped it hard, and said only, "Voices. Grace."

She directed her thoughts. *Grace! The voices are starting. We're beside where the horses go onto the track to work out. On the bleachers to the right.*

She swallowed hard. "They're very faint. Barely there."

He drew her in close, lifted her chin, and brushed her mouth with his. "I'm here, Rachel. I'll keep you safe."

"It's like the sun's dimming. Like clouds slipping over it." It only took a quick look to confirm the sky was endlessly blue. Not a cloud in sight.

Quinn pulled out his phone and set it to video. It would be perfectly normal for someone to take shots of horses from here, so he panned over the entrance, catching all the humans and horses in the area, then he pointed toward the track to record the passing horses and riders.

"Anything yet?" asked Logan as he and Grace took a seat on the bottom level.

"Nothing out of the ordinary as best we can tell," answered Quinn.

Grace's voice was low. "Fill me in silently to start. Then follow my lead."

The voices are very faint. Kind of like a television on in a nearby tack room. It's been steady since it started. Nothing's changed at all, not volume or clarity. But it seems darker out now, like clouds are blocking the sun.

Logan touched Grace's arm and pointed toward the people on the observation stand on the other side of the gateway. He nodded, then she climbed up to approach Rachel and Quinn, holding out a sheet of white paper.

"Hello," she said in a normal tone that would carry to anyone nearby. "We're looking for this young man. His family is worried about him."

They studied the photo and shook their heads.

In a very quiet voice, Grace filled them in. "We'll be speaking to horsemen over by the gap. If you need us and don't see us responding you can always give a yell." She straightened with a smile and a shrug, then joined Logan to stroll away.

Quinn continued to record everything in sight.

Apprehension crawled up Rachel's spine, and she realized the voices were a bit louder. She shivered, and Quinn slipped his arm around her as she sent a quick update to Grace.

"You okay?"

"Louder now and it's spooking me."

He pushed a button on the side of his fancy phone. "I've noted the change so we can check for changes in the video."

She nodded. "Good thinking." An odd sound made her look up, and she spotted a huge bird coasting by, as though riding the breeze. "Look," she said pointing to the sky.

"Red-tailed hawk," said Quinn. "They prey on small animals like mice, rats, and rabbits."

"Oh." She blinked a couple of times. "The voices. They're gone." *Grace! The voices are gone.*

Tension she hadn't known was there, drained from her shoulders and neck. The sensation of relief spread up and over her head as though a vice on her brain had been released. She let her eyes drift closed. "That's hard on a body." Quinn rubbed a hand up and down her back. "But now that it's over, I feel an amazing sense of security. As though all is well with the world."

"Is the sun brighter, too?"

"Gloriously so." She chuckled. "Kind of like the bone-melting relaxation that comes after a seriously amazing orgasm."

"Well then, let me know when you think you've got the strength to stand on your own."

"Okay, not that kind of bone-melting." She tipped her head toward him and frowned. "Do you miss it?"

"Stupid question."

She shrugged. "I don't remember anything about our life together. Maybe we don't have an active sex life."

Quinn couldn't help himself. Simply dropped his mouth over hers and kissed her with all the pent-up frustration he was living with and damned unhappy about. He trailed his lips over her face, tilted her head, and claimed her open mouth with serious heat. Her tongue ended his deep strokes by battling back, warring for supremacy. The hand he rested on the pulse pounding in her throat felt the groan even before the sound escaped her.

When he eased back, her eyes opened and he muttered, "We're good in bed, and every other room in the house. But it's been a while."

She nodded and swallowed hard. He noted her dilated pupils and the flush under her skin. It made him feel better to know she could be suffering, too. Small of him, but it helped all the same.

She wiped a hand across her mouth, then ran both through her hair as she sucked in a deep breath. "Bloody good thing we're already married. So, what now?"

"Find a flat surface, or hell, a broom closet, and ten minutes of privacy?"

She rolled her eyes. "I thought we were heading back to the barn."

He called the bloodstock agent and arranged to meet him at the security gate where they'd parked.

Grace, we're getting ready to leave. Will be meeting Johnson at the East gate.

Quinn's phone buzzed. It was Logan. "Hey."

"Everything okay?"

"Yeah. But we're done here. We'll meet you back at the house."

"Sounds good."

He pocketed the phone and took Rachel's hand. "I'm going to make offers on the two horses, subject to vet approval. That work for you?"

She grinned. "When they retire can we make riding horses out of them?"

"Sure."

"About the mean horse, the one they called Dweezle. I want to buy him."

Ah, his wife the soft touch. "He really doesn't fit into our project." Her face fell. "It would look all wrong if we inquired about him, but we could make arrangements to claim him under a stable name next time he runs."

The grin spread over her face and she bounced on her toes like a kid. "Thank you, thank you, thank you! I know he's awful and mean, but there was something in his eyes that got to me."

"You'll have your work cut out for you trying to win him over."

"I won't expect anything from him. I can find him a place with lots of acres to roam where he can live out his days without anyone bothering him."

"I hope he runs for a low tag."

Her expression went indignant. "You're buying horses for half a million dollars. Surely we can afford a claimer." She winked. "I *could* find a way to pay you back, I suppose."

"There are a few fantasies…"

She quirked an eyebrow, then tipped her chin toward the man standing by their car. "Too bad Johnson's waiting for us or you could tell me about them."

"This won't take long."

She laughed. "You're always wrong when you say that about sex."

He stopped and stared at her.

She put a hand over her mouth. "I don't know where that came from."

"That's twice."

Chapter 17

They'd been reviewing the video from his phone for nearly two hours when Grace came into the living room.

"Logan's doing lunch. Soup and sandwiches. Any special requests?"

"I'm a sucker for grilled cheese with tomato soup, but anything else will do just fine," said Rachel.

"I'll eat whatever he makes."

"Except you hate pea soup," said Rachel, then her eyes widened.

Quinn stared at her. "That's too many times. Twice can be chalked up to book learning, but the comment about sex and this now… I think the memory block is slipping, or eroding, or whatever it does."

She sighed. "Did you ever have that? Bits and pieces that slipped past the block?"

Grace nodded. "But they were always followed by a crippling migraine—the side effect they've managed to get rid of with sophisticated programming and chemicals being used nowadays. I thought you'd experienced nausea?"

"Only when I try to remember. But these other things sort of pop out of my mouth and I don't know where they come from."

"Yeah, you better talk to Kelton."

She pushed the button on the phone, and when the doctor answered, she explained their concerns. He said he'd consult with his team and get back to her. He also advised her to stay in the house until he had some answers.

So the four of them continued to view footage, and in the end, they'd identified twenty-two subjects that could be associated with the mystery of the murdering horses. They sent all the data, plus their conclusions, to Meyers' headquarters.

Once that was out of their hands, Logan filled them in on his part of the investigation and Rachel was gobsmacked. "You can hear other people's thoughts? Like just anyone passing by?"

He nodded.

"Ohmygod. That's so wrong." She fought the growing color she knew was soon to accompany her embarrassment. "Isn't that uncomfortable? I mean, there's stuff you shouldn't hear."

He smiled. "Lucky for me I'm able to switch off my reception, rather like a telephone. And I can also fine-tune. For instance, when we were at the track today. I opened a general channel which gives me kind of a background chatter, plus I consciously tuned into people. I do that by either looking at them and opening the pathway, or thinking about an imaginary connection."

"Just wow," she said, and hoped that meant he hadn't been able to hear her thoughts when they'd first met. And then there was the X-rated stuff this morning when she and Quinn had been in a lip-lock. "It must be embarrassing sometimes."

His mouth quirked. "I don't embarrass easy. And I'm not into voyeurism, so I tend to shut the door if I stumble into something, uh, private."

"Okay, gotta say it, did you hear me today? Were you listening to my thoughts at all?"

The grin spread across his face. "Were you having embarrassing thoughts, Rachel?"

"No. But I was seriously lusting after my husband and that wasn't meant for anyone else's ears."

Logan and Grace both laughed while Quinn simply stared at her.

"What?" she asked. "You knew you were making me crazy."

He shook his head. "You've always been able to surprise me."

"Speaking of surprises, and in the interest of full disclosure," said Grace, "I'm also telepathic with abilities similar to Logan's. But I only pick up thoughts of children, people in distress, or those directed specifically *to* me."

"Good to know. I don't think I have any confessions to make. You're all aware that I hear unidentified voices and that I have a peculiar power in my hands. What about you, Quinn? What don't we know about you? Got any superpowers?"

"Aside from my work in PTSD prevention and treatment, I seem to have a nose for suicidal patients. But I think that's instinct. I'm probably reading body language and hearing the meaning behind their words."

"How *do* you prevent PTSD?" asked Logan.

"Making sure people don't bottle up their emotions and responses to horrific situations is the biggest single key, but there are lots of other factors.

"Like?"

"Research shows that people with other means of expression fare better. Meaning, emergency workers who have families and hobbies to involve themselves when off the job do better than those without other outlets. And in the military, the extension of camaraderie and brotherhood can be an insulating factor."

"That makes sense," said Rachel.

"Extensive debriefing is another key component to healthy recovery from critical incidents."

"What about afterwards? Is there ever a cure once someone has the disorder?"

"*Cure* is a word I try to avoid. Symptoms diminish. And people learn to live with the symptoms and find ways to avoid the triggers that set them off. Plus, there are tons of successful therapies like cognitive, behavioral, chemical, and animal, as well as numerous types of support groups."

"You know," said Rachel, "Dweezle—the horse I'm going to rescue—I wonder if what he's going through is kind of like PTSD?"

Both men looked at her like she'd lost her mind, but Grace said, "Abused animals certainly have issues that could be similar to what people suffer from. And interestingly enough, there are therapy programs that hook up abused animals with people also in need of psychological assistance."

"I remember a program on TV where convicted murderers in prison were given rescue animals to rehabilitate to make them adoptable, or train them to be assistance animals. It was really amazing to see the differences in the men after they'd been working with the dogs for a while."

Rachel smiled at Quinn. "You've got lots of money, why not start up something to rescue people and animals? We could name it after the horse."

"Dweezle?" he said.

"No. The kid said his racing name was, Hopeful Horizon."

"Sounds like a perfect fit to me," said Grace.

Quinn nodded. "Can't do much until this case is wrapped up."

"You called your trainer and got the stuff in motion to claim him though, right?"

"I did, while you and Grace packed away the lunch dishes."

She marched across the room, grabbed him by the front of the shirt, and planted a noisy kiss on his lips. "Thanks." Then, she plopped into a chair and said, "Okay. So what's the next step to get the bad guys?"

"When you were hearing voices, Logan picked up some thoughts that may have been our guy."

"But," Logan qualified, "there was nothing incriminating. If you hadn't let us know the voices were happening, I wouldn't have noticed the thoughts at all."

"I wish they'd get loud enough so I could hear what they were saying."

Both men focused on Grace and she sighed.

"Okay. Might as well get this over with. Rachel, do you have any ideas about the voices themselves? About what they are? Where they come from?"

She frowned. "No. Is it important?"

"Not right now. But you need to know that when the voices get louder, that's when trouble strikes. And when it does, you have the power to change the outcome."

Rachel held out her hands. Stared at them for a few beats, then met Grace's serious gaze. "I remember how it works."

"Kelton made sure your power was undisturbed." The steadiness of Quinn's tone was as important as the words. "You'll have no trouble with it. Instinct will guide you to place your hands on either side of the victim's head and your energy will course through them to reverse the theft of life."

She nodded. "I don't feel any trepidation at the thought of doing that. So I'm good. You say when I can hear the voices clearly, that's when Death happens?"

"Usually," replied Grace. "And I have a theory about that."

Quinn's eyebrows were raised. "Are you—"

"I'm certain Rachel needs to hear my theory. I believe what you're hearing is those already dead."

"Ghosts?"

"Souls who are somehow able to communicate with you as a warning of impending death. Or perhaps they're gathering to escort someone who's about to cross over to their side."

Rachel swallowed, crossed her arms, and hugged her middle. "That's just creepy." She glanced at the others. "Are there other theories?"

"No," said Quinn, and Grace went on.

"I had the idea that if you understood the origin, perhaps you could try to communicate with one of them. Attempt to engage or draw one out to help you recognize the unidentified subject manipulating the horses. Hurting the people."

Logan piped up. "I'd wondered if maybe it was the horses trying to communicate with her."

"I'd rather that than the dead, for sure. But I'm leaning toward Grace's explanation. Creepy, but logical if the dead having voices is anything one can attach logic to."

Grace's phone buzzed, and when she checked it, her forehead creased. "I have to take this call. I'll be back in a minute."

CHAPTER 18

Quinn's lowball offers on the two horses were designed to extend the negotiations, and it worked. Both offers were countered, so they'd go back to the track in the morning, look at the horses again, and hopefully get closer to an answer in the case.

This time, the horses were going to the racetrack to train, so Rachel and Quinn grabbed coffee and tea to go, and perched upon the bleachers, waiting for the phone to ring to tell them when each was coming out. It gave them more time for general observation. And it paid off. They'd just decided to head back to the kitchen for more warm drinks when the voices started.

Rachel grabbed Quinn's arm. "Voices, they're louder. I'm going to update Grace, then try to talk to them." She let Grace know what was going on, noted Quinn had his phone out to record all the action in the area, *and* that he kept a hand on her knee. As an anchor for her, she supposed. She touched his hand and smiled. Then closed her eyes and concentrated on trying to communicate.

You want me to hear you. Speak up so I can understand what you're saying. Nothing changed. *Come on, you guys. You obviously want me to know you're there, why not speak out?* The sound level increased as though they were arguing among themselves. *Do you have a leader? Or at least a spokesman? If you all keep yammering, how am I supposed to hear your message? Or is that it? Do you really want the person to die and join you?*

She waited again, listening to what now seemed like an ocean's ebb and flow. If nothing else, she was having an effect on them. But nothing changed. No single voice rose above the others.

Fine. You don't really want to talk to me, so to hell with you. And she began to hum. It took a minute, but she finally recognized the song and nearly laughed out loud. *When The Saints Come Marching In* was a hilarious choice considering.

She noted the look Quinn tossed her way. She shrugged and muttered, "Winging it. Who knows what'll work?"

His return expression was a mix of amusement and concern. But she couldn't be thinking about that right now because the voices in her head had increased their volume once again.

She stopped humming. *Okay, so now you want to communicate? Tell me what's going on?*

She flipped over her wrist and watched the second hand on her watch sweep around two full times.

Guess not.

She drained the cold dregs of her tea.

"They're being difficult," she told Quinn, and went back to humming. She watched horses galloping by. Admired a pony horse patiently plodding alongside an excited filly dancing onto the track.

And a breath caught in her throat when a voice rose out from the others in her head.

Tick, tock, it's nearly time. Closer to the rail.

Heart thumping against her ribs, she stood and pulled Quinn with her toward the track.

Tell me where to look. Who's doing this?

You have to look. You have to see. Tick, tock, watch the clock.

She repeated the words out loud to Quinn and they both studied the area around them. Horses came and went from the track, people watched, talked to each other, nothing looked out of order.

Tell me more!

Tick, tock, watch the clock. A rider joins us if you're slow.

She spun around, concentrated on the scene. Spotted a clock on the side of the tiny building. A man stood inside. She knew he was the identifier—took the names of the intended workers and relayed the information to the clockers on the roof of the grandstand.

Her gaze swung to where they were positioned. Could barely make out the open windows. Her gut twisted at the thought of someone falling from there. The injuries would be far beyond anything she could fix. So she went back to her visual search of the area close to her.

The mix of horses and people had thinned somewhat. Only a handful of spectators lingered. Two racehorses walked off the track accompanied by ponies, and as they came closer, something in the atmosphere changed. The rider on the pinto stopped to wait for a woman who stepped into his path, and it happened.

The other pony and horse swung around them and the horse beside the pinto lifted off all four feet in a huge buck, kicked out, and connected with a sickening thud. The movement had been lightning fast and it took a moment to assimilate what had happened. By then, the pony rider who'd been kicked in the chest, tumbled to the ground and landed in a heap.

Horses and people scattered, and Rachel sprinted into the melee. As did the first aid attendant shouting, "Don't move him!"

She knelt in the classic position to stabilize his neck. With a hand on either side of his head, she said to the fellow dropping to his knees beside her, "I'm trained in first aid. I'll look after the C-spine for you."

"Do not die," she whispered in the fallen man's ear as she drove energy through her hands. "Death comes up empty this time. Live, dammit."

"Keep very still," the attendant told her as he went through the steps. "He's not breathing. Do you know how to do a jaw-thrust with your fingers?"

"Affirmative," she said as she used her fingertips to push against the base of the jaw and force it forward to open the airway—even though she knew it wasn't blocked. "Airway's open."

"Good." The first aider was searching for a pulse as Rachel shoved another blast of energy into the downed man and was rewarded almost instantly with a low groan, and the rise and fall of his chest. The pulse became visible in his throat.

She stayed in position until the ambulance arrived and the paramedic team took over, then she backed away until Quinn's arms came around her. Warmed by his breath on her cheek and the words, "You did good," she went limp.

"I need to sit down."

"Can you make it to the car? I'll borrow a golf cart if you want."

Grace!

"Right here, sweetie, how can I help?" Grace and Logan had come up behind them.

"I'm okay. I was just going to update you. We're headed for the car before my legs give out."

"Looks like we have a solid lead. So we'll stay and work it for a while, then meet you at the house."

"Nice of you to say so," said Quinn, completely out of context. "She's always the first one to jump in and help out."

Rachel was quick to catch on. "Thanks. I was a first aid attendant years ago, and know it's always good to have a second pair of hands, so I never hesitate." She looked around to see who was listening in, who was too close for comfort.

A young man, maybe in his early twenties, was hanging about, watching them.

"We should get going now. Good luck with your search." They left Grace and Logan and made their way to the car without looking back.

"Voices are gone?"

She nodded. "They crowded and got really loud until I touched the guy, then they disappeared as though a switch was flicked. His heart had stopped. Probably from the direct blow of the hooves. But I don't think the ER will find much wrong with him now besides some broken ribs."

They said little else as they walked, and he kept an arm around her until they got to the car.

Grace, in the car and headed home.

She let her head rest against the seatback and ran it all around in her head, trying to see if there was something she'd missed. "You got it all on your phone, didn't you?"

He nodded. "But it's going to be crappy when I was running after you."

"Points for trying." She smiled. "So, do you have a theory?"

"About?"

"Any of it."

"Well," he said, easing onto the interstate. "I agree with Grace about the voices. I think they are probably from the other side. And as for what's happening, that looked like an accident to me today. If there's a mechanism being used on horses to create a specific action, it must be incredibly precise. That target, the man's chest, left little room for error. Not many horses kick out the same way exactly, not every time at least. So compared to the other possibly faux accidents, this one didn't look to me like a set-up."

"So you think it was a coincidence, a fluke that I was there when a heart was stopped?"

He shook his head. "That's the hard part. It didn't look like a set-up, but I don't believe in coincidence either. So I'm my very own hung jury."

"Maybe the video will give us something more to work with."

"Hopefully. Meantime, do you want me to swing into a drive-through or something on the way back?"

"Sounds good. The healing hands suck all my energy."

Three hours later, Grace and Logan joined them in the den where they were snuggled on the couch, watching an old movie.

"Well, don't you two look cozy," said Grace with a smile.

Rachel blinked a few times. "I must have drifted off."

"Saving lives takes a lot out of a person," Logan said. "Many people with comparable skills are bedridden after expending the kind of energy you do."

"There are other people with my kind of weirdness?"

"I thought you knew about ETCETERA?"

She shrugged. "I don't really know much. At least, not that I remember."

"ETC's comprised of people with extra-ordinary talents, skills, and senses, ranging from elite scientists to ghost-busters and fortune-tellers, to put it in layman's terms."

"Why don't you and Grace belong to them? With your telepathic abilities, aren't you, like, one of them?"

Grace replied, "We've chosen to create an independent entity because it suits us, and leaves us open to work with whoever we choose. But, getting back to what happened today, we have news."

Rachel leaned forward. "Is it over?"

Grace shook her head. "No. But we've got a good idea who's behind it. Now we need some solid evidence. With the help of the racing commission, the horse was quarantined. Then we stayed with him until he was picked up by ETCETERA. The story is that he pulled up bad, as in lame, and has been turned out to rehab. We had him taken from his barn to the vet hospital by equine ambulance to lend credibility to the story. It took some fancy footwork, and thank heavens he was a plain brown horse with no markings, because ETCETERA shipped a lookalike into the clinic, and shipped him out."

"Wow. Impressive."

"Teamwork. Meyers found the replacement, ETCETERA provided the transport."

"They have a horse van?"

"They acquired one on short notice. They're connected to all kinds of law enforcement and probably borrowed a mounted squad transport and did a fast facelift. It doesn't take much to slap on a quick seal. It works like static labeling."

"So the horse that did the kicking has been taken where?"

"To a state quarantine facility. He'll be gone over for implants or devices of any kind. But it will take time because portable equipment will have to be used and that's slow, tedious work. And, I figure he'll have to have regular breaks between exams so he doesn't get overly stressed by the procedures and the amount of time he's required to stay still."

"Wouldn't it be easier to knock him out and get it done quickly?" asked Quinn.

"It would, but we'd need the owner's permission and the FBI as well as IRIA would rather not explain what they were doing."

"So we continue to wait," said Rachel. "Do you expect them to find anything?"

"It seems like a stretch to me. It was a perfectly normal situation and lots of horses would have kicked out at a horse going around his offside."

"It was the way he lifted his head and looked away that had my curiosity. He never seemed to focus on the horse behind him. I thought he lifted up and kicked out blindly."

Logan's eyebrows lifted. "You've got footage? Let's see it."

Quinn lifted the converter and pointed it at the television. "I've only got the one angle, but there's a good view of the incident."

They watched it silently once, twice, and a third time. Then Logan said, "I agree. He's focused on something in front of him, and maybe to the left. But his ears never go back to listen behind him, and they never do flatten in meanness. And that woman deliberately walks in between, as though her goal was to draw the rider's attention from the horses and force the other to go around.

"She's not working alone."

"A killing team. Can you get an ID on her?"

Logan looked up from his laptop with a grin. "Already did. She's a transient worker. Goes from track to track. Never stays long with an outfit. Been kicked off the grounds of two tracks for smoking in barns. She used to gallop, but got grounded after a positive drug test. If you ask me, that's the perfect sort of patsy to pay to stroll from point A to point B when instructed."

"How much you want to bet she doesn't show up for work tomorrow."

CHAPTER 19

Rachel woke up alone. Again. And it was getting annoying. She slid her hand over the sheets and found them cold where he'd been. It matched the chill in her soul. The emptiness in her heart.

With a sigh she heaved herself out from under the duvet and stalked into the bathroom. She had to shake it off. He said *she'd* made the rule before the hypnosis and chemical implants were started. Didn't make it any easier to take his rejection. And deep inside, she suspected that if she'd made such a stipulation, something wasn't right between them.

A kick in the gut feeling went with wondering if he'd leave her after the case was closed. Her reflection in the mirror showed fear in eyes gone dark.

"Think about the way he touches you when other people are around. There's a sense of possession, of ownership. And not in a bad way. The moves are so natural between us if we don't think about it. That's good. Remember the good parts." She grimaced. "And get your ass into the shower."

Once under the hot spray, she thought about relieving the ache. But it wouldn't help her any. It was the emotional pressure, not the physical one she was finding so difficult to live with.

She'd have to have a word with herself about stupid rules when she was whole again and not merely a part of herself. But it wasn't like there was an opportunity for a do-over, and that just sucked.

She rinsed the shampoo out of her hair and finished up quickly. Eager now to not be alone with her thoughts. She needed a distraction and needed it now. Wrapped up in a luxurious bath sheet, she bundled her hair into a smaller towel, and headed for her bag and fresh clothes.

Catching a movement out of the corner of her eye, Rachel whipped around with a scream lodged in her throat. Grace was sitting by the window. "You scared the freaking life out of me!"

She smiled. "You don't look any worse for wear. Did you work it all out?"

"Work what out?"

"Whatever you were going on about in there. For a minute, I thought maybe you weren't alone, but I'd left Quinn downstairs making breakfast so I guessed you were talking to yourself."

"God, I wish he'd been in there with me."

Grace's smile widened. "You had the whole night together. Must be part bunny."

Pffft. "I feel like one, but he's not playing, and it's beginning to get to me."

"No sex?"

"I apparently put a clause in the ground rules before the hypnosis."

"Hmmm."

"What the hell does that mean?"

"Hey. Don't be snarling at me. You did this to yourself. I guess you have to trust there was a reason. One you believed in at the time."

"But I've learned no sex with the man I love is way harder on the heart than sleeping alone. Were we okay?" She swallowed hard when Grace didn't answer. "I'm terrified he's going to walk away from me when this is done."

Grace went to her, wrapped her up in loving arms. "It's going to be okay, Rachel. But you need to say this stuff to him. Let him know you're scared because you can't remember. Let him help you through the worry."

"You won't tell me anything."

"I'll tell you this. The man has faith in you. Through the hard stuff, I've seen him believe. Trust him, trust yourself, and believe in love." With a final squeeze she went back to the chair. "I suggest you get some clothes on. Federal agents are meeting with us in less than an hour to discuss the results of the necropsy."

"Who died?"

"The horse they took into quarantine yesterday for testing. Dropped dead in his stall last night."

"Holy shit."

"That about sums it up." She flicked her hand in a hurry-up motion. "Go. Get dressed."

Rachel tipped her head at Grace. She'd dug her heels in. "What are you doing, guarding me?"

"Nope, hiding. So the men don't expect me to help in the kitchen."

***

They rushed through eating and had finished cleaning up when the agents arrived.

Once everyone was settled around the dining room table, Foley began to read from the report he'd brought along, but Quinn stopped him. "Give us the short, layman's version."

"Sure. The horse was poisoned. The bureau's confiscated all security tapes from the facility, plus they're having the trailer swept for evidence. The racing commission is conducting a random—" he held up his hands to do finger quotes "—shakedown on six barns as we speak. One of which is where this horse had been stabled."

"It's unusual for a horse to drop dead. Poisons generally make them very sick and death is long and painful," Rachel said, then clapped her hand over her mouth, and shrugged. "Sorry, I have an odd and sometimes obnoxious recall button for random information." And now she wondered why she'd have known or studied such facts. She rubbed her wrist.

"This poison was a combination of drugs which have particular reactions to each other. The FBI lab came up with the formula only last month after a series of suspicious deaths on a cruise ship. Due to the nature and variety of the deaths, the FBI feared the ship's passengers had been chosen as lab rats. All those who died had ordered room service at some point in their stay, but neither death, nor illness had occurred immediately after ingesting their meals. Each victim had also used the ship's gym, the spa, and had played the slots. As—you can imagine—had many others."

"I haven't heard anything about this incident, and I'm kept in some pretty exclusive loops," said Logan. "I'm assuming the case is still open and under investigation?"

Foley nodded. "A correct assumption. But because Homeland Security has taken control, very little information has been shared with any other agency. I should also note, we had to fight not to lose this case with the horses to them. They've agreed to shadow for the time being, and *did* sanction the release of information regarding the poisoning components to ETCETERA and Meyers. Three of the six ingredients are everyday items. Sugar-free chewing gum, table salt, and rubbing alcohol. Apparently, the other long-name components will not kill without the basic three."

"Bet the research guys were scratching their heads until it was figured out," said Quinn.

"That's an understatement. I'm sure the shout of eureka was heard across a bucket load of states when they discovered the formula."

"So," said Rachel. "When they were doing the necropsy, did they find anything else? Something that could make the horse kick at that particular person at the exactly the right moment?"

"That, my friends, is exactly why I'm here. The standard procedures would have missed it, but with your heads-up, we sent a special team along, complete with their own high-tech detection equipment and a couple of machines on loan from ETCETERA." The gleam in his eye gave away his excitement. "The nanotechnology department has taken over the items. A minute capsule found at the crest of the neck, imbedded among the roots of the mane, and what appears to be two fine wires the team removed from the heels of his hind feet."

"Why are you frowning, Rachel?"

"I don't understand why they killed the horse. What you found would have gone undiscovered if there hadn't been a necropsy."

Foley nodded. "Speculation by our group is that the poisoning was already started and when you had the horse taken away, it couldn't be stopped. Or, perhaps he was unwittingly given the last element and the death was accidental. Perhaps they'd expected to retrieve the capsule and that backfired."

Nodding, Rachel said, "I'd bet they're pissed to lose what's likely a freaking expensive piece of equipment ."

"Oh yeah, and I'm betting there won't be any mysterious deaths by horse for a while. They'll have to get new hardware," said Foley.

"No."

They all looked at Rachel and Quinn asked, "Why not?"

"I'd wager they've got more than one of those microscopic gadgets and more than one person to operate it. I think they'll hit on the other side of the country next. And it will be soon."

"Premonition?" asked Foley.

She frowned. "Not sure, but it's coming from my gut."

"Okay, so we have to figure out how many people can access a horse, *and* try to predict where trouble will strike."

"Way too many possibilities for a focused investigation."

Rachel tucked her legs up under her. "We can work with what we know." She leaned forward. "I'm betting they're using horses with a predisposition. An animal that normally bucks and kicks would be easier to set up than one of those four-feet-on-the-ground placid types."

"Like Dweezle, the horse you want," added Quinn. "They say he's gotten more and more sour and mean over the years. It wouldn't surprise anyone if he killed."

"Right," said Rachel. "But that's not going to happen because I'm going to fix him. Take the bad out of his life. Give him some kindness."

"What if he's been implanted and they're intending to use him?"

She stared at him.

"You hadn't thought of that."

"No."

God, he hated jerking the rug from under her.

"Maybe we can find a way to buy him right away, instead of waiting to claim him," she said hopefully.

Grace put her hand on Rachel's arm. "We have to remember our goal."

"I know. I wasn't thinking."

"I'm buying a horse from the same trainer," said Quinn. "So I may ask about Dweezle and be straight up about it. I'll tell him my wife has a soft heart and wants to see him made happy by retiring him to our farm."

A lump formed in her throat and she swallowed hard. No freaking wonder she loved the man. It was so hard to sit there and not fling herself into his arms the way she longed to.

"Okay, let's get back to the planning list so we can stop these freaks before somebody else dies," said Grace.

Rachel nodded. "There's a new track called Adeleen Downs southeast of San Francisco. And I have no idea why, but I believe that's where they'll strike next. Some horses will be more vulnerable than others. The big-name outfits have great security, never use transient or day workers etcetera. And some even do their own shipping, so there's not much opportunity for tampering. We eliminate those."

Foley was scribbling on his notepad while Quinn's fingers flew over the keyboard of his laptop.

"We need to involve the racing commission at each track," said Logan. "Makes it easier to access inside information. Ask them to name the ten horses on their grounds that are most likely to hurt someone. Trust me, these people will have the answers."

The meeting went on for most of the morning, and by the time it was done, they'd worked out Plan A and a couple of backups. A dozen more people were added to the team. They would spread throughout the west, infiltrating every single racetrack, but concentrate their efforts on Adeleen. They would stop the insanity.

CHAPTER 20

Rachel changed the radio station again, sat back, and tried to get into the music, but found herself staring out the side window reading billboards.

"Talk to me," said Quinn.

"About what?"

"Anything to engage your mind. Your fidgeting is driving me nuts."

She went still. Slowly turned to stare at him. "Well excuse me for breathing."

He banged the heel of his hand against the steering wheel. "I know you're wound up and feel trapped right now. I get it. But there's nothing we can do to get there any faster in this traffic."

"Did you ever play those travel games when you were a kid—like alphabet, or I spy, or—"

"No. Tell me about the refuge you want to build. Details. Imagine you have unlimited funds and a huge chunk of land. What will it look like?"

She leaned back in her seat and inhaled slowly. Exhaled. "White fences. Miles and miles of white fences. Keeping them painted and looking good will be a chore that can be shared by many and will help with a sense of pride. And of course, most of the paddocks and fields will have double fencing so we never have to worry who's where."

"So it sounds like you'd have colts and stallions?"

"We'd cut the colts, but sometimes old stallions need homes. I wouldn't want to castrate the older guys, but we may have to invest in a few donkeys so they have company. I hate seeing stallions turned out alone. I feel so bad for them. People don't seem to get that horses are herd animals."

"I agree. Okay, you've got fenced fields and paddocks. What else?"

"We have to have barns, of course."

"What if you're in a climate that doesn't really need a barn?"

She tipped her head to one side. "Hadn't thought of that. But even in that case, we'd need at least one barn. A dozen or so stalls for when horses come from the track or wherever and need to have stall rest or need rehabbing. Besides that, without a barn, there's no place to do the rehabbing of people—them working with the horses. So I've circled around to thinking we need a couple good-sized barns."

"Okay. What do they look like? Stalls down both sides? In the middle?"

"First of all, they have to be made of cinderblock so they're as fireproof as possible."

"I've seen burned out cinder-block barns."

"We'll have a super sprinkler system, and no storage of flammables like bedding and hay."

"Good planning. Now the stalls."

"I like the standard set-up with stalls down both sides and a middle alleyway wide enough to drive a truck through. And they'll be big. None of that ten-by-ten crap. I think fourteen-by-fourteen would be best."

"That's big enough for a foaling stall. Are you going to raise foals there?"

She shook her head. "Nope. I won't be creating new lives in a world where there's already lots more horses than homes. But we have to be prepared to possibly rescue a mare that's in foal. Besides, anything on stall rest needs room. I'd have a couple we could take a wall out of to make a fourteen by twenty-eight. That would be the next step up from stall rest, before moving to turnout paddocks."

He nodded. "Sounds like a good plan. What else do you need in the barns?"

"Well, can't have feed storage. That'll have to be a separate building. But there will be a tack and equipment room, a wash-rack and a couple sets of crossties for grooming. Every stall will have two doors, one on the inside, and one on the outside. A dutch door so the top can be opened. Housebound horses will be able to at least see the outdoors."

"Okay, you've provided for the horses. How about the people. Houses? Dorms?"

"And cottages. A mix of all three. Dorms will be apartment-like. With a bedroom, bathroom, and a living area and some cooking facilities. But there will also be a community kitchen and a dining room where meals will be provided."

"So you'll have staff."

"In the beginning, but I want it to become a cooperative kind of place where people who arrive seeking refuge end up working there, helping each other. Everyone will have to work eventually, to earn their keep."

"Makes sense. But you'll need management on the grounds to maintain order."

"Oh, for sure. It'll be years before it's looking after itself."

"So are you sticking to only horses and people?"

She smiled. "Well, I wouldn't mind having other animals. Barn cats are a necessity, and there's bound to be a horse that needs a goat, and well, then there's dogs needing rescue all the time too. So I suppose it will be a rescue center, with the emphasis being my horses and your people."

"Will you live there?"

She swung to stare at him and her gut churned. "I don't know. What about you?"

He spared her a quick look, but his expression was unreadable.

She swallowed hard. "Is our marriage in trouble?"

He flexed his fingers on the steering wheel, glanced over his left shoulder and shot into the next lane.

"Quinn?"

"Not a good time for this discussion."

The traffic was nasty, and they were approaching a stretch of highway thick with directional signs so perhaps it was, as he said, bad timing. But it felt like evasion. Well, God hates a coward. "Do you love me?"

"Christ, Rachel, what do you think?"

"I think you're avoiding answering my questions and you're scaring the shit out of me."

He said nothing, but the muscles in his jaw were moving.

She sighed. "In case you're interested, I love you. I know there's almost nothing about us in my memory, or at least my retrievable memory. But in spite of that, I'm attracted to you and I love you and sleeping beside you every night and being ignored is making me crazy. I'd rather sleep alone than have you not touch me." She fastened her gaze on the passing scenery. "There. I've finally said it out loud and I'm glad. Even if it pisses you off."

"It thoroughly pisses me off that we're doing this in a moving car on a freaking interstate during rush hour."

"Sorry. I have a feeling timing has never been my strongest suit."

"Nail on the head."

"Am I right about anything else?"

"Rachel. Can you leave it be for ten lousy minutes?" he asked, changing lanes again.

"Ten minutes is going to feel like an hour. But okay." She pushed buttons on the radio until she found a news channel. They listened to the headlines, a traffic report, weather then sports, and the whole thing was starting all over again when they rolled up to the gates of a private airfield.

"Stay here," he said. She watched him march across to a lockbox, punch numbers on the keypad. When it opened, he unlocked the gate and jumped back in to drive through. Once they were inside and the gate locked, he drove them to a small hangar with a big padlock on the door.

"Crew should be here shortly."

"Your ten minutes are up."

Quinn's leash snapped. He reached with both hands, grabbed the lapels of her jacket and jerked her over to meet his mouth as it came down with fury and frustration.

He plundered with tongue, teeth, and aggravation, and she met him stroke for stroke and bite for bite, wrapping her hands around his wrists to hang on.

He wanted his hands on her, to slide them under her sweater, spread his fingers across her back and pull her in. He wanted her hands on him, her fingers gripping the back of his neck, sliding down to his chest.

But the sound of a vehicle and one last thread of sanity stopped him. Kept him from dragging her into his lap and tearing at her clothes.

He set her back, sucked in a strangled breath. Their pilot was already unlocking the hangar. "Time for us to go." He went to the trunk, took his time gathering their bags, and reminded himself she'd been the one to leave.

Rachel leaned her head against the seat and let her eyes close. Waited for the thudding of her heart to slow, and for her scrambled brain cells to get their shit together.

Watching Quinn take their bags into the hangar, her gaze locked onto his very fine ass and she sighed. If she was this hot for the man, how could there possibly be anything wrong between them? It wasn't like he didn't want her.

She studied his face as he strode back to the car. Jaw set and eyes hard, that mouth was still sexy as hell. He opened her door with a jerk. She didn't move. Wasn't sure she could.

"We need to get going. Now."

She tipped her head back and stared into his eyes. "You never answered my question."

"The hell I didn't. Come on, Rachel, we don't have time for this crap right now."

Her nostrils flared. "Do. You. Love. Me."

"Yes."

She shook her head. "Why do I hear a silent 'but'?"

The look on his face was far from friendly as he held his hand out to her. "Now, Rachel. You got your answer and we need to get a move on."

She climbed out, pushing past him, and marched into the hangar, not stopping until she was beside the helicopter.

Frustration and fear warred within her. She could feel the space between them, despite the explosive chemistry. It was as though he didn't want to want her and that scared her spitless. How could she fight that? How did a woman go about making him want to stay with her without knowing what had driven the wedge between them?

She sighed. According to Quinn and Grace, she'd made the conscious decision to have her memories temporarily erased. So she had no choice now but to trust the plan and get through the mission before she could unravel the mystery of their relationship.

By the time he set their luggage by her feet, she'd gotten a grip. She met his steady look with one of her own. "All I need is a promise that whatever's wrong between us will be visited with honesty and candor once this mission is finished. Then I'll drop the subject and you can relax."

"You have my word," he said, and switched his attention to the pilot standing on his other side. "I'll get Rachel and the bags inside, then I'll be ready to help you push this thing out."

The man dressed in all black held out a gloved hand. "I'm Richard, ma'am."

She shook his hand. "Rachel. Nice to meet you."

He opened the door and she jumped onto the stout platform and climbed into one of the helo's rear seats.

Once they were airborne, she settled in and tried to concentrate on the details of the incident they'd witnessed at the track. Somewhere deep in her gut, she knew she'd experienced something similar. The pungent combination of horse manure, dirt, and death. The rising nausea warned her she was attempting to resurrect a blocked memory. She had to let it go, work with the facts instead.

Their hours of reviewing the footage had netted a few conclusions. The woman passing between the horses had glanced at the clock several times first, then stepped out with purpose as though a planted distraction. One that caused a simultaneous redirection of attention and pathways.

Unfortunately, none of the video showed them a suspect. No button pusher was seen. And there had to be one. Rachel's thoughts kept going upwards. But they'd reviewed images from the grandstand cameras and netted no information.

And if the trigger had been pushed from an apartment in the area, they'd never get a lead on it. She sighed and turned her thoughts to the horses. The ones Quinn had put offers on. Would they get to save the old gelding? It was so wrong for a horse like that to still be at the track, forced to grind out a living. She'd researched and found out he'd once been a stake horse, at the top of his game. As a three-year-old, he'd earned over a million dollars, and now, at ten, he was running once a week as a bottom claimer, for purses of twenty-five hundred dollars instead of two hundred and fifty thousand.

She'd made one last visit to his stall. Stood far enough away to avoid his gnashing teeth and promised him she's find a way to get him out of there. He'd stared at her as though she was crazy to be standing there. On a parting shot, she'd promised no one would ever call him Dweezle once she got him away from the track. They'd choose a new name, one that suited his new life, one he liked.

Her thoughts wandered to the rescue farm she'd built in her mind. There would be tons of work to do if it was ever to become real. But she believed Quinn would make sure she had the money to do it. Even if she didn't have the man himself.

Circled right back to it, she had. But luckily, they were descending now to the California coast, and she'd have more to do than worry.

Rachel and Quinn met the others at a pretty house overlooking the bay. It was old, but clearly well-loved, with siding the color of sumptuous buttercream, and gingerbread trim in candy-apple red.

They settled into the living room for their briefing. Grace and Logan sharing an overstuffed loveseat, while she and Logan each sunk into an armchair.

When Rachel continued to rub at the back of her neck, Quinn asked her what was wrong.

"Something must have bit me. There's a weird tickling."

Grace's gaze narrowed. "When did it start?"

"Don't know for sure. I only noticed when I was unpacking my bag."

"What exactly does it feel like?"

She thought about it for a minute. "Kind of like fingertips teasing."

Grace nodded. "How do you feel about ghosts, Rachel?"

She shrugged. "I hadn't given them much thought until lately. When it was pointed out that my voices might actually be ghosts or souls or something from a different plane of existence, I started to wonder about the possibilities, but... You think ghosts are playing with me now? Tickling me to get my attention?"

Grace frowned. "I suspect you've been recognized by the other side as a possible conduit. But you say you've never had any encounters."

Rachel rubbed the back of her neck. "Not that I know of. And as for the time period that's been hidden from me, who knows?"

"Quinn?" Grace asked. "You were there for Kelton's interviews before the procedure. Was there anything I missed you would interpret as a possible contact attempt?"

He shook his head. "The voices were a big issue for her, but they were always described as numerous. There was never an incident of a single one. As for physical, that area wasn't really explored."

Grace left her chair and circled the room slowly with her hands held out from her sides. The others watched silently. After one full loop, she went to stand behind Rachel's chair. "Has anything changed? Was there any interruption in the sensation?"

"It speeds up when you're close to me."

"Using my energy. I felt cold, which is often considered an indication of a ghostly presence."

"So what does all this mean? And what do I do about it?"

"I think we need to consult with Kelton and maybe have him send an agent with experience in this field." Grace sat back down. "Then I'm going to do some research on the house to see if I can get a handle on who may be wanting your attention."

Rachel wandered to the window and took in the view. "If we're not going to the track until tomorrow, could we play tourist and go to Fisherman's Wharf for supper? I'd love to poke in the shops and stuff."

"Probably not a good idea tonight, Rachel," said Logan. "Could you wait until tomorrow? We need to lay low tonight. We'll order in, your choice."

She came back to the table. "Chinatown is famous right? Let's have Chinese."

CHAPTER 21

The steely gray and ominous morning sky was a good fit for how Rachel felt. Sleep had not been her friend. She'd lain awake for hours, hoping Quinn would come to bed, but eventually she'd caught on. Her gut-purging comments had kept him away. She'd said she'd rather sleep alone, and he'd granted her that wish. Stupid man.

But she hadn't been alone. Her neck-tickling friend had stayed with her. And that wasn't exactly conducive to sleep either. So now she needed caffeine and hoped the house was stocked with decent tea. Because she needed gallons of it.

Grace was in the kitchen already, and the pungent smell of grapefruit filled the air. Rachel wrinkled her nose at the two bowls with pink-centered halves. "Great, Logan likes them too? No wonder he's perfect for you."

Grace laughed. "He's only eating grapefruit today because it's my turn to make breakfast."

"You call that breakfast?"

"I'll make toast, too."

"Wow. Going all out. But he knew your aversion to cooking before you got married, right?"

"Yep."

"So he made his bed. Speaking of beds, Quinn never slept in mine last night." Rachel was barely surprised the words had fallen from her mouth.

"Problems?"

She sighed. "Yeah. I feel really close to him sometimes, but mostly it's like he's holding me at arm's length. I finally badgered him into saying he loved me yesterday. But it wasn't the magic pill I'd hoped for."

Grace leaned back against the counter. "You've been sleeping together up until last night?"

Rachel hefted herself up on the counter. "Well, yes, but no. He's been coming to bed after I fall asleep and leaving before I wake up." She met Grace's direct gaze. "Yesterday, I told him it was killing me that he wouldn't touch me and that I'd rather sleep alone than feel so lonely beside him, and I guess he took me at my word. He never came to bed at all."

"I'd say you shot yourself in the foot. Men are literal. You can't expect them to"—she finger quoted—"get the underlying message."

"Hmph."

At that moment, Quinn walked through the door.

Grace grinned and said, "Good morning, Quinn. There was apparently a miscommunication between you two yesterday. And by the look of things, you didn't sleep any better than she did. So before we set out on this morning's mission, I suggest you talk it out." Her eyebrows lowered and the smile disappeared. "And I do mean talk. That means you both contribute truthfully and come to some conclusions." She pushed away from the counter. "Meanwhile, Logan and I are having breakfast in bed. We'll see you two in about an hour."

Before she got out the door, Rachel said, "I thought you were taking him some toast, too?"

"Damn." Grace backed up, opened the fridge and looked inside. "This'll make up for it," she said as she tucked a can of whipped cream under her arm and left with a grin.

"Well," said Rachel as the door swung closed. "Why didn't you sleep with me last night?"

He blinked like a confused owl. "You said—" he paused for effect "—you'd rather sleep alone."

"Oh for crying out loud." She thumped a hand on the granite. "You had to know what I meant by that."

"You want me to touch you and I can't right now. Not that way. So I took the alternative and stayed away from you."

"Why can't you touch me? You've admitted that you love me. And I saw the evidence yesterday when you got out of the car. You weren't unaffected by that kiss."

"You made me. . ." Quinn paced the length of the breakfast bar and spun to stare at her. "We agreed there'd be no sex until your memory was back and we'd had a chance to work out what happened between us before. You said you were depending on me to hold up my end of the bargain because you'd have no memory of it."

She reached out to touch him, but he jerked away and strode to the window, stared out over the city.

"Do you have any idea how fucking hard it is to hold up my end? I want to touch you. I want to crawl inside you every fucking night and it's all I can do to stop myself." He spun to face her. "I can only take so much, Rachel, and you've got me at the end of my rope."

"What happened between us?"

"You left me."

"I love you. Why would I leave?"

He shook his head. "That's the question of the century."

Her skin chilled. "Okay. I'll back off."

"You can't. We need to appear natural together until the end of this mission. So in public, I'll still be attentive and you'll still respond appropriately."

"And in private?"

"I'm a man of my word. We'll both have to live with that."

"I may need to ask you to kiss me again, just so I can stay in character. Is that unfair of me?"

"Yes and no, as I fully intend to kiss you in public."

She nodded. "Will you share a bed with me tonight, or is that pushing too hard?"

"I'd rather sleep with you and not touch you than sleep alone."

Her smile was tentative. "I get that now." She hopped off the counter and went to him. Touched his arm. "I'm sorry this is so hard on you. I'd only been thinking of myself." She shrugged. "I guess that was the case when I made you agree to the terms as well." She tipped her head. "I may find there are things I don't like about myself when my memory is restored. Food for thought."

He touched her face. "Remember one thing." He waited until her eyes met his. "I do love you and I do want to stay married to you."

She rubbed a hand over the place where her heart ached. "Good. That's good. But now I'm going to make some breakfast."

He chuckled. "Not your strong suit. May I suggest toast and coffee?"

She shrugged. "Probably a good idea because I don't remember being much of a cook. Grace and I always had that in common. Although I don't think I'd put whipped cream on grapefruit."

"That's not where the whipped cream is going to go. At least that's not where you'd put it," he said with a grin.

She blinked. "I think I'm going to like getting my memory back."

***

The day unfolded slowly. They wouldn't be going to the track until the afternoon. For the races. Logan had picked up the thoughts of someone planning an incident during the third race.

But he hadn't been able to identify the connections. So the four of them would go to the track and see what they could dig up. All the other alphabet groups and agencies would have boots on the ground as well.

It was decided that Grace and Logan would maintain the cover of searching for a missing person. They'd work the grandstand area, searching among race-goers, trying to ferret out the conspirators—and it appeared there were three.

Quinn and Rachel started in the backstretch. Most barns frowned upon visitors during the races, but arrangements had been made for them to view some runners from the first and second races, which would give them a legitimate reason to be in the barn area.

There were few people out and about, and only one or two horses visible when they arrived, the quiet a drastic contrast to mornings at the track. But horses were either resting or being prepared for a race. Preparation that could include standing in boots or buckets filled with ice, or under blankets containing heat coils or magnets. Most often, all food was taken away, as running on a full stomach was not a good thing.

But nerves needed to be quieted, and usually, a nibble of hay would help. Rachel was pleased to see hay nets at every stall in a barn where she knew at least four horses were entered in today's races. She personally hated seeing food withheld. Horses were grazers, meant to continuously eat. Nibble at least.

She sighed. Letting go wasn't easy. Despite her memories being erased, her belief system was intact. As was her inner cop. The one who made her let go of things she had no control over. She could stop Death, but couldn't make sure people treated animals well or even fairly. At least ninety-nine percent of horses at racetracks were well-treated. Some better than the people caring for them. But there was always someone who looked at the fabulous equine and only saw an item. A thing to be owned and operated as they chose.

She recalled a horse she'd met at Paradise, Grace's country estate. An old Arab mare who'd known abuse. Rachel had spent months earning her trust and building her up to a point where she was no longer afraid of strangers. She'd been a show horse with an impressive record, but had endured several bad riders and, eventually, pain from lameness had driven her to lash out at anyone coming near her with a saddle.

Quinn's hand was on her back. Rubbing, and his words finally found their way into her consciousness.

She looked up. "Sorry, lost in thought."

"You'd gone somewhere unpleasant."

She nodded and rubbed her wrist. "I'm back now. Who will we see next?"

"A two-year-old colt. Today will be his first start, but he's had very impressive works. He got the bullet last week. Went six furlongs in twelve."

"Bullet?"

"Fastest work of any horse going that distance, that day. A minute and twelve seconds."

"They must want a bundle."

"He has no paper behind him." She must have looked confused because he then explained, "His breeding is unimpressive, so that helps. But it's a gamble. Before he runs, they want a hundred grand. If he wins the price doubles."

"What if he loses?"

"Depends on how far he's beat and the circumstances."

"If you buy him, will he still run today?"

"That's up to me. I can have him scratched as his ownership has changed. Or I can promise to buy him when the race is over and his current connections will, of course, keep any earnings."

"What will you do?"

"If I want him, I'll have him scratched. No point risking an injury, as my agreement to purchase won't include insurance."

"Is that how we're going to prevent the accident that's scheduled?"

"Possibly."

The colt's trainer, a tall blond woman, met them at the entrance to Barn B, and introductions were quickly taken care of.

She led them to the stall of a quiet chestnut. His groom sat on a footlocker across the shedrow. "Bob, put a shank on Red and take him out the end so Quinn and Rachel can have a look at him, please."

"You want boots on him?"

"Just bell boots," she said then turned to Quinn. "He's in to run today, so I'd like to keep this short. And if he starts to jack around, Bob will bring him right back in so he doesn't spread a shoe, or hurt himself."

"I understand completely."

They watched the colt's action at a walk, observed his good nature as he was asked to stand still, then circle around toward them.

Once back inside the barn, Quinn ran his hands down the chestnut's legs and smiled. "Cold and tight. As expected. I have two more colts to look at, but this one's on my short list," he told the trainer.

"You've only got an hour and a half to make your decision, so we'll put him away and wait to hear from you."

"I'll call you, one way or the other."

"Appreciate that," she said as she closed the screen after the groom had led the horse back into his stall.

Quinn and Rachel moved on to Barn G where they viewed the other colts. These two belonged to the same person, had better breeding than the chestnut they'd already looked at, but their workout times hadn't been nearly as impressive. And the price was the same.

"Why would you consider these over the other one?" asked Rachel.

"Because they have potential for the breeding shed. In other words, if they're successful on the track, they can go on to be sires and, therefore, continue generating revenue. The other colt hasn't got the kind of breeding necessary for that second career, so what he earns on the track is all he's got."

She frowned. "But can't they have other careers?"

"Nothing as lucrative as the breeding shed. If all three colts are completely equal as racehorses, the first would get half as much per foal and probably half the mares the first two would get."

"What kind of money are we talking?"

"That's really hard to speculate. But just for argument, if the first one stood for a ten thousand dollar stud fee, the others would stand for maybe twenty-five thousand. So if they each produced fifty foals a year, Red could generate five hundred thousand dollars. The bay colts could bring in over a million each."

"I bet the chestnut's babies would run better."

He studied her for a minute. "Why do you say that?"

"I don't know for sure. There's something about him. A presence. And his attitude. He's special."

"And the others?"

"They're average. The one with the white socks is cocky, and I like that, but he's got no substance. The other guy, the plain bay, is more serious, maybe even unhappy or depressed."

Quinn's smile grew. "What a fabulous assessment. We'll buy the chestnut colt." He used his cell and informed the trainer he'd be making an offer, then started the process with the bloodstock agent who'd set up the viewings.

"So, now what?" asked Rachel.

"Now we make like we're looking for the bloodstock agent and walk to the far end of the stable area and back. It'll kill some time if nothing else.

Quinn kept his hands off Rachel as they walked. He needed her to be receptive to the universe around her without his interference. But it was hard because what he wanted most of all was to be touching her. For not only the personal connection, but to help ground her in case of the voices. In case Death was lingering, waiting and hungry.

CHAPTER 22

Having picked up no connections in the barn area, Quinn and Rachel decided to take their search front-side —to the grandstand area. They hiked the quarter mile to the security gate where horsemen could pass directly into the public area, stopping to confirm their day passes would allow them to reenter the barn area.

Barely into the shadow of the grandstand, she tipped her head up and sniffed the air. "Fried onions. The smell I associate with going to the fair as a kid."

"Mine's hotdogs."

"There was always a hint of them behind the fried onion scent because they were on the same grill right beside the entrance gate. We'd go through a bunch of the exhibits in the morning, then have onion-smothered hotdogs for lunch."

"Now that's something I didn't know about you. I thought you didn't like onions."

She shivered. "Hate 'em raw, or cooked with stuff, but fried as a topping at the fair? Yum. Add a hefty sprinkle of parmesan cheese and I'll crawl all over you to get to it." She was nearly licking her lips thinking about it.

With a grin Quinn said, "I think we need to find a concession stand. I'm dying to watch you eat something that messy. And I bet you make awesome sounds."

"*I* think you're having the kind of perverted thoughts your mother would cuff you for."

As they followed the scent of food, Quinn spotted a dozen familiar faces. Some from ETCETERA, some from Meyers Security, and even Caroline from Paradise. He wondered if her husband, Sergei, was there as well. He'd never met the man—an independent agent, often utilized by Interpol, ETCETERA, and the FBI, among other agencies.

A tiny woman dressed in a swirly pink skirt nipped in front of them as they approached the food stand. She ordered a chili dog, and while it was being made, she said to Rachel, "I call it a good luck mutt, ya know?"

Rachel grinned. Her mom used to call them mutts, too. "What makes it good luck?"

"I always cash after I've had my daily fix."

"Cash?"

She put her hand on Rachel's arm. "You're new to racing, aren't you?"

"Sort of."

"When someone says they've cashed, it means they cashed a gamble. Had a ticket on the winning horse, or in my case one that finishes first or second because I always bet to place." She winked at Quinn. "You're with her, right?" At his nod she went on. "All the good ones are taken."

When her food order slid onto the counter, she picked it up, then flashed a brilliant smile. "It's going to be a great day. I can feel it in my bones and hear the whispers in my head. I'm Jen by the way. Good luck and see ya around."

Quinn and Rachel stared after her.

"Order, ma'am? Sir?"

Rachel shook off the odd feeling that she should know the woman walking away from them. "Uh, hotdog with fried onions?"

He shook his head. "Toppings list." He tapped the board beside him. "Fried onions at the burger stand down the way," he said pointing.

Just as well. The flutter in her tummy didn't feel like hunger. "Do you have root beer?"

He nodded.

"Make that two," Quinn said as he rested a hand on her shoulder.

A peculiar pain stabbed along her jaw, and she rubbed the area as a single murmuring voice slipped in.

"What's wrong?"

"What do you mean?"

He squeezed lightly and her tight shoulder muscles objected. "Where'd this sudden tension come from?"

"A single voice with a chant-like rhythm. I can't make out the words."

"Let Grace know."

"This morning we established a link which means Grace has access to all my thoughts. Updating isn't necessary."

"Excellent."

"So, now what do we do?"

"We stick with the plan. Avoid the paddock, and find a good spot on the fence to watch the first race."

***

Surrounded by crowd noise while the first race ran, more voices had crept up on her unnoticed. She stiffened and the hand Quinn rested at the base of her neck tightened. "They're very low still."

"Do you have a gut feeling on this one?"

"It's off. If the voices are coming from a world beyond, this group doesn't seem to have a leader. There's no stronger voice than the others, and they seem agitated, like they're all trying to talk at the same time."

"We have someone on the team with the ability to connect with the world of the dead but not gone. Let's see what they can come up with."

Scanning the area, she noticed their new friend, Jen clutching the fence as though needing the support. Her eyes were closed.

Rachel nudged Quinn and tipped her head toward the other woman.

He frowned as they moved closer. "She seems unwell," he said.

Rachel touched Jen's arm and a jolt of electricity shot clear to her shoulder. Her fingers tingled. "I think I've found our medium."

Rachel stared at the woman who'd yet to open her eyes. Was this the reason the voices were low? Was Jen diffusing them? How exactly did this stuff work? She really wanted a chance to ask questions, but understood that now wasn't the time.

The murmuring suddenly increased in volume.

Jen's eyes popped open and stared directly into Rachel's. She smiled slightly before holding up her program and shrugging. "I missed that one. My horse ran fourth."

"Did you bet a lot?"

"My usual two dollars. I guess I'd better get to the paddock and check out the next bunch. Maybe one will give me the wink this time." Her smile was brighter now. "You should come and watch. The horse people always look so serious that it can be comical. And there's always at least one horse that does something naughty," she said as she walked away.

Rachel looked over her shoulder at Quinn. "I think we should go with her."

"Sure, nothing to watch here besides tractors smoothing things out for the next race."

Quinn took Rachel's hand and rubbed his thumb across her wrist. "Let's go then."

The saddling paddock was an odd mixture of flash and calm. True enough, all the people seemed very serious, and tension hung over the area. Rachel grinned as a strapping chestnut danced and kicked out playfully.

But catching sight of a quiet gray in the last stall set her heart skittering. The horse appeared to be calm and quiet, but his ears were flat on his head and his nostrils pinched half-closed as the valet approached with the jockey's tack.

Rachel squeezed Quinn's hand. "Look at the gray."

"Not a happy camper."

"I'm getting a bad feeling about this. He's all bunched up, ready to explode or—" Her breath caught as the horse went airborne, all four feet off the ground, kicking straight out with the hinds.

The sound of dozens of people sucking in a shocked breath reverberated in her head. "Someone's going to get hurt."

"Voices?"

She glanced around, worried that he'd spoken too loud, but there was no one close by. It was as though the angry horse had made people take a step back. "No, it's just obvious. Where did Jen go?"

"I don't know,"

She quickly scanned the crowd, but no Jen. Her attention returned to the groom trying to get the gray back under control.

The valet and trainer again stepped into position on either side of the horse. But as the beast's muscles began to bunch, the valet backed away, shaking his head, and the trainer walked over to speak with him.

The horse was led from the stall to circle the paddock while the discussion continued.

When he was put back into the stall, one of the lead ponies was ridden over to stand in front of him. Another man stepped in to snap a second lead to the gray's bridle.

With a man on each side and the horse and rider in front, the horse didn't seem any happier.

Because the valet had layered the saddle and pads together, he was able to approach and slide the tack into place in one move while keeping all the space he could between him and the angry equine. When the trainer passed the girth under the beast's belly, Rachel held her breath.

"Just the over-girth now," she muttered. The tension in the air was beginning to dissipate, but the horse was no less agitated, and when the trainer and valet were both leaning down to pass the last strap underneath him, it happened.

With a huge roar, the gray leapt forward, tearing away from the handlers, crashing into the pony-horse, and kicking both trainer and valet. Still roaring and kicking out, he catapulted away from the mess he'd made and plowed a path through horses and handlers until he reached the out-gate where he stood, snorting and pawing at the ground.

Two first aid attendants who'd been hovering close to the action dove for the men on the ground.

They were both moving and making sounds that confirmed there'd been no death, but the voices continued to murmur in the background of Rachel's thoughts. She shook out of Quinn's grasp and hopped the fence.

"I'm an off-duty paramedic. Can I maintain C-spine for you?" Not waiting for an answer, she knelt at the head of the trainer, rested her elbows on the ground, and gently placed a hand over each of his ears.

The female paramedic's gaze settled on Rachel's hand position, then nodded. "Don't move."

Quinn had followed her. "I'm trained as well," he said as he knelt and did the same for the valet.

As the attendants went about assessing their patients, setting up oxygen, and calling for the ambulance, Rachel whispered to Quinn, "I don't think either of them need me. But I couldn't take a chance. Where's the horse?"

"The outriders took him away."

Rachel noticed Jen standing at the fence watching them. She gave a discreet thumbs-up, then tipped her head toward the exit. She was leaving? That didn't make any sense, but then again, what did?

When Grace and Logan appeared at the exit gate, Rachel understood. They edged through the crowd to stand behind Jen before the security team started moving people along. The crowd thinned as the other horses were mounted and led out to the track for the second race.

An ambulance was driven into the saddling paddock and once the onboard paramedics took over and C-collars were put on the two injured men, Rachel and Quinn were thanked for their help and they stepped away.

A security officer escorted them back to the public area, and shook their hands. "The track management would like to thank you for your assistance by offering you a table in the dining terrace."

The man's thick accent was niggling at the back of Rachel's mind. "Thanks, but we're probably not staying long." She nodded toward an old man hobbling from the paddock area towards the track. "I'd be grateful if you could extend the invitation to that gentleman instead."

After a long look, the security guard nodded. "I will make the arrangements, Rachel." His smile was warm.

"I know you."

"Another lifetime." He approached the elderly man and they heard him say, "Sir, may I see your program?"

When it was handed over he opened it to the back and grinned. "You have the lucky number, and today's prize is an afternoon in the dining terrace, all expenses paid." As they headed toward the elevators he said, "Oh, I have to keep this program for the records, but a new one, plus a racing form and a morning odds sheet will be brought to your table."

Quinn tugged her in tight and kissed the top of her head. "That was a nice thing to do."

She shrugged. "It was one of those weird things. The words were coming out of my mouth without any thought. As though I was being coached, repeating words that were given to me."

"Did you feel another presence?"

"No. But I felt like the guard's voice, his accent should mean something to me."

"He's married to someone you know. And yes, that makes him part of the team working on this project."

Her smile came with a look of relief. "It feels good to be a bit grounded by that. Thanks."

When they reached the rail, once again, Jen was there waiting for them. "Those guys okay?"

"They've been transported to hospital, but it looks like a lucky day for both of them. The valet's flack-jacket protected him so he's likely only got a couple cracked ribs, and the trainer took it in the guts so there's a good chance several layers of fat protected him."

"I wonder what happened to the horse. Or what will happen to him. If people will treat him badly now?"

Quinn caught the look on Rachel's face and guessed what would be coming. He held up a finger and reached for his cell phone before stepping away.

CHAPTER 23

From her rooftop vantage point, Caroline scanned the paved apron between the track and grandstand as it became crowded with people. Nearly time for the second race. Jen was maintaining her position at the rail, as was another team member, and Sergei had moved to the gate at the winner's circle. If help or a diversion were needed, there were plenty of people to act, with more of the team scattered throughout.

Focusing now on the starting gate, she studied the horses as the field of nine were loaded in and quickly dispatched, bounding out as one, and settling into stride.

Cameras and officials would be concentrating on the race, so she looked elsewhere. She spotted Grace and Logan watching from the small stand along the backstretch, zoomed in and realized their attention wasn't on the race either. They were watching a couple of men having an arm-waving discussion near the backstretch gate and there was a woman standing several feet away.

Caroline switched glasses and powered in to see that the men were apparently having a discussion about the female who appeared to be about fifteen. When she began to ease away, the older man said something that had her stopping in her tracks.

Caroline smiled. That was a reaction to a parent if she'd ever seen one. And to confirm just that, the older man stalked toward the girl, then passed her and she fell into step behind him, making some hand gestures Caroline interpreted as, "I've got to go with him, but I'll be back."

It seemed like a fairly normal interaction until a third man slipped out from behind a barn and had an intense discussion with the young man who did lots of shrugging and pointing.

Grace, there's more going on there than meets the eye.

Affirmative, this one gave us a tingle too. Logan's setting up eyes and ears on all three parties. We'll make sure the girl is safe, and figure out what the other two guys are up to.

Meanwhile, the race had ended without incident, and Sergei had vanished from his position, but Quinn and Rachel were still at the rail, chatting now with Jen.

Caroline called to Grace again. *Anything new from the railbirds?*

No voices, but a growing certainty that something is off about the next race. They'll go to the paddock again to watch the saddling, then if we don't have something concrete to handle, we'll call it before they load in the gate. The tractor's been rigged to stall out, and the race won't be allowed to run if the gate can't be moved off the track.

Ingenious.

Why, thanks. I'll keep you posted.

Caroline searched for Sergei, but not getting a visual, went for their personal telepathic pathway.

Where are you?

Leaving the tunnel, headed for the stable gate.

She spotted him now, walking behind the horse that had won the race and was now headed for the test barn. Urine and blood samples would be taken before he could return to his own barn. *You up to date on the backstretch thing?*

Hang on. He put a hand up as though to rub his head signaling he was getting a transmission through his ear bud.

A line of horses and handlers were now coming toward him from the barn area, and he stepped out of the way. Leaning against the fence, he studied everyone who passed.

When a familiar figure in a blue suit ambled past him, his eyes narrowed, and he lifted his arm to cough into his sleeve—a move to cover speaking into his Bluetooth.

Caroline followed the man with her high powered binoculars and tried to read his lips while he spoke to the groom leading a sideways-dancing bay colt. The young man then used both hands on the reins to steer the colt, and the rest of his trip to the paddock was uneventful.

Sergei walked behind the last horse in the line, and disappeared when they went under the grandstand.

Caroline swung her attention back to the apron area, but Jen, Rachel and Quinn were gone, as were the other team members.

***

Rachel stood back, not wanting to go too close to the saddling area this time. The voices had intensified. "It's building."

"If you focus on the horses one at a time, can you figure out which one is connected to what's going on?" Quinn asked.

She frowned but gave it a go, starting with number one and working through them methodically. First the horse, then each person connected. Nothing happened until she focused on number six. The voices grew louder and she felt pressure around her heart. She gripped Quinn's hand and whispered, "The six horse."

He was a plain bay, as were two others in the race. Quinn studied the program. "Blucher Hall. He's by the same sire as the two and the seven, and he's got the same jockey as was supposed to ride the gray in the last race."

"Where's the chestnut colt we looked at?"

"I bought him so he's been scratched."

She flashed a grin. "Awesome. How about the crazy gray? Any word on him?"

"The commission has him in the quarantine barn. We'll go see him after this race."

"Any chance we can buy him?"

His frown was nearly comical. "We already did."

Rachel grabbed the front of his shirt and dragged his mouth down to hers for a kiss, then whispered, "Thanks. I'll pay you back."

"I'll see that you do." He grinned and reached to drag her back for another kiss—and the world went black.

Quinn's grip turned to steel when she went limp in his hands and he eased her to the ground.

Jen dropped to her knees at his side and laid a hand on Rachel's forehead. "Grace is on her way," she whispered.

***

Grace knelt beside Rachel, pushing Quinn out of her way. "What the hell happened?"

"No warning. She went out like someone hit her off-switch."

Running her hands over Rachel without touching her took about ten seconds before Grace said loud enough for anyone to hear, "Simple heat stroke. Or perhaps low blood sugar. Her vitals are good."

Sergei appeared with a wheelchair, but Rachel was still unconscious, so he simply picked her up and carried her to the first aid room with the others in tow.

Grace updated Caroline and the rest of the team. They were going to Red Alert. The race would be called off in the last moments before the horses were to load in the starting gate. It would play out as an equipment malfunction to delay the race, and after ten minutes, the commission vet would recommend calling the race off as there would be several horses showing signs of tying up—lactic acid buildup that tightened muscles to the point the animal would be unable to move.

With that part of the op handled, Grace focused on Rachel and the paramedics working on her. She needed them gone. *Caroline. I need to get rid of the medics. Can you get me ten minutes?*

Consider it done.

A dispatch came across their portable radios. "Three-five-alpha."

"Three-five-alpha," the paramedic responded.

"Three-five-alpha. Take in Barn D, south side, code three for a forty-year-old male, kicked in the chest, difficulty breathing."

"Three-five-alpha copies Barn D, south side."

"We'll have to split up," he said to his partner. "You stay here, I'll go."

Grace touched his arm. "Sergei here says he's a trained paramedic, as is the lady's husband, so you two go ahead and we'll stay here to wait for the doctor."

He nodded and the two took off with their jump kits.

Grace stepped to Rachel's side and laid a hand on her forehead. "Rachel, I need you to wake up now."

Rachel groaned and Quinn stepped forward, but Logan put a hand on his arm. "Leave her to it." He led Quinn to an alcove at the side of the room.

"What's she doing?"

"Reaching past the barriers. Your lady is fine. She blacked out from extra-sensory overload. It's a fairly common phenomenon, and Grace knows exactly how to fix it. She just needs a bit of space, so we'll hang over here and leave her to work her magic."

Quinn shook his head. "It's fucking hard not knowing what to do, how to help her."

"You don't have to tell me. When Grace and I first met, there was an incident similar to this, and I felt so fucking helpless I wanted to pound something."

"Obviously you got past it."

He shook his head. "Not for a very long time. Grace is an extremely private woman and didn't want to share what she was going through with me or anyone else."

"Well, that certainly sounds familiar. Rachel ran off to protect me and my family."

"If she's anything like Grace, and I believe she is, you've got your work cut out for you. She won't be an easy woman to live with, but oh what a ride you'll have."

"It must be amazing to connect with your wife telepathically. Rachel and I don't have that."

He chuckled. "It is amazing. But it's something we both lived with for a long time before we met, so it's just a part of everyday life for us. No different than understanding the human mind is for you. At least you're equipped to understand Rachel and the basis of her fears."

"Not really. What she needs is a clear explanation of what she's hearing and I think she'll get that from the experts at

ETCETERA. I know she's afraid they'll treat her like a lab rat—"

The sound Logan made was an interesting mix of laugh, snort, and groan. "Funny, that was one of Grace's problems too."

"But she got over it, right?"

"To an extent. But she stays guarded with ETC."

"Her sister is married to the head man."

"Head of the psi department. Sara's a psychologist herself. But Grace remains cautious. We both work for ETCETERA on individual cases and contracts, but we've never become a part of the organization."

"Rachel's concern is that, in order to test her ability to bring life back to the dead, they'll have to kill, and that sends her over the edge."

"No small wonder. It'd freak me out, too. I suggest you, or she, set specific parameters for what goes on at ETC. Set goals and boundaries. Always be there, or if you can't be, have either Grace or me with her as her advocate so she never has to fear what will happen next."

Quinn tipped his head. "I can hear her voice."

"She's been awake for a couple of minutes. And she's fine." He hesitated. "Grace says it's time to leave."

***

Their mission was over. They'd been debriefed by the FBI and Homeland Security, then been politely told to go away. HS had taken three people into custody at the track, and another sixteen across the country. The evil had been stopped and, for that, Rachel was grateful and more than happy to leave it all behind.

Jen had cornered her after the debrief and talked to her about the voices. Confirmed that she'd heard them as well, and they were definitely from the other side, whatever that meant.

On the drive to the airport, Rachel stayed quiet. She'd gotten over the embarrassment of her collapse, but now had to face returning to the ranch in Texas. A place she apparently knew well, although she had no memory of it. There would be people there she was supposed to recognize.

As they drew alongside a small, sleek jet, she chewed the inside of her cheek. Quinn had withdrawn. Was keeping his distance and she didn't know why.

Throughout Grace's explanation of the extra-sensory overload, he'd remained silent, and done nothing more than nod. How had he felt about what happened, who she was inside—with her peculiar wiring and all?

She sighed. For a psychologist, he didn't seem to be a very good communicator.

"Shouldn't I be going to ETCETERA first, to have my memories restored?"

"You don't want to go home with me?"

"That's not what I said. I'd rather face your family and people who know me *after* my memories are back. It's awkward when people know more about me than I do—at least when I'm the subject in question. I could go with Grace."

"Termination of your programming won't happen for three more days and I see no point sitting in the underground of ETC headquarters when we could be home instead."

"Why can't I be—" she searched for a word, "—undone, dehypnotized or whatever, now?"

His jaw clenched and his knuckles went white where he gripped the door handle.

Quinn shouldered the pressure of the secrets and the weight didn't sit well. He'd made a decision on her behalf, in spite of Grace's warning. He'd thought it was a shot in the dark, and Kelton's agreement had surprised him. Now he felt cornered.

"Will it be that big a deal, Rachel? What's a couple more days?"

She heaved a sigh. "I want normal back. I want a past without holes in it. I want to get on with our relationship, and you won't let that happen until I have my memory back."

"We can work on the here and now without the interference of the past."

Tipping her head sideways, she said, "I thought you didn't want to do that."

"I think I was wrong."

"Really?" Her smile started slowly and warmed him as it grew. "Not many men say those words. I don't suppose you'd add an 'I think you were right' to that?"

"How about, you may have been right so I'd like to explore the possibilities?"

Her eyes crinkled as her smile deepened and his heart did a slow roll. "What did you have in mind?"

"How would you feel about a couple of days alone, just the two of us?"

"Where?"

CHAPTER 24

Four hours later, Rachel was watching a sailboat glide over the Pacific as it passed between islands. She glanced at Quinn kicked back in the recliner beside hers. "I could stay right here in this chair for a month."

His eyebrows went up.

"What?"

"The logistics would be a bit of a problem," he said.

With a wave of her hand, she dismissed his concern. "Okay, so I'd have to get up to do a few things, but seriously, I wouldn't have a problem staying here for a long time. Besides this view, all I'd need would be food. And nothing fancy. Toast and coffee. Maybe throw in a case of Girl Scout cookies and a box of apples, and I'd be good to go."

He grimaced. "I'm a carnivore. My family made their fortune on beef. I'd have to throw a steak on the grill every other day. Or at least a hamburger. And I know you wouldn't survive without your baked potatoes."

Something fluttered near her heart. Tears welled and spilled over. Tracked down her cheeks. She closed her eyes. Tried to make them stop, but they kept coming and she didn't have any idea why.

"Rachel?"

When she refused to answer, he lifted her up, and she melted against him.

"Baby, what's wrong?"

She looked away.

Quinn, having no clue what had upset her, simply sat and curled her onto his lap. Snuggled her in and held on, waiting for the silent storm to pass. Kelton had warned him she might have issues once the op was over and she'd be without direction. He should have taken her back to ETC headquarters. He'd selfishly wanted this time with her. Without the past in their way. To build strength in their bond. Strength they'd need to get them through the hard times to come.

Trying to comfort her through whatever had descended on her, he rubbed her back and rained gentle kisses over her forehead, across her eyebrows, down the bridge of her nose. When she tipped her head, their lips met, melded, and the sweetness twisted in him, squeezed his heart, and undid him from the inside out.

Her lips parted. Her tongue slid softly toward his, and the dance began.

He'd intended to work on their relationship without giving in to the chemistry between them, but this *was* them. It was real and it was the here and now. With her arms somehow around his neck, his hands slid up, cupped her face, and she continued to strain toward him.

He tucked her face into his throat and groaned. "Oh, God, Rachel. You undo me."

"Mmmmm." She nuzzled and tasted his skin. Nipped at his ear.

"I will always love you. No matter what."

Rachel leaned back and studied him. "No matter what. That's an odd thing to say. It's as though you expect things to change, to go badly. Is it our past that's going to be a hurdle or something else?" When he shook his head, she said, "I think I have a right to know, Quinn. It's my life, too."

"I've painted us into a corner here. You're flying blind and I've got one wing tied behind my back. I wonder if we should continue and let our hearts lead us, or if we should be getting our asses to ETC as quickly as possible."

"You make it sound like everything is up to you, but I get to have a say in this. Even if I don't have all the facts."

"Don't you see? That's the problem. You're sailing along with only a part of yourself having an opinion."

She shoved off his lap and stood in front of him with her hands on her hips. "Tell me. Tell me what it is I can't remember. I'll believe you."

"It's not my place to mess with your mind."

"Fuck that, Quinn. It's my life and my mind. Tell me!"

He pushed past her to stand at the wide window, his back to her. "You left me. Walked away from our marriage. Tossed our vows to the wind and disappeared."

She sat on the edge of a chair. "Why? There had to be a reason why."

"When you came back, two years later, you said you'd left to protect me and my family. You thought the people dying around you was somehow your fault and you feared for the rest of us."

"That makes a weird kind of sense to me."

He spun and stared at her. "You'd think that? Even now without any background information, you'd think that way."

"My heart says I love you. That means I'd do anything to protect you."

"I don't want your protection. I want a wife."

"Well then, that's going to be a problem. Even without my memories, I know I'm the type of person to want to protect the people I love." She frowned. "And I don't think I like the tone you use when you say *wife*. What, exactly, does that word mean to you?"

He scrubbed at his face. "What we had. I want it back. A woman who loves me, who accepts my love for her, a partner in life. One I can talk to. One I can spend a great deal of time with, saying nothing at all. Someone I know will be there no matter what."

"I was all of that for how long, Quinn?"

"From the minute we met until you walked away from the hospital."

"What hospital? Why was I there?"

He strode to the kitchen. "You want coffee?"

"Sure." She'd wait. For as long as it damned well took. He could stall all he wanted because she'd simply outwait him. She'd occupy herself watching the waves, the boats, the clouds riding a brilliant blue sky.

He set a steaming mug and a handful of chocolate chip cookies onto the table beside her.

She sipped the sweet creamy coffee and munched cookies. "Start anywhere you like."

Carefully placing his mug on the table between them, he plopped into the chair and pushed back until the footrest came up. "My sister's ten-year-old son was in our back yard playing with Chance, the greyhound you'd rescued a few months earlier. You heard voices. Something drew you outside, and you found Dhillon on the ground without a pulse. You laid your hands on him and restarted his heart. You called my sister—Dhillon's mom who's also our resident helo pilot. She picked you both up and flew you to the hospital. Once he was stabilized and she was busy filling out paperwork, you wrote me a note, left it in the bird, and walked out of our lives. You disappeared, and even my family, famous for their investigative skills, couldn't find you."

"How did I manage to evade them?"

His mouth twisted. "You got fake ID, became a master at disguise, and kept moving."

"But I obviously came back."

"You'd stumbled onto the work of someone using horses to kill people."

"The mission we were just on."

"Exactly, which is why your memory was temporarily erased."

She nodded and pushed a few cookie crumbs into a pile on the table. "You're afraid that now the mission is over I'll disappear again."

"I have no way of knowing if you still think you're connected to the deaths you prevent by actually causing them in some way. Until your memories are restored, *you* don't even know what you believe. I'd hoped to spend this couple of days building some comfort between us. Some trust."

She couldn't sit still. She stood and prowled the room. Then, with her back to the window, she faced him. "I give you my word, Quinn, I won't vanish on you."

He sat forward in the chair, elbows on his knees, and his dark gaze steady on hers. "You gave me your word before and it meant nothing. Without talking to me, telling me what you feared, you up and left. Blindsided me." He swallowed hard. "You didn't trust me then so how can I trust you now?"

Well, that hurt. She rubbed her knuckles on her chest while she ran what he'd said around in her head and came up with a question. "In hindsight, did I give you any indication of my fears? Did I try to talk to you? Or would I have gone to Grace because she was my person before I met you? Did you see anything in retrospect?"

"Not a fucking thing."

"Hmm. Well, I certainly owe you an apology because I am extremely sorry for the pain I brought you," she said, wrapping her arms around her middle. "As for an explanation, well, that will have to wait until I have the memories to draw from. And I can only hope there's something that accounts for such bad behavior."

He feigned a snort. "Trust me, you've done all the apologizing and explaining you need to do. All of it was before the procedure."

"But you haven't forgiven me."

"That will take some time."

"What do we do until then, Quinn? Avoid contact, or resume a physical relationship?"

His eyebrows went up. "That's black and white."

"Well it sounds to me like you're not interested in the many shades of gray in between. So I'm cutting to the chase because my heart, in spite of what you think, wants nothing more than you. But my mind sees a problem with that."

"Amen."

She swallowed the lump in her throat and followed her instincts. Went to him, straddled his lap, and held his face between her hands. "I'm taking a risk here, Quinn. I hope I don't regret it." Her mouth settled on his to tease. To urge a response in spite of him.

Quinn held out for as long as he could, wallowing in the softness and love that came through her fingertips, her mouth, and the breath they shared. She was laying her soul bare and he had no defense. The groan came from somewhere deep inside him when he cupped the back of her head, angled his mouth for better access, and delved with his tongue.

When they finally came up for air, nothing had changed, but everything had. Rachel was reassured of the romance between them, while he fought the doubts plaguing him like a slow rolling tape of his mistakes with her.

Now she'd expect things to be normal between them. Fixed. But there was still the trust issue. Would she flee again? In a New York minute if she thought it was what she had to do to protect him and his family. And there lay the problem. The same one that started the whole mess.

He blinked. Wait a minute. Was her fear of being like her mother the root of the problem?

He stroked down her back, then locked his arms around her. "Rachel?"

She nuzzled into his neck. "Hmm?"

"We still need to talk."

"I know. But does it have to be now?"

"I think so."

"How do I do what you want, Quinn? How do I convince you to trust me?"

"We take it back to the beginning and find our way through."

"The beginning."

"Let's start with your mom."

She swallowed hard and tried to wrench away, but he held her firm. "First, we'll consider schizophrenia. How much do you really know about it?"

Her reaction was to go limp, and give him a clinical description in a monotone voice. "Diagnosis of schizophrenia involves ruling out other mental disorders or physical conditions. In addition, there must be an evaluation of symptoms over a period of at least one month. At least one symptom such as delusions, hallucinations, and/or disorganized speech, thinking and/or behavior must be present for a month, with some level of disturbance being observed over six months."

He nodded. "Absolutely correct. But how about in your own words? A layman's interpretation."

"As my mother did, I hear voices no one else hears. Auditory hallucinations perhaps? Am I delusional? The power to heal, is it real or imagined?" She shrugged. "And while medication can effectively control the symptoms, the drugs sometimes cause horrible side effects. This is why so many go off their meds, and the other reason is that they feel well and see no point in continuing to have their minds altered by drugs."

"That's a good thumbnail. Tell me now, how you see your mother's suicide and its connection to her illness." He felt the sudden jump in her heart rate and she sucked in a big breath, let it out slowly.

"Let the words spill, baby," he said as he rubbed her back.

"She said she couldn't take it anymore. Couldn't fight the voices. She was exhausted, never slept because they wouldn't let her rest. She'd pace the floor at night, mumbling, not making sense, and crying because they wouldn't stop. I tried to help her, to sit with her, talk to her, but mine was just one more voice and she'd beg me to stop. To stop the others, too. I'd try to get her to take the meds, but the voices told her they were poison and I was trying to kill her and she'd scream at me to leave her alone. She'd cry and say she knew I'd never hurt her, and then she'd hug me and I could feel her heart beating so horribly fast. Her skin would be hot and red or cold and white."

When she hesitated and shivered, he reached for a blanket from the back of the chair and tucked it around her, wrapping her up tighter in his arms.

"Once, I put her pills in her tea—she always asked for tea when she was cold—and she went to sleep. But the next night, she screamed at me, said I'd tried to kill her yet again. It was so hard to know what to do. We lived in a duplex, and the lady next door called the police a couple of times. That's when she'd be taken to the nuthouse, as she called it, and I'd go into foster care. And when she'd get out and I could go home, she'd be on meds and life would be good for a while. My mom was so cool and nice, and cooked special meals and made fun lunches with notes inside, sewed me pretty dresses, and she'd be singing all the time. But then the home visits would stop, and she'd say she was well and didn't need to take the meds anymore. They gave her diarrhea and other side effects. So it would all begin again."

When she went quiet, Quinn held on, stroked her back, her hair, pressed his lips to her forehead and stayed silent, waiting on her to continue. She'd never shared any of this with him before, and she needed to get the rest out. For both of them.

"She'd been off her meds for nearly six months the last time. Coping somehow for the first few and managing to keep it hidden. But she started to lose track and sometimes forgot to flush when she dumped her pills in the toilet.

"I'd wake up at night to find her standing in the doorway of my room, staring at me, with tears running down her cheeks. She was so sad it would make me cry, too. And she'd crawl into bed with me and hold me until she fell asleep there."

He wiped away her tears. "She loved you."

Her smile was weak, but there. "She used to say I was the only reason she lived. But even that wasn't enough in the end. She got more and more sad and never went to her bed. She'd either walk the house at night or sit in the corner of my room. She said if she could just see me, she'd have something to hold on to. I was sleeping less and less by then, worrying, watching her, trying to soothe her when she'd get all freaked out by the voices telling her stuff. She'd rarely say what they'd said, just that it was bad, very bad, and she was afraid they'd win and she'd have to be locked up again.

"She swore she'd die before they'd take her away from me again. It got worse and worse, and then one day, she was different. I came home from school and she asked about my classes and what university I wanted to go to. All kinds of things like that. What I wanted to be, if I wanted to get married when I grew up, how many kids I'd have, and what my husband would be like. She stared at me as though trying to memorize every word and expression. Then she said she had to go. To protect me. So I could have the life I wanted. She was so certain. So calm. She knew what she was doing and was sorry it would be hard for me at first, but then I'd have a fine life. A career, a family of my own. She was sorry she'd never see my children, but it was best for them to not have to worry. To never be exposed to the crazy lady."

His heart broke for the child she'd been and the horror she'd faced. He wished he could stop her memories, but the therapist in him knew better.

"Then she told me about the voices and how they could never be trusted. How they drove away my father and made her life too hard to live. She also told me more about my gift. How I'd be like her and able to stop Death from taking lives before their time. Then she held me for a long time and said it had to last forever because she was leaving forever and I wasn't allowed to stop her. She made me promise to let her go because she needed to finally be at peace and it was the only way. Then she grinned at me, said, 'enough of this morbid stuff, I'm going to take a long hot bath while you go to the grocery store and get something special for supper. How about pizza and chocolate cake to celebrate?' She stuffed a wad of bills in my hand, kissed my cheek, and sent me away." She shuddered.

CHAPTER 25

"I got halfway to the store and realized she hadn't been talking about sometime in the distant future as she always had before. I raced back as fast as I could and found her in the tub, with the water running.

"She'd slit her wrists, but was still alive. With her last breath she begged me to let her go.

"I touched her face with my fingertips and told her I loved her. She smiled at me and I saw peace in her eyes for the first time ever. And then she wasn't there anymore. I could have put my other hand on her and made the connection that would cheat Death, but her blood was gone and she wanted to die. I just sat there with her for a long time, then I went to the lady next door, and she called 911." She sighed.

"I read her journals, later." When Rachel lifted her tear-drenched gaze to meet his, he'd have given his last breath to take her pain away. "She left me in order to protect me. No small wonder I did the same."

His heart clenched.

"Your life after that. Was it better?"

She shook her head. "Foster care sucks. Not saying there aren't some great placements, but they're never yours for sure.

There's always a chance you'll be moved. So you don't form any attachments if you don't want to get your heart ripped out."

"Do you think your mom should have tried harder? Not left you?"

"She did the best she could and was so very tired. For a long time, I thought I should have tried harder to get her back on her pills. But now, looking back, she needed an adult that loved her and cared enough to stand by her and help her through the treatments, to help her find a way to make the meds work in her life. She was so alone, with only me to love her. I'll always wish I'd been enough for her, but at the same time, I remember I was only a child and not wise enough to see suicide coming and find a way to prevent it."

He nodded. "I think we should take a break. Find some food."

She stayed where she was. "Do you understand me a bit better now?"

He kissed her slowly. "What do you think?"

She slipped her arms around his neck. "I don't want to think right now," she murmured against his mouth, and the kiss deepened.

Rachel settled in with a groan. While their tongues dueled, his hand slipped up under her sweater to caress her breast, tease her nipple, and send fire straight to her core. She slid a hand to his back and dug in with her nails as she strained to be closer still, and was thoroughly shocked when he shoved her off his lap and stood.

"We need food."

"I need you." She didn't want food. She wanted him. All of him, now. She was tired of him holding back. Felt like a teenager necking on the couch. They'd yet to make love, and her body was on freaking fire. Sure, there was much to be said for anticipation, but there came a point…

Following him to the kitchen gave her too good a view of his fine ass, and she sighed when he bent to look in the fridge. She finally averted her gaze and stared out the window at the windswept arbutus trees with shreds of red bark hanging from them.

"Soup and sandwich work for you?"

"Whatever," she said.

"You gonna sulk?"

"Maybe."

He took her by the shoulders and turned her around. "If we make love before all this stuff is out in the open and talked about, we'll lose ground. Trust me, I want you bad, but it has to wait."

"Were you this noble when we got married? This determined to do what's right?"

His grin was a bit twisted. "Yeah. You said it was an endearing quality."

"I was obviously an idiot."

He laughed. "Find a pot and put on the soup while I build a couple of sandwiches."

She looked at the can on the counter and murmured, "Comfort food. Grilled cheese and tomato soup. My mom's go-to meal." She looked at him. "Did you know that? Had I told you that?"

He shook his head. "Until today, you've never spoken of your mother."

"Wow. That was stupid of me. My childhood has so much to do with who I am. Who did you think I was?"

He stared at her for a moment before turning to the cheese and slicer. "You were a woman who'd been through hell and found her way out. Grace had filled me in that you'd been the one to find your mom when she committed suicide, and you'd spent years in the system. You'd come to Paradise on a sort of field trip for foster kids. Ended up working there in the stables where I met you years later."

He slid the sandwiches onto a grill. "I met a strong woman. One with shadows behind her eyes sometimes, but a smile that took me out at the knees. You knew how to live, how to laugh, and you had the kindest heart I'd ever encountered. Barn cats followed you around. Horses watched you."

He framed her face. "I saw the woman I wanted to spend the rest of my life with. The face I wanted to wake up and see every morning. The heart I wanted to lay claim to. Sometimes I felt like one of those cats following you around, hoping you'd give me a pet or a smile. You were my everything, Rachel."

"And I left you." She pulled away, went through the motions with the can opener and pot. How could he forgive her for leaving? For not being who he thought she was?

As though knowing exactly where her mind had gone, he asked quietly, "How long did it take you to forgive your mother for abandoning you?"

Her hand stilled and something in her gut twisted.

"How long, Rachel? A week? A month? Years?"

She shook her head. "I honestly don't know. It was just gone and I didn't know when it'd happened. I wasn't mad at her anymore." She switched the burner to low, and spun to glare at him. "If you're trying to make a comparison to me leaving you, you're way off base. There is nothing remotely similar."

"You left me for my own good. You don't think that sounds similar?"

"She *killed* herself. Ended her life. There was no going back. No making up for past mistakes."

He nodded. "True. But somewhere deep in your psyche, there is a connection. Like children who are battered moving on to become a batterer. It's what they know. You understood, and were taught that it was worthy to protect a person the way you tried to protect me and my family."

She opened her mouth to protest, but closed it again. Intellectually, she agreed with his argument. Didn't mean she had to like it or even agree with him out loud. She gripped her bottom lip with her teeth while she thought about the options. He knew she knew, so it could end there. But she needed to do something more.

"You're right, of course. But having acknowledged that, and seeing clearly now what happened, I'll apologize one last time and ask you if we can move forward instead of rehashing the past."

Quinn wanted to say yes. But he knew better. He understood the human mind and how it worked. Rachel had far more work to do before she'd be fully aware of her own reflexes and how to counteract her natural impulses. Besides that, there was the fear buried in the hidden memories. Her fear that she was schizophrenic.

"How about a compromise instead?"

"As in?" She backed up to lean against the counter.

"We move on in our relationship and continue building trust as you work through the past."

Tipping her head like a curious dog and crossing her arms in front of her she said, "Therapy? Marriage counseling?"

He sighed. This wasn't going to go well. "You have more than your mother's suicide to work through. There's stuff you don't remember right now. Stuff that needs tending before you'll be emotionally whole."

"You think I need a shrink. Fuck you." She reached over and shut off the stove before storming out of the room.

Well, that was about what he'd expected. Teach him to get into professional mode at the wrong time. But it was more than that. He needed to throttle back because he was the wrong person. He was too close to her.

He found her on the wide deck, leaning against the railing, staring at the ocean.

"Rachel?"

"Don't talk to me, Dr. Meyers. I'm not in the mood for analysis."

"I'm sorry."

"Lots of sorry flying around here, isn't there?"

"I think we should head for ETC. You can get your memories back and then see where we're at."

"Sounds good. Not like I'm going to convince you to make love to damaged goods."

He had her in two strides, spun her and kissed her like it was their last. He sunk in, and she met him stroke for stroke. She grabbed the bottom of his shirt, peeled it up over his head, and tossed it aside as he did the same with hers. The clasp of her bra popped easily and he pushed it away as his hands caressed and teased.

"Quinn," she said when his mouth left hers to graze down her throat. "If you're planning on stopping, do it now."

In answer, he took her mouth again and slipped a hand inside the waistband of her jeans. She unbuckled his belt and dropped his fly before he stilled her hands. "Not this way." He swung her up into his arms and carried her to the master suite, laid her on the bed, and followed her down.

With his mouth paying homage to her breasts, he dragged off her jeans, dispensed with her underwear, and he slid down. She gasped at the first touch of his tongue, dug her fingers into his shoulders while he teased. Went limp when his teeth sent her crashing over the edge, and her heart sang.

He worked his way back up her body, nipping at heated flesh, stoking the flames before rising over her, looking for the answer in her eyes before he nudged at her entrance and was welcomed in.

When they lay spent, it took all the energy he had left to roll them so she'd be sprawled over him instead of wearing his weight.

She snuggled her head on his shoulder and they drifted off to sleep.

***

When Rachel woke, she was alone. And it was dark. She swung her feet to the floor and listened for a minute. Quinn was talking to someone. She grabbed her clothes and headed into the bathroom for a quick shower. Looking in the mirror as she dried off, she noticed whisker-burn over much of her body. She'd already acknowledged that making love several times throughout the night had left her sore and looking like she needed a nap. "But happy," she said with a grin and dressed quickly.

She found Quinn in the kitchen alone, and before she could ask who had been there, he swept her up in a kiss that had her system humming all over again.

When they came up for air, she said, "What's burning?"

"Shit." He grabbed a frying pan off the stove and took it to the sink. "Eggs." Then over his shoulder he said, "Grab the rest from the fridge."

With a loud sizzle and a puff of steam, the pan was rinsed and ready for a second try. He broke four eggs into a dish and whisked them with a fork.

She peeked in the oven where potatoes and bacon were staying warm. "Who were you talking to?"

"Grace."

"She called?"

"I called her. I'd promised before we parted that I'd keep her in the loop about our plans. She wants you to call her later."

"Why? What did you tell her?"

"That things were going okay and you were looking forward to getting your memory back. She's going to offer to go to ETC with us."

"As a mediator?"

He cocked his head. "Do we need one? I thought we worked a lot out last night."

She shrugged. "I thought so, too, but in the light of day, with clothes on and space between us I feel less confident."

He grinned and pulled her toward him. "Then let's get naked so you're more comfortable."

"Works for me," she said, undoing the button on his jeans.

Grabbing her hand to still it, he groaned. "We need food first."

"Really?"

"I'm trying to be mature and responsible right now and you're not helping."

"Sue me," she said, leaning against the evidence of his arousal.

"Here," he said, handing her the spatula. "Scramble the eggs while I set the table."

She gave in with a grin, glad she was keeping him on edge. The man was way too serious sometimes.

CHAPTER 26

She fought the urge to squirm under Kelton's gaze when he asked her if she had any concerns about the procedure. "I just want to get it over with so I can get on with my life."

He nodded. "Then let's get on with it." He addressed both Grace and Quinn. "As you both know, I'll need you to leave the room during the induction, but you can watch on the monitor in the office next door. Once Rachel is ready for the reversal procedure, you can come back into the room, but it would be best, less disturbing for her, if you wait until she is waking up."

Grace rose and kissed Rachel on the cheek before leaving, but when Quinn leaned over to do the same, Rachel grabbed his hand and said, "Wait."

"What is it?"

"Was I this scared the first time?"

"No."

"Why is it different now?"

"Because we've worked through some things that effect how you may react to your memories. I can't tell you all will be perfect when you wake up, baby, but I'll be here for you and we'll make it work." He kissed her then and she let go of his hand.

Once she was alone with the doctor, she said, "Let's get this done."

He nodded and asked her to recline her chair. Using a remote, he started a taped induction. The one he told her she'd chosen herself the first time around.

She felt the warm voice wrapping around her, soothing her, and her eyelids began to droop as the tension left her body.

Quinn watched the monitor. There was no sound, of course, but he knew the steps and could imagine the words. She went under quickly, and once she was ready for suggestion, Kelton activated their audio.

The process was lengthy, and the doctor was thorough. The chemical implants had already been removed, so this was the last step before she was fully herself again.

"Why are you so worried, Quinn?"

He grimaced. "I love her, and it scares hell out of me that she could decide not to continue our marriage."

Her smile was slow but warm. "She's not going to forget what's happened between you over the last few days. She loves you, too, so relax."

"I want her to start therapy. And she's balking."

"Hmmm. Is it a deal-breaker?"

"Of course not."

"Make sure she understands that. And a bit of advice between friends?"

"Sure."

"Don't push. Give her time. She's got a lot of baggage, and I think you're the man to help her unpack, but you have to be patient. You two dove into marriage long before you knew each other. Now you have an opportunity to rectify that mistake."

***

Rachel opened her eyes and reached for the handle to set the recliner upright.

Kelton was sitting behind his desk, studying her. "How are you feeling, Rachel?"

She thought about it for a minute. "Much more relaxed than before we started. Are we done?"

"Yes."

The question she'd planned to ask herself the moment she awoke popped into her head. *Why did I leave Quinn? Death. It was dogging me. Followed me to the ranch and two people had to be saved. I had no choice but to protect them by leaving. Taking the Grim Reaper with me.*

"Rachel?"

She blinked to orient herself.

"Do you have any questions for me before Quinn and Grace join us?"

"No. How long have they been waiting?"

"Two hours, twenty minutes."

"It took longer than you expected."

"Yes. We had discussed that possibility."

"What was my stumbling point?"

"As you predicted before the first procedure, you were resistant to suggestion. So I was very careful to be certain that each one was well seated before I moved on."

When Quinn and Grace came through the doorway, Rachel's heart kicked up a notch. She wiped her palms on her jeans and steeled herself. For what, she didn't know.

Grace came right to her, touched her shoulder, and smiled. "You okay, kiddo?"

"Sure," she said, trying to sound nonchalant.

"Good. You ready to blow this popsicle stand?"

"Yes." When she stood up, Quinn stepped in front of her. She met his gaze and didn't know how to respond to the concern she saw there, because she was just as worried about what would happen next. Even though her memories had been restored, she hadn't had a chance to work through the melding of the last weeks with the past she'd recovered. She managed a smile. Probably an odd-looking one, but it was the best she could do, considering.

Kelton's voice interrupted. "You're free to go, Rachel, but I highly recommend you stay for a few days and work with our rehab department to make sure there are no problems with assimilation."

"I'd rather leave. I'd like some time to myself now."

He nodded. "As expected." He then addressed the other two. "Don't push. Rachel needs to work at her own speed. Pushing will only backfire on you by creating confusion."

***

Unanswered questions and anticipatory tension made the flight from ETC's underground headquarters to Grace's country inn feel more like hours than minutes.

Rachel wanted to fold herself into Quinn's arms when he caught her as she hopped out of the helicopter, but he stepped back and she was left standing alone, feeling horribly isolated.

Caroline waved from the waiting jeep and, with a grin, Rachel marched right over and gave her a huge hug just as the helo lifted off and disappeared into thickening clouds. "It's so damned good to see a friendly face I recognize for a change."

"Do you remember seeing Sergei at the track?"

"The voice I knew. The accent. That was Sergei?"

"Yep. And I was on the roof, in the steward's room watching over the whole place."

"I never saw you, did I?"

"Nope. Only Sergei and Jen."

"I met her at the hotdog stand. But I don't know her, do I?"

"I guess not. Grace met her when she was on that first op with Logan. She's a real gem. Training and experience to envy for sure, and a really great team player."

"Is she ETC?"

"Nope, freelance like us."

When Caroline stopped in front of one of Paradise's small homes, Grace said, "This is yours for as long as you want to stay. Likewise, you're free to leave when you wish."

It was where she'd lived when she'd worked for Grace. "Thank you." Rachel reached across the seat back to touch Grace's shoulder. "Thank you from the bottom of my heart. You're always there for me." The lump in her throat prevented her from saying anything more.

Quinn echoed her thanks, took Rachel's hand, and they walked toward the bungalow together. She remembered it well. Two small bedrooms, a bathroom with a huge soaker tub, and a great room living area that was filled with kitchen appliances, a field-stone fireplace, and a couple of comfy couches.

Once inside, they stowed their gear, and she wandered around, opening windows to draw in the fresh country air. Hoped it would help her deal with Quinn's watchful gaze. He'd been hovering silently, yet she could almost hear the gears grinding.

She threw herself onto the couch and hugged a brilliant blue pillow against her middle. "You have questions."

"I do. But more importantly, you have things you want to say."

Her teeth came together. It would be unreasonable to yell at him for being obliging, accommodating. But she wanted to yell. Instead, she chose her words carefully. "I'm still too angry."

"Getting it out would help get rid of it."

Her nostrils flared and her jaw ached. "Screaming at you would do me no good and I can't think of how it would help the situation at all." She jumped to her feet and tossed the cushion at the couch. "I need to get out of here. To walk it off."

She stormed out the door and headed east on the path she'd used to walk to the barns years before. It would take nearly thirty minutes to get there, but she didn't care, at least she had a destination. But ten minutes into her hike, she was drawn to one of the smaller offshoot trails, one that led through the woods. Only suitable for being on foot, as the branches above weren't cleared for the height of a rider, Rachel had used it before as an escape from her own thoughts. And now, it worked every bit as well.

The songs of tiny birds flitting around seeped into her consciousness and she smiled. What was it about birdsong that was so distracting? And why did it cause her to open her eyes and see her surroundings? Bark peeling back where bucks had rubbed their antlers, the beauty of a bright orange fungus attached to a decrepit stump, and then there was the smell. The dank earthiness of just that. Earth. Dirt. Overlaid with the freshness of green. It entered as simply an odor, but settled at the back of the throat with a presence of its own.

She could always find peace in a forest. Even when she'd been a girl afraid for where her life was going, for what was happening to her mother, she'd been able to slip into the woods behind their rented house and feel the peace, the balance that came from the surroundings.

A tiny bird flew past her to settle on a branch only inches beyond her reach, and as it sang its staccato tune, she watched what appeared to be its mate land nearby and begin to sing an answer. Looking around, she spotted a log she could sit on to watch the antics of the feathered couple, and they didn't disappoint. While the male's dance wasn't as fancy as some, he fluffed and strutted with as much determination as any other male would when presented with an almost willing partner.

The tiny female had a few things to say herself, then she flew off, and the male followed.

"Pretty simple stuff for your feathered friends," said Quinn.

She jumped up and spun toward him. "You scared me half to freaking death."

"Sorry, I thought you'd heard me come up while Romeo was pleading his case."

"I guess I was too engrossed in the show. Do you think she's going to accept his excuses?"

"Excuses for what?"

"For why he was late for supper of course," she said, grinning.

He tipped his head. "Does this mean you aren't mad at me anymore?"

She ran her fingers over the fine edges of a fern. "It means that I can't stay angry in this kind of atmosphere. Besides, what's done is done, and I have to find a way to accept that you thought it was okay to ask me a question I've never answered before. That you have a whole piece of me now that I'd never shared before."

He didn't say a word. Kept his gaze fixed on hers.

"Why did you do it, Quinn? Why did you ask me about my mom when I'd so adamantly avoided the subject throughout our earlier relationship? What made you think it was all right to ask me when I was missing the part of my memory that would have kept me protected?"

"Protected is an odd word to use."

She shrugged. "I'd kept stuff to myself on purpose and I don't think you can claim to not know that." She spun away, continued down the path.

"I didn't expect you to answer. I was surprised." He was behind her, following but not making any attempt to touch her or even draw alongside.

"And you couldn't resist seeing how far I'd go, what I'd say next?"

Silence stretched for several beats. "The woman I married, was ridiculously in love with, had walked away from me, and here I was being offered information that could help me understand what had driven her to what I saw as an extremely injudicious decision. I did what any man would do. I grabbed the ball and ran with it."

A lump formed in her throat and she stopped. "That is so fucking unfair," she said as she faced him. "How can you spin things around so fast that I suddenly feel sorry for you?"

He grabbed her shoulders and got in her face. "I don't want your pity, Rachel. I want a partner. One who's willing to participate in the repair of our relationship."

She jerked away. "Yeah, well, it's gonna take some time, Dr. Meyers. You know how I feel about shrinks and their couches."

"No freaky furniture. I think walk and talk will be the best fit for us. I don't care if we have to cover every square inch of this place. We're going to cover ground both literally and figuratively until we get this shit figured out. We're worth the effort."

"Okay." She sighed. "I'm in as long as I'm talking to my husband, not my therapist."

"Deal." His smile faded. "I noticed Grace put us in a cottage with two bedrooms. If it's better for you to have your own space and not share a bed with me..." He shrugged. "I'll give you your space."

"Oh no. You're not taking that away from me. I need our physical connection."

"Good answer," he said and drew her back toward him. "Truce?" He lowered his mouth to hers, but hesitated, only a breath away.

"Truce," she said and closed the gap to meet him in a kiss that made something move in her chest.

CHAPTER 27

"Which way today?" Quinn asked as he stepped out into brilliant sunshine.

Rachel pointed to the road. "If we start toward the inn, there's a couple of paths along the way."

He locked the door and followed her down the driveway, noting that she'd stuffed her hands in her pockets and wrapped the down-filled vest around her as though donning armor.

Yesterday, when they'd arrived, she'd been thrilled to find the pair of bright red vests with the word *Paradise* splashed across the back. She said she'd always worn one when she'd worked here years ago and seemed to find a level of comfort in wearing it now.

"So, Doc," she said as he caught up with her. "What's the topic of discussion today?"

"Up to you."

"No way that's going to work because I don't want to talk about myself or anything touchy."

"Okay, then I'll ask this. Why don't you want to talk about yourself?"

She twisted her mouth back and forth and huffed out a breath. "You don't mess around, do you?"

"Nope."

"Secrets. My life has been full of secrets and I'm always afraid of being found out."

"Found out?"

She wiped a palm against her hip, then stuffed the hand back into her pocket. "That I'm a fraud. I'm not the person the world sees. Never have been."

"Who do you think you appear to be?"

"A normal person. One without a ton of baggage. A woman who is comfortable in her own skin, is bright and cheerful and confident."

"For starters, *normal* is a word I never use. It's a useless term with a totally ambiguous meaning. It means something different to everyone, so we'll toss it out as worthless. And everyone has their own baggage. Again, a catchall word without much worth.

"Talk to me about the other stuff. Why don't you feel comfortable in your own skin?"

She hesitated as though having trouble coming up with the words. "Sometimes I have an odd feeling of detachment from myself. As though I'm here in this body, but it's not really mine. Like I'm going to wake up one morning and find out I'm someone else. That even sounds crazy to me when I say it out loud."

"Is there any time you feel this more than others? I mean, do you feel that way when you're doing something specific, or at a particular time of day?"

"It's always after. After I've done something where I was totally absorbed in the experience and forgetting about what I looked like or sounded like or how anyone saw me. When I realize I've forgotten to be concerned about being judged."

He fought the grin back to a slow smile. "Sex?"

"Yep."

"So having said this out loud, what do you think it means?"

"I'm terrified by the moments that I slide into an experience."

"When you allow yourself to simply be."

She stopped. "That's true, isn't it? When I let myself go, I become someone I don't know."

"Oh, I think you know her."

"There it is. *Her*. As though I'm more than one person in here. And that scares me spitless."

"Why?"

She held out a hand that shook. "Look at me. I'm terrified I might have inherited my mother's mental illness."

"That's craz—" He caught the word and reached to grab her hand. "It's wrong-thinking, Rachel."

"Schizophrenia runs in families. I've done my research, Quinn."

"And I've done more. I didn't get my degrees from cereal boxes. I did long, hard hours of study, and spent the best part of five years in general practice before I specialized. I've seen and heard nothing in your behavior or what you've told me that causes the smallest red flag to appear."

"You're biased."

"I've been closer to you than anyone else in years. Well, besides Grace. And even your disappearing act doesn't suggest anything but a rational response to misinformation. That you may have—in my estimation—misinterpreted what was going on doesn't tell me you've got a mental illness."

She sighed. "I kept my mom's condition a secret because I didn't want it to play a part in our relationship, but now it does. Anytime I make a bad decision or seem to be going an odd direction, you're going to wonder."

Quinn took her by the shoulders, and shook her gently when what he wanted to do was make her teeth rattle. "You're wrong. I don't know how else I can convince you."

Closing her eyes so she didn't have to see the frustration in his, Rachel said, "I want to be tested."

"There are no tests to be passed or failed. I think it would be more useful for you to work with ETCETERA's specialists. Talk to people who hear the voices of the dead. Compare notes and see that you're not alone in this experience."

Opening her eyes, she turned away. "How can I be certain they won't work their magic and convince me to become one of them? What happens when they want to explore the power in my hands? Investigate the way I stop Death?"

"Maybe instead of you going to ETC, we could get Jen to come here and talk to you. She's able to communicate with entities on a separate plane. She was there at the track when the voices took you down. Maybe she can enlighten you about what was going on."

"Then I'd be letting yet another person inside my head."

"Jen's already been there. When you blacked out, she was the one who made sure you were okay."

She shook her head. "Back to the different people inside me."

"Tell me about them. Or better still, let me tell you about the facets of Rachel as I know them." He rested a hand at the back of her neck. "Come on, let's walk awhile."

He slid his arm across her shoulders and drew her in as they strolled along the trail. "There's strong Rachel, the one who can handle anything that comes her way. Then soft Rachel, whose heart is bruised by unkind words, and bleeds when she sees others suffering. The smart woman in you knows what I'm saying is all true, but the sensitive one is uncertain about my ulterior motives."

When she started to speak, he stopped her. "Sexy Rachel bats her eyes at me from across the room, but sensual Rachel makes noises in the back of her throat when her mouth is on me." He tugged her around and kissed her gently. "Sweet Rachel hates my job, but would never say anything about it to me or anyone else, and the caring woman you are would be reaching out to each and every one of my patients to help them cope with the pounding hearts and sweaty palms making their lives difficult." His hands slid down to cup her butt and ease her into him. "The public woman would be mortified if someone came down this trail and caught us making love, but there's a devil inside you thinking about going for it anyway."

She unbuttoned his shirt and pressed her mouth over his heart. "I love you, partly because you get me. Even if I think you don't really know me, you get me."

"So, do you see what I mean about all the facets making you a whole?"

"I do. And while I'm here with you, it seems so straightforward that I'm almost embarrassed. But. It's when I'm alone with my thoughts…"

"What thoughts are the hardest?"

She shook her head and headed them back the way they'd come. "It's like feeling whole and in control in the daylight, but at night, sounds creep in, the wind comes up, and the lights flicker."

"You could use an inner dialogue to help you through the darkness."

She laughed. "Great, now you're encouraging me to talk to myself."

"When you're not hearing the voices, how do you feel?"

"Fine. Normal." She held up her hand. "I know, that's not a word we're going to use, but my normal is how I usually feel. Like my mom when she was on meds. She'd think there was nothing wrong with her. She was all better and didn't need the drugs anymore. And then her voices would come."

"We're pretty sure your voices are coming from the dead." He tipped his head. "Did your mother have power in her hands as you do?"

"She said she did, but I never saw anything. My father had something extra as well."

"As in?"

"He could find things, fix things."

"What happened to him? Why wasn't he a part of your life?"

"He disappeared. According to my mom, he did the classic, going-out-for-cigarettes and never came back."

"How old were you?"

"I hadn't been born. He ran off when she was only six months pregnant."

"Do you know any of his family?"

"Mom said he was an orphan. His mother died when he was ten and he had no dad."

The dead-end in conversation left them without much to say for a while, and for the first time in ages, their silence was comfortable. They simply held hands and strolled along, content to be in each other's company for as long as it could last. The rich scent of leaves and prickly pine needles seemed stronger now with the sunlight filtering through the tangled weave of branches. More intense somehow, as though taking over for their lack of words.

Rachel smiled at the thought and chuckled.

"What's so funny?"

"Us. Me. I don't know any other woman who would feel this comfortable surrounded by woods and rodents and insects."

He gave the ground a cursory look. "Rodents and insects?"

"You've got to know they're there. Even if you don't see them."

"Now isn't that an interesting segue?"

She tipped her head in question and he repeated her words back to her. "You've got to know they're there, even if you don't see them. In relation to your voices. They belong to souls. The essence of people who cannot be seen, or even heard. The voices aren't audible, but somehow, you have the reception necessary to know that they're there."

Her smile grew slowly. "A very nice interpretation. I hate to be repeating myself, but again, the word *comfortable* comes to me. There's nothing frightening about the voices that way. They've become explainable, even though, ultimately, there isn't a scientific explanation for the possibility of invisible entities who were once human beings. Nor a way to comprehend them walking among us. But it works.

"And accepting that as a reality lends credence to the knowing of other. Takes away the uncertainty of the unexplained."

"Isn't it really like faith?"

"How so?"

"People have faith, of whatever variety, and believe in something they can't actually see or put their hands on. And somehow, even without proof, that brings them comfort."

She nodded. "Are you a believer?"

"I believe in many things I can't see or touch or hear."

"What about religion, Quinn? We didn't get married in a church because I said they made me claustrophobic, but did you do that just for me? Did it matter to you?"

He hesitated. Gazed up into the trees as though searching for the sky, then ran his hands through his hair. "Although we did go to Sunday school as kids and it was a good experience, I have a bit of a problem with what I see as abuse of organized religions."

"Are you Christian?"

He sighed. "I believe in a higher power. I believe in an afterlife, in the strength of soul, in the power of the universe and ordinary people. I don't believe in retribution and the notion of people going to hell. Being married in the church or not was a non-issue to me. I…"

She felt the pressure of the words he'd left unsaid. "What was important to you was the words. The promises we made to each other. The promises I broke."

His mouth opened and closed while he clearly struggled with what to say.

"We're doing honesty here, Quinn. Say what you're thinking. I can take it. Let me just say—to put the words out there—I know I let you down."

He shook his head. "The words are redundant."

"Cop-out. You'd make me say them if this was reversed."

His mouth twisted. "You're the therapist now?"

"Yeah. Looks like the tables have turned."

"I'm a man of my word. So I expected no less from you. I felt betrayed. I felt like you should have come to me with your worries and concerns rather than running away. I hate that you were doing it to protect me, without ever letting me know what was wrong. But I get it now. I understand a lot of what happened and why. I still don't like it, but some of the blame falls on me for marrying someone I didn't know. Someone I assumed had the same kind of understandings and basic beliefs I did. Assuming anything is a huge mistake. I know better. But the feelings I had, and I suppose a slight worry that you may not want to stay with me and marry me, led me to make rash decisions."

The sick feeling in her gut was accompanied by a clutch of fear that made her voice sound thin. "Marrying me was a rash decision."

"Rushing into marriage. We'd only known each other for weeks. We should have taken the time to learn what we're learning now. Shared our history, our beliefs, and what made us who we are today."

That helped to smooth the inner trembling. "I don't know much about you either. Why did you become a psychologist when most of the rest of your family went into the military?"

He fixed his gaze on hers. "For a layman, that was an amazing choice of question."

"Why?"

"Because you poked your finger right into my weak spot." He hesitated, then shrugged. "I was expected to go the way of the rest, and my family was astounded when I said I wanted to go to college instead. My argument was that I could enlist afterward, and I was, of course, told I should enlist then and get my education later through the services."

"So what happened?"

"I applied for scholarships and went to college."

"As a psychology major?"

His laugh was half-hearted. "Nope. I majored in kinesiology, with a minor in communications. I was looking at physiotherapy as a career."

"What happened to change your direction?"

"My dad, his brothers, and his buddies. He was Special Forces. A career man. And I watched him change as I grew up. Saw the changes in his mates and my uncles. The effects on their families. And I wanted to make that go away. I wanted to fix the men who came home different. I thought I could learn how to heal their minds." He shrugged.

"And?"

"It doesn't work that way."

"But your practice is successful. You told me yourself you make a difference. Your programs are being duplicated by groups around the country."

He grimaced. "That's true. But nobody is fixed. I can make them better, but I can't make them who they used to be. That's the thing with the human mind. It can't be taken back to a previous condition any more than a broken leg can. The scars are always there. So men and women, the kind who believed themselves invincible, discover they're far from it, and many don't cope well. They're not used to leaning, to depending on others for guidance. Some become angry with themselves, some become furious with the world around them, and yet others are crippled by flashbacks and nightmares and hide for fear something triggers the horrendous memories and forces them to relive the terror only they know."

"It must be hard for you, too."

"Not being able to fix the people who've made that leap of faith and show up in my office expecting to be miraculously freed can be exhausting, but nothing like what they're going through."

She'd never seen his vulnerability before and it made her heart ache. He was a fixer. A man always ready to step in and make things right. This might be her only opportunity to ask the question. Broach the subject she'd watched his family skirt around. "Will you tell me about your dad?"

His shoulders came up as he drew a tight breath and tears stung her eyes. "Wouldn't it help if I knew? Your mom talks about him as though he's off on a mysterious mission, but from bits and pieces of emotion and whatnot I get from you and your sibs, there's something darker there. Can you tell me?"

Seeing the instant tension in his jaw, she was tempted to take back her request.

When he spoke, his voice was low and filled with something she didn't recognize. "He was a Green Beret, as one of my brothers was, and two of my uncles. He left on a mission nearly ten years ago and hasn't been home since."

"He's missing in action?"

"No. He's on medical discharge."

She frowned. "He's in a hospital?"

They'd come upon one of the many benches along the trail and Quinn sat. With his forearms resting on his thighs, his hands hung limp between his knees. "My father was in a VA hospital for a long time, recovering from injuries he sustained in the failed extraction of civilians kidnapped in a foreign country. He was badly burned while trying to rescue a woman and a child."

Sitting beside him, she rested a hand on his back. She needed to touch, be connected while she waited for him to continue.

There was no humor in his laugh. "He'd been living with post-traumatic stress for years. Refused any kind of treatment. But the last incident pushed him over the edge, and, coupled with the pain of the burns, he got hooked on prescription drugs.

"He was living in a motel close to the Rehab Center, doing five hours of PT a day while they worked on atrophied muscles and the taut grafted skin. And my mom was right there with him every step of the way. But the pain and flashbacks tipped him over the edge, and he started drinking. They had a huge blow-up over the pills and whiskey one night and he took off.

"When we found him weeks later, living on the streets of Seattle, we did an intervention and I got him into a residential treatment program. But he left there after only a few weeks. Vanished as he was well-trained to do. I haven't seen him since."

She shook her head. "Your mom—"

"He calls her almost every week. She's asked us to leave him be. Says he's doing the best he can, considering what he lives with. She's afraid to push him—afraid he'll commit suicide like his brother did."

Rachel slid her arms around him and rested her head on his shoulder. "I'm so sorry." There was little else she could say.

Quinn was grateful for her warmth and her silence. The weight in his chest was no less, but at least now, he didn't feel alone with it. He pulled her closer and held on. She was no longer a girl he'd met and fallen stupid in love with. She was a woman with a history. Experiences that made her both weak and strong. No different than he was.

It had been years since he'd talked about his dad. About the man he'd worshiped, the man he could do nothing to help in spite of his success with others—the men he held together while they walked the miles they needed to in order to find what worked for them, what would help them lead lives that weren't haunted by a continuous fear of what might set off their internal demons. All he could do was help the ones he could reach. And it would always burn that there was nothing he could do for the one he most wanted to help. The same as it burned that his father never asked to speak to him, but had contact with both

Angie and Gage. James Meyers wasn't unaware of what his son went through because of him.

"I wonder if I'd have run away if I'd known about your dad."

His fingers caressed her throat. "If I'd known about your mother, I wonder if I'd have handled our marriage differently. Or would my need to fix you have driven you off as well?"

She gripped his wrist, hard. "Look at me." When his head came up, she said, "We can't change the past. Only today. All we ever have is today. And I, for one, would like to have a today with you. One that doesn't revolve around our before."

"The past won't go away by ignoring it. Our choices along the way have made us who we are."

She sighed. "I know that. But I want to be more than what made me. I want to be the woman who grew from what happened in my past. I want you to understand that my choices are made with wide open eyes. By talking to you about my fears, they've become less. Less of who I am, and even less of who I want to be."

"Then I'm going to push the envelope. You said before that you didn't ever want to have children. And when I'd ask you why, you'd say you just weren't into kids. Couldn't imagine being a mother. Was that true, or was it because of the fears attached to your mom's illness?"

Rachel fought the sudden desire to get up and walk away from the conversation. Instead, she closed her eyes, leaned back, and took a minute to respond. "I—"

She stopped, ran her hands over her face, clasped them behind her head, and stared up into the sky. "I'm not sure. It's all interwoven. Sort of a chicken and egg thing. Would I like to have kids? I really don't know if I could say yes, and go for it."

"What if you found yourself pregnant, accidentally?"

The smile came unbidden. "Then I'd become a mom." And although she could feel the pressure of fear, she also felt the sparkle of wonder that came along with the possibility. She grinned at him. "Don't tell me you've been poking holes in the condoms?"

His responding grin warmed her inside. "Nope. I'm too honest. And that's way too much like Russian Roulette." He shook his head. "I don't think either of us is ready to have kids right now, but I come from a big family, and I'd always thought I'd be a dad, someday. Of course, we all play dad to Angie's son."

"I remember being surprised when you told me you didn't know who his father was. Does anyone?"

Quinn chuckled. "Nope. We were all shocked when she announced she was pregnant. My brothers and I were all ready to go out and hang a beating on whoever it was, but she wouldn't tell. None of us even knew she had a boyfriend, and she wasn't the kind of girl to screw around. But she said she'd had a one-night stand with a guy from out of town and there she was, *eighteen* and pregnant. My parents were shocked, but supportive. And she's never divulged who Dhillon's father is." He stood and held out his hand, taking her into his arms.

She sunk into a kiss that began as sweet, but the slow tangle of tongues became more, and passion built until Quinn stepped back, keeping her at arm's length. "Know any shortcuts back to our cabin?" His voice was low and laced with gravel.

Swallowing hard as she saw the storm in his eyes, she said, "No. But we could run."

His eyebrows went up, he slung an arm across her shoulders. "Not up to running at the moment." Lifting her hand, he ran his teeth across her knuckles.

Her heart turned over when she saw the expression in his eyes and it was all she could do to stop herself from wrapping herself around him. How, she wondered, had she lived for two years without that look?

That blatant unguarded love.

CHAPTER 28

Julia stared at the man standing in the doorway of her office, and without breaking eye contact, she stood and walked to him, lifted a hand, and touched his face. He turned so his lips grazed her palm and she choked out some of the words screaming in her head. "You're home. You're really here."

When he squeezed his eyes closed, her heart lurched. No. Please, no. "You aren't staying."

"I can't. Not yet. I came to see Quinn. I have a fence to mend."

"He's not here."

"I know. I thought about leaving, but I had to see you first." He folded her into his arms and his voice was warm by her ear. "I couldn't go without holding you."

"Why?" She shook her head. "No. You don't have to explain. I'll stand by my promise. I'm here. And you know, anytime, anywhere, I'm yours."

"It's a big step for me, love, to come here, to speak with Quinn. I owe him an apology. It's a step closer to what has to be."

When he eased back, she could see tears on the cheek she'd known for what felt like forever. Lines of age were interwoven with the scars now. But, at least this time, there was the color of health in them again. And his eyes didn't have that haunted look she'd grown to expect. But he was safe here. Her office was one of the few places that held no ugly memories. "Can you stay with me a while?"

Lines deepened around his eyes as his smile grew. "Yeah, but my friend could use a drink."

Her heart thudded and hope drained away. "James—"

"No, Lia, not for me, for Swagger." He tipped his head down and she saw the dog leaning against his leg. She was so used to dogs belonging to family and workers being around, she hadn't paid any attention to the one James had arrived with. Who was she kidding? She wouldn't have noticed a camel. Her husband was standing there, in their house, for the first time in so many years she'd stopped counting. Almost stopped hoping.

"Swagger helps me more than the booze or the drugs ever did. He understands what I need, when I need it. I joined a special program. We rescue them from shelters, they rescue us."

He hadn't said a word. Called her every week, but hadn't let on that there was hope. Hope he could maybe come home. But then she understood. There'd been hope for so long and each time it had fizzled out, and another piece of her heart had shriveled up.

But look at him now. He was as close to the man she'd once known as she'd seen in so long. So very, very long. She shook herself and stepped to the kitchen area of her office to fill a cereal bowl with water for what looked like a black collie cross.

James waved his hand and the dog ambled across the room and swagger he did, making her smile.

"Well-named."

James' smile was the one she'd seen time and again when someone commented on one of his children. A mix of pride and wonder.

Tears burned her eyes. She crossed back to him. "Come, sit with me?"

He closed and locked the door, then led her to the pink sofa and drew her down with him. He sighed as he wrapped her up and just held on. "I miss you so goddamned much."

With her face buried against his throat, his words, his heartbeat, and his arms surrounding her, she did something that rarely happened anymore. She let her guard down, opened her mind and let him in to wander, to see what she'd seen—the faces, the laughter, the family he had left behind when the nightmares, flashbacks, and uncontrollable rage had taken over his life.

She savored a feeling she'd missed. There was nothing like the comfort that came with the love of her life slipping into the most sacred part of her, sharing her mind, her thoughts and her memories.

"Dhillon's growing up so fast." His voice was gruff as he slid his fingers into her hair and tipped her head back. "He looks a lot like you when we met."

She'd been ten, he'd been eleven, and she'd hated boys. Until James moved into the apartment over the garage with his mom. She hadn't been able to resist his charm. They'd become fast friends. They'd begun tripping around in each other's minds at twelve, but hadn't stepped over the edge and become more than friends until ten years later.

"You saying I looked like a boy?"

"Yep. You had a good throwing arm, too. I remember thinking, what a waste on a girl."

She smiled. "You were always jealous." He smiled back and seemed to sink deeper into the cushions when his canine companion laid down across his feet.

"Damn sure. You could always out-throw me, but you couldn't catch worth shit."

Laughing softly she said, "Those were the days."

"And they got better and better, didn't they?"

His lips grazed her forehead and she lifted up in answer, met him halfway, and tenderness soon became passion. She absorbed him like a drowning woman gulped air. Slid her hands under his shirt and shuddered as the familiarity overwhelmed her senses. Home. It was like coming home. To where she belonged. With him. Her other half. Truly.

Chapter 29

Quinn reached for his vibrating cell and hesitated when he saw the display. His mother's private line. If it was important, she'd use a company phone. Rachel was still sleeping so he grabbed his pants and crept out to the kitchen.

He flicked on the light over the stove to cut through the darkness of the room.

"Mother?"

"Quinn. How are you and Rachel doing?"

He set the phone on the counter and dragged on his jeans but didn't bother with the fly or button. "Fine. What's up?"

"I…"

Leaning against the wall, he rolled his shoulders to release the new tension. "What's going on?"

"Nothing, really. I just needed to call."

"Trouble sleeping?"

She chuckled. "I had a nap this afternoon, so I'm wide awake now and thinking about you two. About what you're going through."

When Rachel stepped into the room, he took her in his arms and said, "Say hi to my mother. She's worried about us."

She kissed his chin. "Hello, Julia. We're fine. Even better, we're making progress, so no need to worry."

"Wonderful. I'm sorry to bother you. I guess you were probably asleep."

"As you should be," said Quinn. "We'll call you tomorrow, okay?"

"When are you coming home?"

He kissed the tip of Rachel's nose and when she slid her hands to his open jeans, he said, "Soon, Mother. Now go get some sleep."

"You, too."

"Soon," he said and disconnected. "But first, I'm going to make love with my wife, ever so slowly."

Rachel's voice was husky. "And, here, I'd been hoping for wild monkey sex."

"Well in that case…" He grabbed her, tossed her over his shoulder. "Let's get on with it."

As he marched toward the bedroom, she slid her hands inside his jeans and over his glorious ass.

"Hey."

"Mmmmm. Making the best of an awkward position."

He dropped her onto the bed and came down after her, his hands capturing her wrists, his mouth on her throat. "Mine," he murmured.

Rachel arched upwards and his mouth descended to her breast. "Mine," she echoed.

He grazed her with his teeth before biting down just hard enough to have her sucking in a startled breath. Using his tongue, he soothed, then teased some more, going back and forth while she arched to his mouth.

"Quinn." She tugged to get her arms free.

He released her, slid his hands down her body, caressed his way to the sweet spot at her center, and began the torture of not quite touching. Had her rising up off the bed in anticipation until he caressed the soft skin behind her knees, lifted, and slid lower.

"Look at me, Rachel."

Her brilliant blue eyes opened, then went glassy as he pushed her over. With a long slow moan, her body convulsed, and he slipped inside.

***

In the morning, they tossed around the idea of going on a road trip instead of flying to Texas. It would give them time to talk and be together without the pressure of his family watching over them. But they decided to stay a few days longer at Paradise instead, then fly home.

Nearly a week later, they climbed aboard the Steed. They'd barely settled into the back seats and donned the black helmets when Angie's voice came through the built-in headphones. "Get strapped in. Sixty seconds to lift off."

Rachel's stomach did the little twist she hated. Was Angie still mad at her? Would she continue to be a problem? Might as well bite the bullet instead of wondering. "Hey, Angie, good to have you at the helm."

"Hey, kiddo, we're set," added Quinn.

"Hang on," was the only reply as the bird lifted off the ground.

When Quinn took both of Rachel's hands, rubbed slow circles on the palms with his thumbs, then lifted them to his mouth, the discomfort in her belly smoothed out. She stared into his eyes and wished they didn't have the bulky helmets in the way because she wanted to kiss him. Bad. She'd recently become helplessly addicted to his lips, his taste. And she still wanted more. Would it always be like this? Likely not. Love was supposed to grow stronger than the lust eventually, but she had a feeling that would be a long time coming.

Not that she wasn't happy to just be in his company, but there was a constant underlying desire that never seemed to dim, no matter how many times in a day they made love. She couldn't seem to get enough of him, and he apparently felt the same way about her.

She tipped her head to rest it on his shoulder and he slipped a hand up to touch her throat. She caught the groan before it escaped. No point entertaining Angie, or more likely, make her uncomfortable. They used to be friends. But Rachel realized now that they'd both held back, protected much that they hadn't wanted to share. Angie had never talked about Dhillon's father, or even her pregnancy. Rachel had, of course, shared nothing about her mother or life in foster care.

Quinn knew most of it now. And she felt lighter somehow. Understood herself better for having said the words out loud. For having him ask her how she'd felt about stuff. Holding back hadn't been an option once she'd started to open up. And he'd talked more about his dad, too. And about his role in the family. He carried the weight of everyone's well-being. Self-assigned for sure, but still, it was there and it wasn't light.

A family filled with alpha males and females had troubles like any other. She had little reference, but suspected the Meyers had bigger issues than most due to the members and their responsibilities outside the family compound.

Eve was a medical doctor, but she was also doing research on specialized healing methods, Gage's long stretch of perfectly resolved missions had gone down in flames when he'd kidnapped a woman who would eventually become his wife. He still blamed himself for her close call with an organized crime group called the Minnows. She'd cheated death more than once on her own without his help, and that was hard for a hero to take.

Quinn had a similar problem. How did an accomplished healer reconcile the fact he'd failed two of the people he loved? She and his dad had both slipped out of his hands. She sighed. Couldn't imagine what it must be like for him. And that's when the light bulb came on. Wasn't that exactly what terrified her about her healing power? What if she wasn't successful and it was someone she cared about?

Quinn hated that Rachel was growing tenser by the minute. He slipped a hand to the back of her neck and worked the knots as they formed. He wanted to pull off their headgear so he could talk to her, but the Steed was designed to internalize the sound of the monster engine, so they needed the protection of the helmets.

He twisted in his seat to look into her eyes and smiled, but the grimness of her expression didn't change. "What's our ETA, Angie?"

"Fourteen-thirty."

An hour. Such a long fucking time when Rachel was distressed and he couldn't talk to her and find out what was going on in her head. So he went for the tried and true. Slipped his hand up under her jacket, tugged the T-shirt out of her jeans and the heat of her skin warmed his hand. Further evidence of how cold his hand must have been was her swiftly indrawn breath.

With a small smile he ran his fingertips around the edges of her bra, then let his thumb drift back and forth across the lace. The vibration of her groan made him grin. Maybe an hour wasn't such a long time after all.

***

Rachel's tension resurfaced as Angie set the Steed on the helipad beside her house—an instant reminder of the day Rachel had run away. Back then, the Steed was housed at an airstrip nearly a mile away, and the six minutes it had taken Angie to get there and get airborne, could have been critical to Dhillon's survival.

Rachel and Quinn unbuckled and stepped onto the concrete pad. "Thanks, Angie," she said.

Angie tugged off her helmet. "Take my SUV. Keys are in it."

Rachel hesitated. "Thanks, but I need to work out the kinks so walking will be good for me."

With a shrug, Angie took two steps away and stopped. "Damn." She turned back. "I need…" She stuffed her hands in her back pockets. "I want to thank you. For back then. For what you did. You saved my kid's life and I'll always owe you for that." She huffed out a breath. "And somebody recently reminded me that life is short, and the people who belong to us are everything. You're Quinn's, so you're mine by default." She snorted. "I guess that didn't sound very nice. I'm sorry. I'm just not very good at this people shit." She took a deep breath. "But Quinn is more than my brother. He was kinda mine before you came along. Not in a creepy way, but he always had my back."

Angie looked up and met his gaze. "And he's the center-pin of this family. He's the glue that holds us together, no matter what. He looks out for us and we owe him. Owe him, big. So between you and me, well, it's the bridge and the water, ya know?"

Rachel didn't know what to do. Angie was standing there looking all prickly, but sounding like she needed a hug.

Quinn knew. "C'mere, shithead."

Angie threw herself into his arms and he muttered, "Bridge? Water?"

She shook her head. "You know what I meant."

He reached over and drew Rachel into the fold. "My two favorite women, and you're both work."

"What does that say about you?" asked Rachel.

"Glutton for punishment, but I'm going with bigger-than-life hero?"

Angie grinned. "The first for sure." She stepped back. "My kid'll be back any minute so I need to get some food on the go. He's become an eating machine."

Rachel touched her shoulder. "Thanks. For everything."

"No sweat." She scooted off toward her house without a backward glance, but left the gate open for them.

"Nice to see the Steed's new home," she said. "Doesn't she need help to get it into the hangar?"

"Nope, the hangar comes to the pad." He pointed at the ground. "See the tracks? The cover slides into place automatically. And she has a control inside the house, as well as a remote, so if she gets a call, by the time she gets to the pad, the copter's all ready to go."

"Freaking awesome set-up."

"Angie's own design."

"Says her proud brother."

"Yeah, she can be a real pain sometimes, but when she's not—"

"She shocked me today. I've never seen that side of her. Gotta say, she wears pissed off and feisty better than she wears humble."

"I can't figure out what made her speak up. Way out of character," said Quinn.

"It was nice what she said about you, though."

He raised his eyebrows. "She called me glue."

"In the nicest possible way." She grinned and slipped her arm through his. "It feels good to be walking home with you as though it was just any other day. I wonder how long it will last."

Chapter 30

She'd barely stepped through the doorway when he spun her around, put her back against the wall and leaned in so only their mouths touched. Force became tenderness, drawing her in, steeping them in an ache so sweet, it drew a long slow hum from her throat.

Sliding his fingers into her hair, he feathered kisses on her eyelids, and her hands came up to rest on his chest. "I love you so much more. Now that I've been honest and shared my past, it's added a whole new level to how I feel."

He used his teeth to tease the sensitive spot where her neck met her shoulder and she nearly sunk to the floor. Would have if he hadn't wrapped an arm around her waist and dragged her against him. His hands slid down to cup her butt and lift her, pressing her against him as she locked her arms around his neck.

"I want you, here and now. I'd planned a perfect night. We'd start slow, build and layer, share words…" When he lifted, she locked her ankles at the back of his waist and he reached for the button on her pants. "I don't want to wait. I want you now, but…"

Dropping her feet to the floor, she popped the button on his jeans and ran the zipper down. "I want you too. I want you now." She took his mouth with hers, plundered with her tongue, and he met her stroke for stroke while her hand slid around him, and released him from the confines of the fabric. Cool air washed over her heated skin when he pushed her shorts to the floor, hooked his fingers in her panties and sent them down as well.

His hands came up under her shirt and pushed it off over her head to leave her standing naked but for a lacy bra. He teased with a fingertip inside the edge as he pushed it down and her breast came free. He watched her as he repeated the process on the other side. "I love the way your body responds to me," he said as his grazing thumb sent an orgasmic shudder through her.

While he lowered his mouth to replace his hands, he unclipped the bra, and she had to let him go to pull her arms free. Her fingers trembled as she fought to drag his shirt over his head. "I need your skin."

In response, he straightened to tug off his clothes, then picked her up again. When she wrapped her legs around him this time, his fingers found her dampness and stroked, bringing her to the edge before lowering her to wrap around his arousal.

All thought was gone as he drove her. Sent her over and made her climb again before he came with her.

They lay crumpled on the floor, fighting to get their breath back, and she suddenly got the giggles.

He opened an eye and raised the same eyebrow. "What's so funny?"

"Your socks."

He lifted his head and looked. "What about them?"

"You're naked, except for socks. It looks funny, that's all."

"Hmph. At least they're both the same color."

She smothered a chuckle and grinned, loving that he remembered her habit of wearing mismatched socks. It shouldn't be important to her, but it was.

With her head resting on his shoulder, she said, "This floor's getting cold. I guess we should get up."

"Hmm. I think I can stand now. Come on." He helped her up and they leaned on each other as they climbed the stairs to their room. "We need a shower."

True enough, but she figured he had more sex in mind, and she had no problem with that either, but she needed to clarify. "Hot water, okay?"

He groaned. "We'll come out looking like lobsters."

"Then you go ahead. I'll have mine after."

He tightened his grip on her. "I'll boil with you."

By the time they made it to the kitchen for supper, Rachel was surprised she could still walk, considering the state of boneless satiation she'd been in for most of the afternoon. For someone who'd spent most of her life not asking questions and staying under the radar, she was way outside her usual comfort zone and feeling just fine as she asked Quinn, "What was so different, coming home?"

"What do you mean?"

"We made love lots when we were at Paradise, but you're different since we walked through the front door today. Why?"

Being on this side of the questions had him stuffing his hands in his pockets and struggling not to shuffle his feet. "Home is different. It's real. And mine."

He went back to the task of setting the table, but she stopped his progress by stepping in front of him and gripping his arms. "Look at me, Quinn."

He met her gaze and couldn't help but smile at the serious expression she wore. He sighed. "It was here that I missed you the most. Here that I worried about you. Here that I wanted my hands on you, wanted to make love with you. This is where I imagined our reunion."

***

Quinn lay in the dark, listening to Rachel breathe, not touching her. He needed a moment for himself and she was dead to the world. Exhausted as he was, but sleep was eluding him. It felt good to soak up the ambience, the presence of her in the room. Hell, she made the whole house feel different. But not exactly in the settled way he'd dreamed of.

There was still uncertainty. Yes, he loved her with all of his heart and soul, but no, he still didn't trust her completely. Would he ever? That was a worry to him. He needed to get back to work. There were men depending on him. Men who trusted him completely.

But his wife didn't. The thought rolled around uncomfortably. He turned his head to study her. The pale green light coming from the clock-radio washed an eerie light across her skin. Making her look a bit otherworldly. And wasn't that a curiosity that he'd already ousted the word *ghostly* from his vocabulary. He'd never actively believed in life continuing after death on a different plane, or other type of existence. But neither had he disbelieved. It really hadn't been something he'd put any thought into. And now, here it was, a part of his life. Rachel's connection to what he now thought of as the other side left him no choice but to accept that there were way more possibilities than he'd ever considered.

He'd blindly accepted Grace and Logan's extra abilities, and on the surface, he viewed Rachel's gift the same way. So why was it nagging at him now?

Perhaps being grounded here in his own home. Acknowledging the differences between what he'd expected of a reunion with Rachel and what had actually happened. Or was it more connected to the future, to not having a clear picture of what would be?

He could fix that. Rachel had a vision. She wanted to build a rehab center for horses and he had people who needed the same thing. They could work on it together. But without him taking over, and he knew that part would be hard.

And then the bottom line. What he'd been circling around the whole time he'd been lying here, thinking. What would happen the next time she heard the voices? Would she panic and run again? He didn't think so, but he didn't know for sure and that gnawed a hole in his gut.

"What's wrong?"

He loved how she sounded when her voice was soft with sleep and his smile came unbidden. "Nothing, exactly. I still need time to work everything out in my head."

"It will be okay, I promise." She reached a hand toward him and he took it, laid it over his heart.

Her breathing leveled out again as she went back to sleep, and he lay there for a very long time awake, but no longer unsettled. He had to let go of the need to control each and every detail of their lives. He would go back to work on Monday, help the clients who needed him, and help himself by leaving Rachel here. She hadn't been out of his sight in weeks, and it was time he stopped hovering.

As he'd say to his patients, "One step, one day, or one minute at a time, pal. Break it down and get through it."

***

Twelve hours later, at his desk in the city, he reminded himself again about those steps. He went to the window and stared out across the concrete landscape. He had three more clients to see before he could leave. And they were all more important than his worries, so he stuffed his thoughts into a mental file, and considered the man about to arrive.

A paramedic who'd attended one too many preventable accidents where there'd been nothing he could do for the victims. What a shame the service he worked for hadn't provided any kind of support for its employees. If this man had been properly debriefed after those ugly shifts, there was a good chance he wouldn't be debilitated now, unable to sleep at night for the nightmares—the bloodied corpses of helpless victims that plagued him. And he wouldn't be suffering every time he heard a certain ringtone, the one he'd heard coming from a phone still clasped in the hand of a dead teenager who'd been driving down the interstate on his way home from a ballgame.

No, the man shouldn't be living his own version of hell, and his family shouldn't have to be constantly worried that he'd do something awful, something permanent, to end the horrors that refused to allow his mind to relax, to rest.

When the door opened, Quinn took in the facial expression and body language of a survivor. "How's your day going, Jacob?" he asked as they moved in unison toward the pool table.

This man needed all of him. One hundred percent of his attention to get through yet another day on the planet.

***

After his last client left, Quinn stood alone once again at the window, rolled his shoulders to loosen the taut muscles, and allowed his mind to wander back to the subject of Rachel. Would she be more comfortable with the voices and his insistence that she wasn't suffering from what had killed her mother if she had a therapist of her own? Possibly. But getting her to see someone would be next to impossible. And as her husband, shouldn't he be supportive of what *she* wanted and not pushing her toward something *he* wanted?

He'd leave things alone for now. Work with her on the project. Get their day-to-day life back onto a smooth and trusting path. Which reminded him: dinner at the big house tonight. With Julia and whoever else she'd bullied into attending.

He shook his head. That wasn't fair. She wasn't a bully. She was a demanding mother and family leader. Life had made her that way and she didn't back down unless she had to. Luckily, her children had learned how to cope with her, just as they'd learned to respect her. She was a hell of a matriarch.

A knock on his door had him swinging around in time to see it swing open, but there was no one there. Movement had his gaze dropping toward the floor, and he couldn't help the smile that took over his face. A puppy. A big-footed black and tan puppy was being shoved through the door by a pair of hands he recognized as his wife's.

He crouched down and called softly, "Come on, puppy."

The critter's head came up, and appearing to forget about what was pushing at his backside, he got that happy puppy look. The kind that would garner cute captions on social media.

Quinn held out his hand and the pup came to him, all smiling face, clumsy paws, and wriggling body. Managing to keep his fingers away from the needle-sharp teeth, Quinn said, "Hey, big guy, no eating hands."

"He's a she. And she has no manners yet," Rachel said, crouching down to rub the round belly when the puppy flopped onto her back.

"Hey," Quinn said as he leaned over to kiss his wife hello. "I thought you were staying on the ranch today. Making plans with Julia."

"Spent the morning locked indoors doing just that. But then your mom decided we should come to town."

"And where did you pick up this little charmer?"

She stood, leaned against his desk, and crossed her legs at the ankles. The view was spectacular, but he needed to stand. Where he could reach her mouth.

He tucked the pup under his arm. "If that was meant to distract me, it's working." His lips met hers, tasted, teased, then moved on to her jaw. "I've missed you today."

"Me, too."

The puppy whined.

"So is this a visitor, or a new member of the family?" He set the antsy critter on the floor and let it toddle about, sniffing at the carpet. "Does she need to pee?"

"Nope, I didn't bring her in until she'd gone. Didn't want her to mess up her introduction. Can we keep her?"

He smiled. "What is she?"

"Pure mutt. A kid had a box of them at the grocery store."

"And you only bought one? I'm impressed."

When she looked away, studied the ceiling for a moment, he laughed. "How many?"

The look on her face was half laugh, half embarrassment. "There were only three left. If I'd taken only one, she'd have been lonely. If I'd taken a second to keep her company, I'd be leaving one behind, all sad and without her sisters."

"So we have three puppies?"

She nodded.

"I'm curious. Why did you bring in this one in particular? I mean, to show me. Is she the cutest?"

"She was the first one to pee. I left your mom in the parking lot with the other two."

He laughed and drew her in to hold on for a minute, reveling in the woman she was, and rocked her back and forth.

"I love you, Quinn Meyer. With all my freaking heart, I love you." She held his face in her hands, and rained tiny kisses over it while his fingers slid down to her butt to pull her closer.

"I hate to interrupt." Julia's voice held repressed laughter. "But there is a bit of a problem here."

The puppy they'd forgotten to watch was headed out the door dragging the purse Rachel had dropped on the floor. Laughing, Quinn grabbed the delinquent and carefully removed the handle from between razor sharp teeth.

"A bit of a klepto, this one."

Quinn's part-time receptionist showed up then with another puppy in her arms, one with a death grip on a pad of sticky notes. "I think it runs in the family."

"Oh, dear," said Rachel.

"I'm done for the day. How about we get this motley crew home?"

Julia's eyebrows went up, but there was a twinkle in her eye. "I certainly hope you're referring to the canines in the room."

Quinn's only response was an expression identical to his mother's.

The ride back to the ranch was quieter than expected. The puppies fell asleep in the back of Julia's SUV and were no trouble at all. Even Julia nodded off in the backseat while Rachel filled Quinn in on the progress they'd made on the plans.

"I still need a name," she said.

"For the puppies, too."

"True. We need to name them before Dhillon gets wind of them."

"You don't want puppies named after hockey equipment?"

"Well, with Puck and Stick already taken, I'd just as soon not have to stick my head out the back door and yell, Jockstrap."

Quinn laughed. "We need a new theme."

"Not a sport."

"How about states?"

"Or presidents," Julia added in a sleepy voice.

"Hmmm. We could just use regular girl names," said Quinn.

"Think about where they're going to be and what will happen when we call them. Will several Susans answer? I want them to be part of my project, but I guess Faith, Hope, and Honor would be too much?"

"How about flowers? Rose, Orchid, and Camellia."

Rachel smiled. "That could work. But let's not decide until we know them better and can base their names on who they are."

"Okay," Quinn agreed. "What about a name for your ranch?"

"I've been thinking about that one for a while. And I think, especially if we blend the horse rescue with PTSD rehab, I want to call it Heroes, or Hero Ranch. But like the dog names, I need to see what really fits before I commit."

CHAPTER 31

The whole family had showed up for dinner at the big house—at least everyone not on assignment.

Unwilling to put the sleepy puppies in the big crate with a fluffy cushioned bottom, Angie and Eve each snuggled one on their lap, while Dhillon played on the floor with the one not quite ready to pack it in yet.

"We should find a way to bottle puppy-breath," said Angie. "They could pump it into prisons and make all the bad guys mellow out."

"Farts work the same way in school," said Dhillon and earned himself a scowl from his grandmother. "It's true. Everybody shuts up and tries to hold their breath."

Angie rolled her eyes, and when Quinn opened his mouth to speak, her eyebrows lowered and her mouth became pinched. He shrugged.

"Even after puppy-breath goes away, dogs are helpful for improving mood and being in tune with people," said Rachel. "These three are destined to be the first of many we'll be hoping to place within my new project."

"Dogs to keep the horses company? Aren't goats a better choice? They can cohab quite comfortably with horses. Eat the same food, etcetera."

Eve had a good point. And Rachel ran with it. "Great idea. We'll rescue some goats, too. But the dogs are for the humans coming into the project."

All heads swung her way and she swallowed hard to fight the initial wave of panic. "Things have expanded on their own. Sort of. What's the point of stopping at horses and a few goats? We're creating a rescue center for humans *and* animals. They will support each other. While treatment will, of course, be a huge component, there will also be residential spots for those with other reasons for needing help. Old race-trackers, the homeless, etcetera."

Gage was shaking his head. "You could be opening a huge can of worms, Rach."

"I'm not going into this with rose-colored glasses. Well, not exactly anyway. I have a plan. We'll start small and bring residents in as the building progresses. Kind of like building a town. And hopefully, we'll be able to sustain ourselves."

"Broad statement. What exactly does it mean?" asked Gage.

"Boy, you guys are tough."

"And successful, so don't let them scare you. They're trying to help," said the matriarch, with a telling glance around the table.

"Julia and I spent the day working out some of the business plan, and a ten-year timeline."

"Holy cow. I'll be old before it's finished."

Angie gave her son a quick grimace. "I won't be old, so neither will you. You'll be in your twenties, and trust me, pal, that's a long ways from old." She turned to Rachel. "What will you have in ten years? As in the land, buildings, people and all. What's the goal?"

Quinn smiled. "Yeah, what exactly will we have?"

Her smile grew. "There will be a residential compound not unlike a resort, with a lodge sort of main building and a collection of cottages. I expect to have a permanent occupancy of around twenty-five, and room for another twenty-five visitors.

"Everyone will have responsibilities of some kind, whether it be mucking stalls and working with the horses, or weeding the gardens, or helping prepare the food grown in them."

She smiled at the puppy now falling asleep on Dhillon's lap. "We're going to work with a rescue group who train service and companion canines so all the residences will be pet-friendly. As well, we'll have stabling for up to fifty horses. I hope most of the horses, once rehabbed, will be able to live outdoors on pasture with a great deal of freedom, but the barns will be needed for transition and therapy."

Gage was nodding. "Sounds like you're going to need a big chunk of land, Rachel. Have you started looking?"

"I've given Rachel the Spencer place," said Julia, and there was a collective gasp.

"I thought that was in Dad's name." There was an edge of disbelief in Eve's tone, but Angie remained strangely silent.

"It was."

Well, there was a non-answer. Quinn wanted to push, but the subject was dropped when Consuelo rolled the dinner cart into the room and began insisting the puppies be put in their crate before plates went on the table.

He studied his mother and recognized the closed expression. She wasn't going to say anything more on the subject. She'd know that he'd eventually see the deed, the exact date his father had signed the property over. It was odd that she'd gone outside of the family policy of having everything co-owned. A policy borne from years of men going off to war or on a mission they might never come home from.

The Spencer place had been what he understood as his father's last property purchase, and he'd been going through a spell of paranoia at the time, refusing to put anyone else's name on the deed with his. Perhaps this was a good sign. Maybe he was recovering. A cold chill ran up his spine. Or maybe he was clearing up his affairs. Maybe he was taking those same steps his brother had. Making sure things were tidy when he left for the last time.

Suicide was Quinn's ultimate enemy. The one that drove him on, relentless with his clients and his family when it came to debriefing and taking care of each other emotionally.

The rising fears were quelled by a hard glance from his mother. She followed it with a small smile and a shake of her head.

As his stomach settled, Rachel whispered in his ear, "She said you'd worry. Said I should tell you he's okay and not going to do anything stupid."

He squeezed her hand and managed a weak smile for his mother. "Thanks."

***

Six months later.

The Spencer place bordered the ranch's southeast fence line and hadn't been inhabited for over twenty years, so there was plenty of work still to be done. But look how far they'd come.

Rachel's heart caught in her throat as she watched her husband approach. Bronze skin covered chest and arm muscles not unfamiliar with hard labor, and low-slung faded jeans covered the finest ass she'd ever seen. She couldn't seem to get enough of the man. Had she been like this before she'd run away? Hard to say. She'd been so preoccupied with what she'd feared was the progression of a terrifying illness.

Cupping the back of her head, he drew her in for a fast, hot kiss, and she had to grab on as her knees threatened to leave her on the ground in a heap.

"Hi." The gravel in his voice washed over her, let her know he wasn't unaffected by her either.

"Hmmm." She gripped the waistband of his jeans. "Anybody else here?"

He tipped his head toward the barn. "Nathan, Gage, and Tyler are in there."

"Too bad."

He gripped her wrist as she stepped away. "What were you thinking about a minute ago?"

She grinned. "How long it would take me to get your pants off."

He groaned. "Unfair. But I meant before that. You were thinking heavy thoughts." His grip loosened and he raised her hand to kiss the palm.

"Wondering." She stopped.

"Wondering what?"

Her gaze locked on his. "If I'd always loved you this much. I mean before I left, when I was so caught up in the fear."

With his hands looped around her waist, he asked, "Any conclusions?"

She shook her head. "I can't imagine anything so bad right now. Nothing that could possibly drive me away from you."

Before he could respond, there was a shout from the barn. "Quinn! Let the woman go and get your ass back to work."

Quinn flipped him the bird, but Gage laughed and sauntered toward them. "You bring us food, Rach?"

"Cooler's in the back. Consuelo didn't know how many were over here today so she filled it."

Gage hauled the cooler out of Rachel's pickup and carried it toward the barn. "Too hot out here in the sun. 'Course, you lovebirds can stay out here and bake your brains if you like."

"Speaking of lovebirds, how's Cass feeling?" Quinn had a soft spot for his pregnant sister-in-law. He'd been part of her rescue a year or so ago when the Minnows were hell-bent on getting their hands on her.

"Morning sickness is starting to ease off, thank God." Gage shook his head. "Not like she'd admit how awful she was feeling, but it was hard to watch. Harder to be her. But she's tough. Won't let me hang around for the worst of it. Kicks my ass out of the house at daybreak and says I can't come back until after lunch."

"She helped Consuelo build the sandwiches." Rachel nodded toward the cooler. "Said she put something special in there for you."

"Yeah?" He set it down and opened the lid. Poked around for a bit before coming up with a clear bag with two cans of ginger ale and a sleeve of soda crackers. He laughed, snagged the phone off his belt and wandered away, completely forgetting about the food.

"Let's take this inside," said Quinn.

Rachel followed him into the barn.

She was impressed with the progress they'd made in the cavernous space. A long alleyway down the middle was flanked by two rows of box stalls. She'd designed them with half walls of concrete topped by mesh, giving the horses full view of each other. And the stall fronts would be mesh from floor to ceiling and the concrete covered with rubber matting.

They set the food out on the long wooden table the guys had built for the barn's lunch room. Checking the big fridge and finding it a bit low on sodas and water, she went back to the truck for the cases she'd brought.

When Gage ended his phone call, he helped her with the load. "Cass says hey."

"I'm going to see her later. She's helping me with the shopping."

"Where are you going?"

The instant tension in his voice had her laying a hand on his arm. She understood his concerns. Cass had been chased down and nearly killed by the Minnows and was still a target, so she rarely left the ranch. "We're shopping online. Not going anywhere but the boardroom."

When he lifted an eyebrow, she grinned. "Big wall screens, six computers. We're doing a buying blitz for the main building. Linens, window covering, carpets, the works. Julia and Eve are helping too."

"What? No Angie? She's an online shopping addict."

Rachel frowned. "She can't come. Said she had something she had to do today and took off in the Steed early."

"Hmmm." Gage set the cases on the floor and Rachel unpacked them into the fridge.

"Quinn," he said, "do you know what Angie's up to today? Rachel says she took off in the bird."

Quinn shook his head. "Nope."

"Hmmm."

When Tyler and Nathan, the youngest two brothers, wandered in from the farthest stall where they'd been working, Gage asked, "You two have any idea where Angie was off to this morning?"

"Nope." They shook their heads.

Quinn studied Gage for a minute before asking, "What's the problem, Gage?"

He shrugged. "She's been secretive lately. I'm wondering if Dhillon's father is sniffing around."

"Have you tried asking her what's up?"

That earned him a scowl. "Of course not. You know what she's like about that subject."

If Quinn had been close enough, he'd have given his brother a finger flick to the side of the head. "I meant, did you ask her *generally* what was going on, without bringing up the subject of the father thing?"

"No."

"Well, maybe one of us should."

"You're the talker. You do it. But do it soon because something's up. I can feel it."

"Sure it's not just a pregnant wife that's got you on edge?" asked Tyler. "I guess you're cut off until the puking stops." He laughed and Nathan joined in.

"Idiots." Gage raised an eyebrow at Quinn. "You sure these two are ours? Maybe the parents found them under a bush somewhere."

Quinn glanced at the two younger men who appeared to be clones of Gage ten years ago. "Yeah, right." If there was anything his parents had done consistently was produce children who were all stamped the same. The girls were tiny but tough redheads like their maternal grandmother and the boys were all the image of their father, tall, dark, and physically gifted with natural athleticism.

"You're itching for another mission so you can get out of barn-building, Gage," said Nathan.

"And away from a wife who spends half her day with her head in the toilet," added Tyler.

Quinn stopped himself from verbally slapping the two of them down and waited instead to see what Gage's reaction would be.

Surprisingly, it was a grin. "You puppies have no idea. I have a gorgeous wife with my child growing inside her. The last thing I want is to spend any time away from her." The grin faded. "But I'm worried about Angie. The last time she was secretive like this is when she was pregnant with Dhillon."

Rachel put a hand on his arm. "I think she's okay. Whatever it is she's up to, there's no worry involved. She seems happy. So why not just relax and wait it out? She'll let you in when she's ready. And she's not stupid. She won't get into any kind of trouble without asking you guys for help."

"Rachel's right," said Quinn.

Gage nodded and changed the subject. "How come you didn't bring the girls, Rach?"

"Funny man. Three half-grown galloping puppies don't belong in this construction mess. Coordination isn't their strong suit."

"Well, considering their names, I'm not surprised."

She shot Gage a look. "Don't play innocent with me. I know you were part of the male conspiracy."

Quinn laughed. "They were supposed to be a joke."

"Right. And then they started coming to their names." Rachel shook her head. "My own damned fault for taking so long to decide."

Tyler grinned. "I think Mary, Curly, and Flo suits them."

Rachel's bland stare made Quinn laugh. "Careful, guys, she brought us lunch."

"Thanks, Rachel," Tyler and Nathan chimed in unison, making her laugh.

"Time for me to head out and slay the market," she said, rubbing her hands together and heading for the door. She turned back. "Maybe I'll convince Julia to do some redecorating in the main house while we're doing such a big order. You guys won't mind pink sheets will you? And some pretty flowery curtains?" She laughed and left them groaning.

Quinn caught up with her at the truck. "We good for tonight?"

She stepped into him, pressed her whole body against his. "The gear is all ready to load as soon as you get home, and Julia's good with the girls staying over. Dhillon's doing a sleepover, too, so they'll be well entertained."

His mouth closed over hers and her lips parted instantly. While their tongues tangled, he walked her backward to press her against the truck and she yelped. "Hot!"

He jerked her clear and smoothed his hands up and down her back while apologizing profusely.

"I'm okay. Come back here." With a firm grip on his waistband, she tugged him against her.

His hands slid to her ass and lifted her for just the right connection before kissing her again, deeper, longer, with the kind of passion that begged for more. A lot more. And when she ground her hips against him, he groaned and buried his face in her hair. "Maybe I should book off early."

She shook her head. "I've got a shopping spree to get through first. I'll see you in a couple of hours." She pushed on his chest and he kissed her once more, hard and quick.

"Later. We'll finish this later."

"Damn sure."

CHAPTER 32

After three hours, they'd had enough virtual shopping, and were now sprawled on loungers on the patio, under the thatched sun shade.

"What's going on with Angie?" asked Rachel, watching the reactions of the three women.

Cass rested the cool glass of iced tea against her forehead and sighed. Eve glanced at her mother, and Julia reached for the pitcher to refill her glass which was only half empty.

"Don't all speak at once."

Eve opened her mouth, then closed it again.

Julia ended the silence. "What do you mean?"

"Quinn's worried about her." She left it at that to see where they'd go.

"There's nothing to be worried about."

"She's flying off on her own. Leaving for hours at a time, and he wants to know what she's up to."

"She's working on a project for me."

Rachel waited for more, but it wasn't forthcoming. "And?"

"That's it. There is no *and*."

Eve had an odd look on her face, so Rachel tried her. "Anything you'd like to add? For Quinn's sake?"

"She's happy. Whatever she's doing, she's happy, so tell him not to worry."

Obviously, they weren't going to say anything more, so she gave up. Angie was a grown woman, and Quinn would have to be satisfied with the answers she'd managed to drag out of them—thin as they were.

"What was the delivery date on the flooring, Rachel?" asked Cass.

She considered the subject change and the corner of her mouth quirked. "Flooring comes next week. Furniture the week after." The main building was coming together quickly. It'd taken a month to put up, and in only four more weeks, it would be ready for the first residents to move in.

"I sure wish you'd let us throw a grand opening bash."

She shook her head. "The point of the place is low-key and relaxed. The last thing we need is glitz and publicity."

"What about your house? When will it be ready? We can at least have a housewarming for you there."

Actually, she and Quinn were going to warm it just fine all by themselves tonight, even though they wouldn't be moving into it for months yet. Gage had asked them to stay on the ranch until after Cass gave birth. She needed people around her to make up for not being able to be seen in public once her pregnancy was visible.

"How about next weekend? Just family though. No outsiders, okay?"

Cass grinned at Julia's perplexed expression. "I think Julia had other ideas."

Rachel winced. "I love that you want to do this for us. But the new house isn't all that far from the main building, and I don't want to have outsiders on the property if we can help it.

Haven is supposed to be exactly that and I don't want an opening or party to mar the promise of the name."

Julia's sigh was somewhat exaggerated, but she nodded. "I understand what you're doing. I'd thought this would be the one time, because there wouldn't be any residents, human *or* animal, to be disturbed."

Rachel chewed on the inside of her cheek. Her mother-in-law wasn't wrong. Maybe she should consider it.

"And," Julia continued, as though she'd seen the chink in the younger woman's armor, "if you're considering corporate support, this would be the opportunity for showing off your vision."

"I hear what you're saying, and you're probably right. But I'm still not sure. Quinn and I will talk about it while we're away, and I promise an answer when we get back."

Julia nodded, barely concealing a smile. "And you, Cassandra, how are you feeling today? Any better?"

Cass shot a grin at Rachel as though to say, *My turn for the hot seat.* "Much better. I didn't even need any crackers and ginger ale this morning. Chances are, your son's going to get lucky tonight."

Eve nearly choked on a mouthful of iced tea.

***

When Quinn came through the door at the end of the day, he was surprised to find himself looking for a puppy welcome. He missed the scrabbling of toenails, the thumping of bodies, and how they bumped each other into the wall rounding the corner. And there was silence instead of the mixed whines and yips of excitement. He missed his girls.

But when he spotted Rachel standing in the doorway to the kitchen, his heart leapt and all thoughts of puppies evaporated. In two strides, he had her in his arms and squealing as he planted kisses all over her face.

When she finally managed to push him away, he laughed as she straightened her clothes. "You're wasting your time. The clothes are coming off."

"Not until you take a shower. You've got sawdust stuck all over."

He grabbed her hand and dragged her toward the bedroom. "Come help me get it off."

"So you can play water games?"

"Damn sure. You teased me at lunch and I've been waiting all day for retaliation."

Standing face-to-face in the bathroom, Rachel was thankful for his western-style shirt with snaps as she ripped it open, then went for the button on the top of his jeans. "Lose the shirt, cowboy." She was dragging off his jeans before he could blink, and shoving him into the shower. "Get a head start on the sawdust and I'll be there in a minute." She ducked his reaching hands and scooted away, leaving him alone.

He had his face in the spray, rinsing off a layer of soap, when hands slid around his waist. With her mouth on his back, her breasts pressing into him, and her fingers gliding over his abs, heaven wasn't far off. He braced his hands against the wall and absorbed the pure pleasure for as long as he dared, then spun around, lifted her, and her ankles locked at his back.

Home.

***

On the night of the Haven unveiling, Rachel found it odd, to see the place filled with people. Not that she didn't hope for it to be fully occupied, one day, but the fanfare and the noise felt so wrong in such a tranquil setting.

"You okay, Rachel?" Logan's hand squeezed her shoulder. "You've got a faraway look on your face."

"Hmmm." She let her gaze drift around the great room. "So many people. And they all seem to be talking at once. I was wishing I was outside, but I promised Julia I wouldn't run away. I don't do social very well."

"You and Grace have a lot in common." He tipped his head toward the hallway to the left, one of three opening off the great room. "Last I saw, Julia was heading that way."

"Dining hall and kitchen areas. She's probably gone for a snack. Have you seen the spread of food in there?"

"Maybe I should check it out. Want to come with me? You'll still look like you're being social."

She slipped her hand into the crook of the arm he held out, glad for an excuse to get out of the noise. And she didn't dare complain. The people were talking about Haven, the dream and all the good they could do here. A room filled with people willing to contribute in one way or another, be it a straight-up monetary contribution, advertising, referrals, or even government assistance and recognition of their programs, was a good thing. There were dozens of therapists in the room, professionals eager to be part of the treatment and housing for those suffering from PTSD and other disorders that would benefit from the kind of experience Rachel was determined to deliver.

"And to think, it all began with a horse," she murmured, then stopped to stare at the tables filled with food. "There's hardly anyone here. Why is it still so loud?"

"What do you mean?" What began as curiosity, quickly became concern. "What's wrong?"

"Voices," she whispered. "I thought it was all the people, but it's the voices."

He gripped both her arms as though afraid she'd fall, and she wasn't sure she wouldn't. "Quinn."

"I've told Grace, she'll bring him." Logan guided her to a chair. "What can I do to help?"

"Angie, too. We'll need the helicopter to evac whoever is about to die."

"Do you know how soon it will be?"

"They're loud, getting worse, so it's close. Did Grace answer you?"

"Yes. Quinn's coming. He'll be here any second. She's still trying to raise Angie."

Quinn was suddenly there, crouched in front of her. "Angie's on her way. She's bringing Dhillon with her. He'll stay with Julia. How bad is it, baby?"

She tried to smile, but couldn't pull it off. "Bad. Soon. It'll be soon."

"Do you have any idea where? Do you want to go back out to the main area, where most of the people are?"

"No. I'll stay here. Where's Grace?"

"She says she's keeping watch over the great room, and she's sent Gage and Cass out to the gathering on the patio."

"What about the barns and other buildings?" asked Logan.

"I've sent word to Security to up their vigilance. Told them I'd had an anonymous tip about a possible intruder."

Rachel nodded, pressed her fingers to her temples as the pressure built. When her heart bumped, then started to race, she exhaled hard. "Now. It's now—"

A scream rent the air.

She jerked to her feet and was on the move, flanked by the two men, headed for the huge kitchen area attached to the dining room.

The chef lay on the floor with a screaming woman standing over him.

Logan grabbed her and hauled her to the doorway, effectively blocking the entrance for anyone else. Quinn and Rachel went to their knees. She at the man's head, he at his chest.

Rachel was preternaturally calm now. She placed one hand on either side of the man's head.

"Is he…?" Quinn whispered, and she nodded.

Concentrating on the drive of energy through her arms, she became deaf to anything going on around her. She blew a breath across the face below hers and silently chanted, "You will not leave here yet. You will not die. I won't let Death have you. Not tonight. Tonight you are mine and you will not leave."

Quinn watched expressions blast across her face, and in the interest of looking like he was doing something useful, opened the buttons of the white jacket. He stared at the man's chest, willing it to rise. *Come on, man, she's giving you a chance to live through whatever's happening to you.*

His own breath, which he didn't realize he'd been holding, whooshed out when the chest in front of him rose. Thank God. And Rachel. Her skin was stark white and her mouth was trembling.

Eve slid to her knees beside them. "What happened?"

"Don't know. We found him down like this. Don't know if he fell or what."

"Rachel?"

Her voice was barely more than a whisper. "His heart had stopped."

"Did you…?"

She nodded. "Took a long time. He didn't want—"

"To come back. Angie's on her way. We need to get him to the helipad," said Quinn.

CHAPTER 33

"Home sweet home," said Angie as she worked the controls and landed the Steed alongside her house.

Quinn squeezed Rachel's hand and said into his mic, "A freaking long night. Thanks for being there, kid."

"Glad to be useful."

"Kind of screwed up your movie night with the kid."

She snorted. "Got me out of another horror flick. Did I tell you he was going to make Julia watch it with him later?"

"She texted me that the party broke up as soon as we lifted off, and she was headed home with Dhillon to watch a movie. I bet she wished she'd stayed with the others to clean up instead."

They removed their helmets and stepped onto solid ground. The usual country silence was magnified by the dark and the canopy of brilliant stars. Quinn draped an arm around each woman. "Good work tonight, team."

"He's not going to make it," said Rachel.

"All the magic in the world can't make a man want to live. According to his doctor, he'd been scheduled for heart surgery twice and backed out. You gave him that one last chance, and he didn't want it," said Quinn.

"I bet they lose him on the table."

He nodded. "Probably. I wish Eve had come home with us. It'll be hard on her if they don't save him. Especially hard because it was her miracle drug that kept him alive on the ride in."

"Everyone pitched in and did the best they could. So I think we should all be able to sleep tonight. You okay being alone, Angie?"

"Not enough night left to bother sleeping. I've got a bunch of paperwork waiting for me." At the sound of an impatient bark, she grinned. "And Chance for company. I'd better go let him out. Catch you guys tomorrow."

Strolling the paved roadway in the starlit night helped them to unwind. To let go of the what-ifs and the frustration that had wormed its way in.

"There will be men and women, people like him, in our programs, won't there?" asked Rachel.

"Yep."

"I'm not going to like that part. Can—"

"Counseling change their minds?" He rubbed at the tense muscles in the back of her neck. "There are many we'll be able to help. But there will always be the others. The ones who won't be reachable." He sighed, thinking of his father. "The most successful are those who want help. And likewise, my failures are pretty much those who are pushed into a program and arrive kicking and screaming."

"I was hoping the connection with the animals would give a bit of incentive to those who don't think they want or need help."

"It's a good plan, baby. The best. And you'll be there to see people get their lives back. Rejoin their families, become useful members of society again. But unlike the power in your hands, it's work, not magic."

"The connection between a human and an animal can be magic, Quinn. That's what I'm counting on. I'm not ignoring the possibility of loss, but I'm being optimistic about my chances to change the odds. Twenty-two suicides a day is a horrible statistic. I can't stand by and not try to change it."

He took her in his arms and stood there holding on, reveling in the beat of their hearts so close together, the lemony scent of her shampoo, the heat of her pressed against him. "I love you."

Her hands moved up and down his back as though to soothe. "I love you, too. And I love that we can work together for the souls who need us."

"I need us."

"Yeah, me too."

They walked on, hand-in-hand, silent until the lights of home became visible. "I guess there's no way we'll be able to sneak in without waking up Grace and Logan."

"Nope." And as if on cue, the girls started to bark in the backyard.

"They're outside."

And that was because Grace and Logan were there, too, snuggled together on one of the oversized lounge chairs.

Once the three dogs stopped jumping around Quinn and Rachel, they sprinted back to Grace and Logan to sit obediently on the patio.

Grace laughed. "Nicely done, ladies. But *stay* doesn't mean it's okay to run off and get silly, then come back to where you were supposed to be."

Quinn rubbed their heads. "They tend to only forget themselves and their manners for brief interludes these days. Their training is coming along quite nicely but for that."

Rachel crouched in front of each one for a quick hug. Once she stood, Grace gave them the signal for release and they went wild, running about like school kids at recess.

"They're priceless," said Logan.

"And amazing considering their age," added Grace. "We did the control switch a few times and they're quite comfortable with changing handlers. They work as well separately as they do in a group."

Rachel grinned. She was so freaking proud of the training they'd done with the girls so far, and all three looked like they were going to be awesome companions for residents at Haven.

Grace leveled a gaze at Rachel and said quietly, "You gave a man a second chance tonight, Rachel. If he dies, it's not on you."

"I know. I just wish…"

"Don't we all."

Logan got up and headed indoors, saying over his shoulders, "Stay put. I'll be right back."

When he returned, he had a platter of food. "The party broke up pretty quick after you took off, so we brought some of this back with us. I'm willing to bet you've had nothing but bad hospital coffee since I last saw you. Eat." He set the tray on the table and dragged some chairs into place.

"Thanks," said Quinn as he urged Rachel to sit beside him.

Picking their way through fancy sandwiches, a pile of giant shrimp, and chunks of cheese, Rachel thought, *This is nice, it's home.*

Grace met her gaze and nodded.

"How do you feel about having to use your powers again?" asked Logan.

"Okay," Rachel said and meant it. "This was a normal death. Not a perfectly healthy ten-year-old boy, or a person injured in some freak way. The man was a walking time-bomb. According to his assistant, he's rescheduled his bypass surgery several times over the last year."

"What happened after we left?" asked Quinn.

"People were understandably subdued, and Julia handled the questions very well. The fact that no one witnessed either the man's collapse or Rachel's intervention was fortunate."

"Thanks for that, Logan. You did a great job guarding the door, and thank heavens you were there to call on Grace and get help started on all fronts." Quinn smiled at Grace. "And thanks to you for all you did." He tipped his head. "The four of us make a dynamite team. You ever want to sign on with Meyers, or with Haven, we'd be glad to have whatever time you could give us."

Grace's smile blossomed. "You have a great project going here and if you need me for something, don't hesitate to call. Now that Logan and I have moved out of the house and into Paradise, it's easier to get away on a moment's notice. Caroline's there to take Milo and Careless whenever I need her to."

Quinn's phone vibrated. It was Eve. "Hey, bro. Looking for a ride home and Angie's not picking up."

"Did he"

"Yeah. The team called it about thirty minutes ago."

"Shit." He sighed and let it go. "Angie said she wasn't going to bed, but she must have shut off her phone. I'll drive over and get her for you."

"I hate to be a pain, but I've got patients today."

"No worries. I'll head over there now."

He stuffed the phone back into his pocket and told the group what he was up to.

"I'll come with you," said Rachel.

"Come on, then."

They didn't talk about the death of a stranger, the man they'd fought to keep alive. They didn't speak at all—until they arrived at Angie's house.

The helipad was empty.

Quinn's stomach clenched. Something felt wrong about this.

"Maybe she got a call from the field."

"We don't have anything going on."

"I'll call dispatch anyway, see what's up." But when she did, they informed her there'd been no callout. No request for Angie or the Steed.

Quinn dialed the main house and discovered his mother was already up. "What's Angie working on?" he asked after a perfunctory hello.

"Well, good morning, Quinn. Angie doesn't have an assignment. Why are you asking? And in the middle of the night?"

"It's four in the morning. Night's over. Eve's trying to reach her for a ride home, but she's gone and so's the bird."

"Don't fret about her, Quinn, I think she's seeing someone and doesn't want to share it with the family yet."

He ground his teeth. "You're not worried at all?"

"She's a mother. Her son is on a sleepover. She's likely headed off to visit her man friend. Leave her be."

"She'd have to log the trip," he muttered more to himself than to Julia, but she was quick to comment.

"Do *not* go spying on your sister. She's an adult. Leave her alone."

He sighed and said, "Fine. I'll drive down and pick up Eve."

"That's silly. Angie said she'd be here for breakfast with Dhillon and I. I'll send her then and she'll still get there before you could. Go and get some sleep instead. I'll call Eve and let her know. How's Rachel doing with last night's ordeal?"

"Fine. She's doing fine."

"Good. Why don't you bring her and join us for breakfast at eight?"

"We have Grace and Logan staying over, so some other time."

When she finally let him go, he realized she'd managed to diffuse the anxiety that'd been riding along the edges of annoyance. He shook his head and said to Rachel, "She's up to something."

CHAPTER 34

Rachel stood back to admire her handiwork. The brass plaque looked good despite the warning printed on it. But the insurance company had been adamant. Potentially dangerous horses had to be kept in a quarantine-like setting. Isolated from anyone who was not specifically assigned to work with them.

Dweezle—she hated that name and couldn't wait to change it—would be safe in here while he was rehabbed, a project she was taking on herself. His one-acre paddock had a six-foot high wire mesh fence. And there was a full screen at his stall door so there was no chance he could reach over and bite someone. Likewise, no one could touch him, and Rachel hoped that would eventually make him feel safe. The paddocks and stalls on either side of him would be occupied by Donald the miniature donkey, and Bonnie the goat. Calm and steady companions, they'd both been rescued from abusive situations years ago by the Meyers family who'd paid to sponsor them at a local shelter.

She so looked forward to seeing the horse moving freely around his space. He'd spent months at a world-renowned vet clinic where he'd been checked over completely. His entire body scanned, searched for an electronic implant of any kind before he was left alone to let down from his life on the racetrack and wait for Haven to be ready for him.

Rachel hated that he'd been fitted with a humane wire muzzle before loading onto the van for the final leg of his journey. But it was a necessary precaution while he was being handled by strangers.

Worry niggled at her. She'd wanted to make the trip with him, but Quinn had balked. Hadn't wanted to let her go alone and he couldn't rearrange his schedule to go with her. Was it all about her safety? Of course not. It would be a long time before he'd trust her completely and she understood that. Didn't like it, but understood.

In the meantime, there was more work to be done in the other barns. Stalls needed to be bedded down for two horses she'd agreed to take the night before, sight unseen. She'd received a call from a local rescue group who were picking up two dozen pit bulls seized from a fighting ring, and had discovered two emaciated horses on the same property. It was amazing to be able to make a difference to a couple of horses she'd never met, and she pushed away the worry of what it would be like when they were full and she had to turn horses away.

She shuddered and reminded herself not to borrow trouble.

"Hey, Rach!"

She spun to see Gage and Cass coming out of the building that housed all the machinery.

"You done already?" asked Rachel.

"Naw, but the smell of the oil was getting to Cass, so she wants to hang with you instead of me."

Rachel noted the other woman's lack of color. "Morning sickness still?"

"No, that seems to be over finally. The smell of anything like gas or diesel has always bothered me. Besides, Gage isn't much for conversation when he's working on that stuff."

Rachel nodded. Quinn was the same when he messed with machinery. All manly concentration. "Come on. I'm headed to the kennel to spring the girls for a while. I hate locking them up, but it's safer for them right now."

They took the three dogs to the main lodge, grabbed cold drinks from the kitchen, and settled on the patio in the shade of a ginormous yellow umbrella to watch the canines romp.

Curly had the Frisbee and was playing keep-away. But the other two were crafty, flanking her and alternately diving at the florescent orange toy. When Flo finally got it, she galloped right to Rachel and dumped it into her lap. Slobber and all.

This was their last day here for a while. Tomorrow, she'd be driving them to a compound outside of San Antonio where their service training would begin in earnest. They'd be based in their new location for three months while they underwent intense situational exposure and evaluation.

Rachel's wish was to have the three of them as permanent Haven residents, to be a part of the daily lives of the men and women who would be staying there, short- or long-term. The trainer's experience was with both service and support dogs— those who were taken to where comfort was needed. People needing post-disaster assistance, hospital patients, and rescue workers always found a great sense of security in the presence of her trainees.

She'd warned Rachel that because the girls would be part of a long-term residential rehabilitation program, one or all of them could become attached to single individuals as they would have a need for the stability of one master.

This possibility, in the end, garnered them funding as a pilot training project.

At first Rachel had balked, not liking the visual of Mary, Curly, and Flo being prodded and poked and experimented on, but she'd been assured that Melinda, the trainer, would be fully in control of the project. The only requirement for the funding was the need for meticulous record-keeping and contact with the dogs for eighteen months.

Funding, she thought, was such an interesting concept, one Julia had introduced her to early on. People would pay a great deal of money for the kind of services Haven was offering. But Rachel wanted to serve the folks who didn't have the money to buy what they needed. And those who didn't think there was any kind of help for them.

So she'd let Julia lead the charge and had gone along on many a meeting to seek charitable contributions. Big corporations had forked up the cost of a one-year stay in exchange for one bed, for four months of the year. And she hadn't even had to specify what months would be made available.

After each meeting, they'd gone home and debriefed with several family members, everyone brainstorming yet more ideas. The project had grown exponentially.

Because the operating costs would be covered by sponsorship and the land had been donated by Julia, they were able to sink a ton of money into the buildings themselves. The original dream had been expanded. Big time. Between the main lodge, sixteen cottages, and four houses, they had room for sixty guests and forty staff members.

Cass rubbed the happy dog leaning against her chair. "Days like this, I miss Blue."

"Blue?"

"My blue heeler. When we left the ranch in Washington, he went with Connie and Jared. To wherever they live now."

"Why didn't you bring him with you?"

"I was on the run from the Minnows and couldn't have a dog with me."

"But you brought the cats?" Rachel couldn't imagine traveling with cats. They seemed so unsuited to cages and such.

"Actually, it was Gage who brought them along. I'd had Blue for about ten months, but Harris and I had been together for years." She grinned. "I knew I loved Gage, but when he told me he had Harris at his place waiting for me, well, I was over the moon. What guy does that?"

"What about Merlin? I thought he was yours, too."

"He adopted me when I was in the safe house." She glanced over her shoulder. "Did you know he talks?"

Rachel's eyebrows went up. "Talks?"

Cass nodded. "I'm still never sure if it's him, or the words I imagine he'd be saying, but I swear that cat speaks to me telepathically."

Rachel heard voices. Apparently the dead communicated with her. How could she doubt that Cass had a talking cat? She shrugged. "What kind of stuff does he say?"

"Up until recently, it was silly stuff. Mostly sarcastic. But I didn't realize I was pregnant until he pointed it out."

"Seriously?"

"Yep. When Merlin flopped on the floor in front of me for his tummy rub and I said, 'Gee, pal, your belly's getting pretty big. I might have to get you some of that fat cat food,' he harrumphed and said, 'you're one to talk.'

"I remember putting my hand on my stomach, and even though it was flat as a pancake, I knew. There was a life growing inside me." She rubbed the now very visible baby bump. "I grabbed my calendar and counted the days. I was a week overdue."

The thought of an accidental pregnancy made Rachel's mouth go dry as the desert at noon. She reached for her cold drink and swallowed a big mouthful. She was careful. To a fault. She even knew when she was ovulating and avoided sex for a couple of days. And Quinn understood her fears.

***

Quinn stopped in the doorway and stared, his heart thumping in his chest. Was love supposed to randomly hit this hard? He didn't know. But the love he felt right at this moment was nearly overwhelming. He ached with the need to put his arms around her and simply hold on while inhaling the scent of her.

Instead, he stared, wondering what it was that made this particular view so powerful. Rachel was leaning back in a plastic lawn chair, with her feet propped on an upturned five-gallon pail. The white cat curled in her lap was staring at her as she read a book aloud. Both the cat in her lap and the horse on the other side of the screened wall appeared to be as mesmerized by her voice as he was.

He allowed himself to stand there and absorb her presence. Take in the emotion in her voice. He'd never met anyone like her. He remembered the wash of emotion the first time he'd set eyes on her. She'd been at Paradise when he'd delivered a retired racehorse to Grace.

She'd stood back while they unloaded the mare, silent, quick to look away each time his gaze landed on her. But when

Caroline introduced them and she lifted long lashes, he saw exotic eyes he wanted to fall into. Eyes as blue as the Texas sky. But what he saw went so much deeper. He'd been held captive since the moment they'd met.

The big gelding's nostrils flared, his head lifted, and he stared at Quinn. The cat took in Quinn's presence as well, and a smile ghosted Rachel's mouth. Without looking at him or changing her tone, as though she was still reading from the page, she said, "Merlin suggested I read aloud. And everyone appears to be enjoying."

Quinn's lips quirked. "Merlin's a pretty smart fellow."

"Yes. Cassandra brought him over. Apparently he wants to be a part of Haven."

"We're still talking about the cat, right?"

She smiled. "Yes."

"I know Cassandra has a special connection with him. How about you?"

"Well, I was just sitting here enjoying my book, spending time with Henry. I simply can't call him Dweezle so I've been trying out other names to find something that sticks. Anyhow, I was hanging out to help him get used to me, and this voice came out of nowhere saying, 'What's the book about?' When I looked around and saw no one, I thought it was random voices again. But it didn't sound anything like them."

She shook her head. "That's when Merlin sat up and stared at me and I heard the voice again. This time he said, 'Read it. It'll help the horse get used to your voice.' He curled up in my lap as soon as I started to read aloud. And Henry came over by the door and hasn't moved since."

It wasn't the first Quinn had heard of the cat talking. Nor was it the first time he'd experienced the wisdom of the feline. He'd be a good fit for Haven.

"How's it going with him?" he asked, tipping his chin toward the horse.

"He's more relaxed and he likes the story—or at least the sound of me reading. And impressively, he doesn't seem to be bothered by your presence, so I don't think he has an issue with men in particular."

She got up and undid the latch on the feed chute to drop another ration of pellets into the tub in the corner of the stall. Then she stood close as Henry ate and lifted his head occasionally to check her out. Most noticeably, his ears stayed forward and he seemed unworried about her presence so close to his food.

"How long have you been with him today?"

"Since noon."

He looked at the folded blanket in the chair. "Not the most comfortable spot. If you're going to continue doing long hours with him, I'll haul a recliner or something over for you."

"Actually, I was thinking about dragging a couple of lounge chairs over and we could stay over. It's his first night and I don't want him to be lonely. The donkey will be here at noon tomorrow so it's just the one night."

In the barn. He had meetings early in the morning. But she was right. Horses were herd animals. And this one was a special case.

CHAPTER 35

Quinn woke up stiff and sore. The lounger was comfortable enough for an afternoon siesta, but a whole night? Not for his frame. Rachel looked comfortable, snuggled into her sleeping bag on the chair beside his. Even though their chairs were touching, he felt ridiculously separated from her. He wanted to slide over closer to her, but there was a white ball of fur in the way. It seemed Merlin had staked his claim.

At a muffled sound, Quinn glanced toward the stall. The big gelding stepped toward the feed tub as though asking for breakfast, so Quinn climbed off the cot and flicked the latch so pellets would tumble into the tub.

"Thanks," said Rachel.

"Sorry to wake you, but he was asking for breakfast."

"He looks more relaxed today."

"He does." Yet why did Quinn feel like something was off-kilter? "What's wrong?"

She shrugged and rubbed a hand over Merlin, who then graced her with an outstretched paw spread wide and a huge yawn.

Quinn considered his options, but decided not to mess with the cat. Instead, he picked up his wife and cradled her on his lap on the other chair. Merlin curled back into a tight ball as though ready to settle in for a day of sleep.

"Now, what's up?"

She laid her head on his shoulder and sighed. "I don't know for sure. I guess I'd expected something profound to happen with this horse. As though I was the key to his recovery. I took him out of what I thought was a toxic situation and provided him with care and comfort and still, he refuses to connect with me."

"Interventions don't always work." He'd taken his father off the streets, put him in a safe place where he'd be cared for and rehabilitated, and it hadn't worked.

"I suppose whatever happened to him can't be undone overnight or with a new setting."

"Truer words."

She put a hand on his chin and made him look at her. "Your mom says your dad's getting better, Quinn. You started the process. Then he went a different path than you'd intended."

He rested his forehead on hers. "You're spooky intuitive sometimes."

"It's because I love you so much. I hear your heart and feel your pain."

"You're going to have people like this horse at Haven, you know. People like my father who don't want help."

"I know. You've been warning me all along and I expect trouble. I just hadn't expected it from a rescued animal."

"You're looking for gratitude. Instead, you'll have to earn his trust the same way you will with the human rescues. It's all part of the process." He checked the time. "Speaking of which, I've got a couple of early meetings so I need to get a move on. Is there anything else I can get you?" He'd stocked the tack room fridge the night before and had brought her a change of clothes.

"Nope. I'll just hang here until the van arrives with Donald."

"You're going to leave after the donkey—"

"Gets here? Not right away. I'll stay for an hour or two, then check back in as the day goes by. But I'm not looking for magic now, just a settled pair."

"Don't give up on magic, baby." He pressed a soft kiss beside her ear. "Never give up on magic."

Her change of tone was subtle. "I'm destined for lots of heartache in this place." She sighed. "We'll have failures along the way. That much I know. But I'm counting on the successes to carry me through the hard times."

"We'll carry each other through the rough stuff." And they'd debrief properly, talk through what had worked and what hadn't, make plans for changes. He'd look after her and allow her to look after him. He would. Or at least he'd try.

"Have I told you lately how much I love you?"

"I'm always happy to hear it again." He groaned as she shifted on his lap and put pressure in the right spot. But he could hear sounds of action outside and was certain someone would be walking in on them any minute now.

Rachel grinned at him and as though reading his mind and said, "The tack room door has a lock on it." She slid off his lap and held out her hand.

***

Rachel and Merlin watched Donald meet his new roommate. The donkey pressed his nose through the mesh and twitched his upper lip in invitation, but the thoroughbred—currently test-driving the name Frank—maintained his dignity by not moving closer.

Thankfully, Frank's ears never went back, a good sign, and he didn't appear to be the least bit aggressive while they snorted and blew at each other.

Donald lost interest in the horse and came to the door of his stall to visit with Rachel who rubbed at the base of his long fuzzy ears. "You're a cutie, aren't you?"

He's butt-ugly.

She swung her gaze up to the cat perched on the wall between the stalls. "What did you say?"

Merlin said nothing, but made his way down to her and settled on the door ledge. Donald poked his nose toward the cat.

Merlin placed a gentle paw on the donkey's nose. *Careful, fluffy.*

Rachel snickered and Merlin gave her a dirty look.

"I think it's time for me to get out of here and let all of you get to know each other. Assuming you're staying, Merlin?"

By way of answer he hopped back up onto the wall between the stalls and settled in as though not planning to go anywhere, so she used her cell phone to update the security guard.

"I'm leaving the quarantine barn now, so I'd like you to bring up that camera and maintain a watch. The horse, donkey, and white cat will be there. Give me a shout if anything unusual happens."

"Will do. Have you programmed the feeder?"

"Yep. Pellets will drop every hour, and they've both got access to their paddocks for grazing."

"Sounds good."

***

Quinn jingled the keys in his hand as he waited for Angie to uncover the helicopter. If she didn't speed things up, he wouldn't have time to confront her about what was going on.

Julia had told him to leave it alone, but he couldn't. Couldn't stand by and watch his sister repeat a mistake. Not that Dhillon was, but getting pregnant had been.

Once the cover was back, he jumped onboard and donned the communication helmet while she went through her prefight checks and eventually prepared for takeoff. He glanced at his watch again.

"Relax. I'll have you in town by eight, as requested." She maneuvered the craft off the ground, and as they slid forward over the fields and picked up speed, she added, "So relax, would you?"

"I am relaxed."

"You're wound up like a ten-day watch."

He circled his shoulders and tipped his head from side-to-side to release some of the tension. "We need to talk."

"You say that, but it sounds like a Quinn lecture coming on."

"I'm worried about you."

"Don't be." Her voice had chilled.

"You're sneaking around like before."

"Back off."

"You ended up pregnant with a fatherless child. I don't want to see you hurt like that again."

"Back the fuck off."

"Angie—"

"No. You don't get to do this. You don't get to stick your nose into my life this way. I know what I'm doing."

"If you're seeing someone, why don't you bring him around for the family to meet?"

"So they can vet him? I don't think so."

"We're family, Angie. We care about you more than any stranger can. We only want you to be happy. And safe."

"I know what I'm doing. And I'll share as soon as I can. In the meantime, I mean it. Back off." She blew out a breath. "Don't you have enough to do worrying about Rachel?"

He opened his mouth and closed it again. No point in telling her he wasn't worried.

"How's she doing, anyway?"

Telling her to back off and mind her own business wasn't a good idea at this point. "She's doing okay."

"What about you? Getting more comfortable leaving her behind when you have to go to town yet? Or is that part of why you were so wound up this morning?"

"I'm not worried about her bolting anymore, if that's what you mean."

"Why not?"

"Because I trust her."

"You trusted her before, too. Look where that got you."

"It's different now. Before, we were all about sex and both of us being what the other wanted. But we hadn't shared who we really were."

"Intimacy is hard, but oh so worth it."

He squinted at her. There was something underlying there that he'd missed before. Something settled. "This guy in your life. He's for real, isn't he?"

"No changing the subject. We're talking about *your* relationship. What made you look deeper this time around?"

He thought about glossing over the question, but something in her tone reminded him of sitting in his office doing an interview or consultation. His mouth moved from a smile to a grimace and back again. She was good. And he needed to talk about what he was going through. He shook his head. Angie flipped things around on him. Always had. From the time they were kids, she'd known how to get to him and he'd never figured out why he opened up to her.

"I begged her to tell me why the voices were so frightening. What was behind the fear? And she agreed to confide in me as long as I, too, would share a piece of me. Something about me she didn't know. Next thing I knew, I was telling her about Dad. About how I'd failed him."

"You didn't fail him."

"I drove him away by trying to get him to conform, to take treatment."

"You're an idiot. Good thing my hands are busy here or I'd hit you. Dad needed to do it on his own. He was already depending on his sons to keep his ranch, his security business, and his family safe and cared for. No way could he depend on you to look after his mind, too." She sounded like she wanted to stomp her foot. "Look at me."

Her green eyes were sharp and deadly. "You need to get over yourself. You can't save everyone. Just the ones who want your help. And you can't take it personally if some don't. Didn't they teach you this shit in shrink school?"

He couldn't stop the smile. "Shrink school?"

"Have you ever heard the line, 'Doctor heal thyself'?"

"Yeah, they taught us self-help, but at the same time, there's a stigma even among shrinks, as you so nicely call us."

"Well, do it. Get yourself some help if you can't get over your God complex."

"Ouch. That's strong."

"Not really. You're a mere mortal, Quinn. Stop trying to be perfect. Hey, have you read that book yet?"

"What book?"

"The one about imperfection."

He shook his head.

She grinned. "Bro, you've got some learning to do. I'm going to send you some links for her talks and her books."

"I don't have time for that stuff."

"Oh, trust me. You need to make time." Her grin spread ear to ear. "I'll make you a deal. You listen and read, and I'll let you in on one of the secrets I've been keeping."

"You play dirty."

"Should make you proud."

"It does. Now, you can get this buggy up to speed? Enough dallying so you can pick my brain."

"Tables turned. You'd planned on getting me to talk so you could fix me, keep me from making a big mistake, and instead—"

"Don't rub it in, pipsqueak."

Three clients later, Quinn's soul finally settled—he was indeed born to help people. Leaning back in his chair, he propped his feet on the desk and dug into a sub sandwich while listening to an amazing woman, a fellow Texan, reveal the kind of vulnerability that made him want to squirm in his chair. But he rode it out. And in the end, sent Angie a text.

LISTENED AS PROMISED. BOOKS ARE DOWNLOADED.

Her reply was quick. IMPRESSIONS?

LATER.

***

The warm glow of success washed over Rachel. Frank and Donald were halfway down the paddock, grazing with only the fence between them. Merlin strolled along the rail she was leaning on and bumped her forehead with his.

"They look like pals already," she said, and though she was looking at the cat and saw no mouth movement, she'd swear she heard his voice in her head.

The Odd Couple.

She nodded. "That's it. I'll call them Oscar and Felix."

Beats the hell out of Frank and Donald.

She scowled at the cat. "A name change will help them leave behind the bad memories of their past."

Hadn't she done that when she'd run away? Taking on a new identity had been critical to remaining hidden, it had allowed her to *be* someone else. To leave the past behind and move on to a different life.

It had also helped her avoid the self-recriminations, the guilt of running away. But maybe it was time she faced the reality of what and who she was.

The two equines happily stuffing their faces with lush grass made her smile. They lived in the moment, but it was colored by their pasts. Any experience they had was seen as fresh unless tainted by a memory.

What they needed were new memories to take the place of the painful ones. Wasn't that what she needed, too?

She checked the door latches to make sure all was secure and headed for home.

CHAPTER 36

Three weeks later

"No," said Rachel.

Her mother-in-law's mouth opened. Closed.

First time she'd ever seen the woman speechless. "I won't lie to him, Julia."

"Well, hell. I didn't see that coming." She tapped her fingertips on the edge of the foil- wrapped casserole dish. "It's such a good plan, and it's a surprise, not a lie—"

"Keeping the truth from him is what I did before." The paper heart was still attached to the front of their fridge. *Love, trust, and respect bind us together… forever.* "He's just learning to trust me again and I won't jeopardize that. Even for a good cause." She held up her hand. "Months ago, you told me I needed to do the work to save my marriage. This is me doing the work. You'll have to find another way."

"I must say, you're frustrating. Yet I have to respect your position. Can I at least put this in the fridge?"

"Of course, and thanks. I'll call Consuela later to thank her." They'd have it tomorrow. Tonight, she had other plans.

"With Haven consuming all my time, her offerings have been a godsend."

Julia suddenly smiled. "You're on your way back over?"

"I am." She'd only nipped home for the change of clothes she'd forgotten this morning. She'd been distracted. "It was too blessed hot for jeans and boots once morning chores were done."

"How are the horses settling in?"

"Quite well. We removed a bottom section of the fence so Oscar—the donkey—could slip underneath and go into Felix's paddock whenever he wanted, and they've become inseparable. It's cute to see him using the horse for shade."

"What about the two skinny horses?"

Rachel thumbed her phone to find a photo. And held it out to share. "They should look better than this by now."

"But there's definite improvement."

"They're not beefing up the way I'd expected."

"You've had Doc check them over, I'm sure."

"Actually"—she glanced at the clock—"he's coming by again today and I'll probably ask him to pull blood so we can see if there's something we're missing."

Julia straightened. "Then I'd best get out of your way and let you get back."

She hadn't meant to push Julia out the door. "No rush. I have a few hours to kill so I figured I'd paint the trim on bungalow number three." She grinned. "Orange for this one."

"I like the turquoise on number two. Reminds me of the ocean." Julia was lost in thought for a moment. "Could you ask Quinn to call me?"

"Of course."

Without another word, she slipped out the back door.

Rachel sighed. Standing up to Julia was uncomfortable, but she'd done it. Stuck to her convictions. In the end, the woman would find a way to surprise Quinn. Angie or someone else would play along, and everybody'd be happy.

In the meantime, today was their anniversary. And she had plans for her husband. Plans that didn't include his mother, Rachel thought with a grin.

Plus a surprise of her own.

***

Damn it. Rachel's truck wasn't in the driveway. Quinn hated how empty the house felt without her. Did it remind him of when she'd been gone, or was it because he'd grown to depend on her presence?

He dug out his phone and texted a note to himself, a reminder for when he talked to his therapist, a colleague he bounced stuff off of. He was glad Angie had pushed him into finding someone to help him get a handle on what she'd called his God complex—his need to fix everything.

Since he had the phone in his hand, he pushed speed dial and waited for the sound of Rachel's voice.

"Hey."

"Hey, yourself. I'm home."

"I wish I was. The vet's running late, so I'll be a while."

"No worries. I'll throw something on for supper. How long will you be?"

"Guessing about an hour." She hesitated. She'd cook tomorrow instead. "Consuela sent over a chicken pot pie. Why don't you toss it in the oven for an hour?"

"Sure."

"And your mother wants you to call. Oh, gotta run, Doc's just coming through the gate. See ya shortly."

He hoped she hurried. He touched the box and the bag on the seat beside him. He had plans.

But first, Julia.

She answered on the first ring.

"Quinn?"

"Hello, Mother. Rachel said you wanted me to call."

"Oh, I had a question for you, but Gage was by earlier and he had the answer, so I don't need to talk to you now."

"Okay." There was something odd in her tone. "Everything all right?"

"Better than. How's Rachel?"

"Fine. Still hung up at Haven, though."

"Oh well, I'm sure she'll be home shortly. Well, bye, then. I'll see you sometime soon, I'm sure." She had a weird sort of laugh in her voice. Almost as if she'd been drinking.

He held the phone out and frowned at it for a second. "Uh, yeah. We have a Meyers meeting at ten tomorrow morning." It wasn't like her to forget details.

"Right. Bye now."

"Bye." Well, *that* was a first, his mother sounding like a ditz.

After shoving dinner into the oven and setting the timer, he took a quick shower, put on jeans and a T-shirt, and was opening his laptop on the kitchen table when a flicker of movement had him spinning toward the window.

His stomach bottomed out.

Both man and dog stared back at him as he slowly rose to his feet. His father looked good. Healthy, like before. Tanned and fit in his signature black T-shirt and pants. One hand rested on the dog leaning against his legs.

As though he'd forgotten to breathe for a minute or two, Quinn suddenly sucked in a huge breath. Swallowed. And without taking his eyes off the pair in the yard, made his way to the sliding glass door. Opened it all the way.

"Would you like to come in?" he asked, amazed his voice actually found its way through the thickness in his throat.

"Why don't you come out?"

Quinn maintained eye contact as he closed the distance between them.

Eyes so like his own stared back. "This is my friend, Swagger."

Noting the Service Dog vest, Quinn said, "Would you like me to greet him, or not?"

James smiled. "You're my son. Swagger needs to know you." He unsnapped the lead and gave a hand signal.

Quinn crouched to meet what suddenly became a black bundle of energy. "You seemed so dignified a minute ago," he said, ruffling the long hair.

"He's like me. A chameleon."

His father's call name had been Chameleon because of his ability to blend no matter what the situation. The dog returned to his side.

"He lets go and has fun, but remains tuned in to what's going on with me. Spooky sometimes, but good. Really good for me." He waved a hand toward the back gate. "Creek down the way still have fish?"

"Don't know."

"We could check it out."

They walked in silence for a while, Quinn dying to ask him questions, yet terrified it would push him away.

"You must be wondering why I'm here."

"I'm just glad you came."

"I fucked up pretty bad the last time I saw you." He shrugged. "Can't change that. But I can be sorry it happened. Sorry I didn't appreciate what you were trying to do for me."

"I only wanted to help."

"I know. And as different as we are, we have that in common. It's what drove me. Why I specialized in extractions. I could get in, get the target out. Make what was wrong, right again." He shoved his hands into the pockets of his cargos. "I didn't get that when you wanted to go to school. I didn't understand that the book learning was taking you somewhere I'd want to go. Taking you to the place where you could help. I get it now."

Quinn had no words. He'd become who he needed to be without his father's validation. And now that he had it, nothing changed.

"I met your wife recently."

Shock rattled through him. "She never said."

"She didn't know. We weren't introduced, more like I was in a room where she was."

Quinn's nerves jittered as things slid back into place. If she'd known, she would have told him. He knew that. But that split-second feeling of betrayal had his gut churning, and had him sliding his hand into his pocket to touch the gift they'd share later.

"She's a pretty impressive woman. Reminds me of your mother."

Quinn laughed. "Seriously?"

"The kind of backbone and determination you don't see in a lot of people, let alone in a woman." He held up a hand. "No point gettin' on your horse about prejudice and all that crap because I'm telling it how I see it. Shouldn't have to be politically correct with my own family." He stopped when the trail they were following opened to the bank of a small creek. He stared into the water.

"I listened to your wife talk about her vision for Haven. Selling her idea to another woman with a backbone, founder of the Service Dog program I work with. If I hadn't already signed over the deed to the Spencer place, I'd have done it then. I like your Rachel, son."

"I'm partial to her myself." He turned his wrist so he could see his watch. "She's due home in about twenty minutes. Will you stay and meet her?"

He smiled. "I will. As I have a proposition for the two of you."

Swagger seemed more relaxed as they wandered back toward the house, trotting ahead, checking over his shoulder now and again as though making sure his partner was still following, still okay.

"How long have you had your dog?"

"About a year now. He's helped me more than I thought possible. Senses when I need his support. Wakes me up when I'm having nightmares, intervenes when I have a flashback. Knowing I won't find myself belly-down under a parked car gives me a new freedom."

"How frequently are you bothered by symptoms?"

The ear-splitting smile went clear to his eyes.

"What?"

"My son, the therapist."

Quinn sighed. "Sorry. It happens. But hey, I see a therapist, too."

"What the hell for?"

He grinned. "As Angie put it, my God complex needed to be taken down a notch."

"Girl never pulls her punches."

"I—" He'd almost said he was worried about her. But the last thing he needed to do right now was heap worries on his father. "Yeah. She's a good mom though. Dhillon's a great kid."

"I know."

Quinn couldn't help the twinge of jealousy.

James sighed. "Yes. Everyone but you. The chasm was too wide to bridge easily. Can you understand that opening myself to you was the final step? Today is like—" He rubbed a hand over his face. "It's like jumping out of a plane for the first time, and trusting my chute's properly packed. The others were like practicing how to tuck and roll."

"Jesus." He wanted to stop. Face his father. Look him in the eye, but the man had picked up speed, striding out as though being chased. Swagger was glued to his side.

They marched in silence all the way to the gate. When Quinn reached over for the latch, he wasn't surprised to see sweat beaded on his father's face. "Take a deep breath. You're doing fine."

"Ha. There you are fucking fixing me again." He held up his hand. Took a long breath in, exhaled. "Thanks."

Quinn swung the gate open. James stared at the house for a moment, then set his jaw, and headed toward the patio. "Can we sit?"

"Sure." Quinn hung back.

James grabbed a chair and set it against the wall. Settled in. Swagger sat, resting his chin on his master's knee.

Quinn dragged a chair over so he was slightly to his father's left as opposed to directly in front of him, and Swagger could place himself between them without more than a step or two.

"Want something to drink?"

James smiled. "Not the kind of thing you'd normally ask me. It's okay, I've been dry for a long time, and no, I don't count the days. Not part of my life anymore."

"Happy for you."

"Wouldn't mind water or a soda, though. Parched all of a sudden."

"Me, too."

He was into the kitchen and back out in less than thirty seconds with a couple of cans of soda. Passed one over and popped the top on his own. Frigid bubbles burned a path down his dry throat.

"It was easier with the others because I hadn't fucked up as badly with them. I owe you an apology." He stroked Swagger's head. "You did everything you could to help me, and I tossed it all aside. I was angry at the thought of my *boy*, the son who dared to not follow in my footsteps, thinking he knew what was best for me." He sighed. "Not proud of that. But I own it. Took me a long time to admit to myself I'd behaved like an ass, but I had. There was so much I could have done differently, but... I couldn't have done any of it differently. I had to go through it the way I did. But I'm sorry."

Quinn leaned forward with his elbows on his knees and his hands clasped together. He wanted to speak, but words would never get past the lump in his throat. He swallowed hard.

"I'm sorry I disrespected you. Sorry I couldn't be the man you wanted me to be. I hope you can forgive me."

"You are the man I want you to be, you're my father." He cleared his throat and his voice grew stronger. "I forgave you some time ago. I only hope you can forgive me for trying to force you in a direction you weren't ready to go." He held out his hand, and James took it, held it for a beat too long, then both men were suddenly on their feet, holding on to one another.

CHAPTER 37

Rachel fastened both top and bottom latches on the stall door. "So you're saying I'm fussing unnecessarily."

"No. I'm saying you're doing a good job. They're putting on weight in a slow steady manner. Any faster would be too hard on their systems." Doc slipped the vials of blood into the insulated drawer in the back of his truck. "We'll run these to be sure there's nothing else going on, but I don't expect to see any abnormal results. Likewise, I don't expect the other samples to show any evidence of parasites."

"All right then. Thanks a heap for coming out. I know you must be busy."

"It's been quiet lately, but Meyers surprised me today. Wanted ultrasounds on all the in-foal mares." He shook his head. "Mustn't have been paying attention when Julia called last week. Thought she'd said one mare, not all of them."

And that, thought Rachel, confirmed her suspicions.

"No worries, Doc. Quinn will have supper ready by the time I get home."

He opened a cooler drawer and dug out a plastic container. "I'll have mine on the drive home." He hopped into his truck and with a wave was off.

She drove out behind him, and slowed to make sure the security gate closed behind her before booting it down the road.

Julia had set it up. Kept the vet busy so he'd be late getting to Haven. She pulled up to the family gate, input the code, and was less than a mile from home when the silent Special Ops helicopter settled across the roadway in front of her and shut down.

"Oh for-crying-out-freakin-loud." She slammed into park, jumped out, and stormed toward the Steed. "Move this tin can out of my freaking way!" she yelled when her sister-in-law opened the door.

"Julia—"

"I've had my fill of your manipulating mother today," she growled.

"She sent me to confess. Apologize."

"I don't want her apology, I just want to go home." *And I want to scream, rant, and rip my freaking hair out, but I'm not going to do that.*

Angie rolled her eyes. "Not hers, mine."

"What?"

"The apology is mine, not hers. I need you to listen, okay?"

"Fine. Listening." She crossed her arms.

"Dhillon's heart stopped for a reason that had nothing to do with you. I shouldn't have blamed you and I should have told you this over a month ago, but when I found out, I felt stupid." She shrugged. "Still do. He inherited something rare from his father."

Rachel didn't know what to think. Didn't want to think right now. "Fine. Thanks for telling me. Now *please* get that bird out of my way. I need to go home. I don't care that Julia wants to slow me down. I have to get to Quinn."

"But—"

"Angie, he's your favorite brother and he *needs me right now.* I need him." She pointed at the aircraft. "Go."

Angie wheeled around, climbed into the helo, and in the time it took Rachel to jump back into her truck, the Steed was fired up. Lifted off.

Anybody else got between her and Quinn, she'd run them over. Well, maybe not, but still.

Luckily, the rest of the drive was uneventful. She ground to a halt beside Julia's SUV, shut off the truck, and just sat still, trying to get a grip. If Julia was there with James, she didn't want her temper to get the better of her.

Ludicrous. She'd been in such a hurry. And now she was stalling. Took a deep cleansing breath.

She climbed out and headed around the back, pasted a smile on her face, then stopped dead in her tracks and backed away until she was around the corner, against the wall. She leaned her head on the siding, pressed her fist over her grin, and tears tracked down her cheeks.

The image of the two men was imprinted on her mind. Not a simple one-armed man-hug. Nope. A father and son who loved each other, who *forgave* each other. It was everything she'd wished for. Her throat burned.

"Rachel?"

She stepped into his arms and clung. Couldn't help herself. The day had been such a rollercoaster ride and now she was back where she belonged and everything was okay.

"What's wrong, baby?"

She stepped back, grinning at him while she mopped away the happy tears. "Nothing. Absolutely nothing," she said with a laugh.

He kissed her hard, then took her hand and dragged her around the corner to meet his dad and the dog who'd apparently alerted them to her presence.

"You look so familiar," she said once they were all seated. "Must be the family resemblance."

James smiled. "We crossed paths a while back, but it was only for a moment. At the Service Dog Center when you were selling your idea to run an assistance program out of Haven. I passed you on my way to get Swagger from the playroom."

"I remember the SDC director explaining about the dogs needing a place for downtime away from their humans and responsibilities."

He nodded. "I confess to eavesdropping that day. I was impressed by your big heart and your gumption. My son obviously has good taste."

The light bulb came on. "Julia sent me there because of you."

He shrugged. "That and it's a good operation. Solid people running it."

"She tried to get me to lie to Quinn. She had a plan to get you two together tomorrow morning, and even though I wanted the meeting to happen, I wouldn't do it." She met her husband's steady gaze. "I won't lie to you, even if it's for a noble cause."

James laughed. "About time somebody in this family gave my wife a run for her money."

"I knew she'd find another way, which obviously she did." She shook off the dregs of annoyance threatening to resurface. "Did she manipulate you into giving us the Spencer place?"

His laughter grew. "You are a perfect fit for this family. No, it was my idea after she told me she was thinking about giving you two a corner of the ranch to build your horse rescue. I thought about all that land sitting unused and figured it would be good for my healing process. Animals I could be around and help without any expectations."

After she'd planted the seed, thought Rachel.

"I suppose now's when I should be asking if I can be a part of your Haven. To help with the animals, not the people. I don't do people too well yet."

"We'd be happy to have you with us. And thank you again for the property. It's allowed us to expand from my vision to Quinn's…" *Shit*.

"Relax. I'm comfortable with discussion of PTSD treatments. It's a part of my life. And not a hidden part."

"Well, good. Because it's what our lives revolve around and we want you to be in our lives again," said Quinn.

"You're not stepping away from Meyers Security?"

"Of course not."

James nodded. "Good work on the racehorse case, by the way. But too bad about the information blackout. No credit where it's due."

"I'm glad they took it all under. The last thing the public needs is to have more crazy ideas planted in their heads. We stopped the murders and the abuse. What the government does with the knowledge they've become privy to is their business. I just hope it's used well," said Rachel. "And to move on, supper's ready. Will you stay and eat with us?"

"Sure."

"Indoors or out?"

"Either works for us," answered James with a rub on his dog's head.

"Let's go in then," she said. It would feel less like he was poised to leave if they were indoors. "I'm sure you're aware we have one of Consuela's chicken pot pie's in the oven."

He smiled. "I was also informed you'd have dinner for Swagger since you use the same brand of dog food as we do at the SDC. Julia's nothing if not thorough." The smile became a grin. "She means well. You always have to keep that in the back of your mind. That way Quinn will never have to post your bail."

"Good point," Quinn had a puzzled look on his face and he deserved an explanation. "Your mother managed to waylay the vet and hold me up at Haven so your dad would have an opportunity to meet with you before I got home. And she sent Angie to land the Steed in my path to slow me down."

"Tell me you didn't drive into the Steed."

"I was very civilized. I allowed Angie to apologize to me. Then I sent her on her way."

"Apologize? Angie?" Quinn's eyebrows went up comically.

"For laying the blame on me the day Dhillon collapsed. Apparently, his heart problem is congenital. Information she's since obtained from his father."

Quinn and James both stilled. Her gaze tracked back and forth between the two of them. "That's all she said."

"You didn't ask how she got the information."

"No. And frankly, it didn't much matter to me what she was saying. I was more concerned with getting past another Julia obstacle and getting home. I was concerned, okay?"

***

Hours after his father left, after they'd made plans together, Rachel dished up ice cream and chocolate sauce for a late dessert. "You want whipped cream on top?"

"No."

"Oh, I thought as you'd brought it home, you must—"

"It's our anniversary. I had other plans for the whipped cream."

"Oh. Well then." She lifted the spoon from the jar of sauce and chocolate slid off in a thin line. "Maybe you'd like some sauce, too," she teased.

He took the two dishes, set them in the freezer, closed the door and grabbed her hand. "I've waited long enough. Come with me."

He tugged her all the way out to the pretty bench in the back corner of the yard where fairy lights twinkled among the tree branches the way she'd imagined when they'd installed the bench so long ago. "When did you—"

"This morning after you left for Haven. I was going to take you out to dinner tonight, and bring you back here for your present."

"It's a lovely present, Quinn. Thank you," she said as her lips found his, sunk in for just a few beats before pulling away. "I have a present for you, too."

"The lights weren't the gift."

"They're still lovely, and you put them up for us, so thank you."

"I didn't do wrapping."

"Me either. Mine's only words. I didn't buy you anything."

They sat side by side for a moment, touching from shoulder to knee. Hands held together. Rachel lifted her chin, her eyes sought his. "When I married you, it wasn't with an open heart. I held parts of myself back, and I said I would never have children. I never told you why. But now you know. It was my fear of a child being forced to live through what I did.

"But my heart is open now. And I don't have what my mother did. I want to do everything I can to put us in a place where we can have children, Quinn. That includes working with ETCETERA, as long as you're willing to stay beside me throughout. I will learn to deal with my healing powers, and learn more about the voices. I think Grace is probably right, and they're from a different plane of existence. Even if they are the same as my mom's, I'll do whatever I need to do to live a good life and be a good mother. I want us to have kids, Quinn. Lots of them."

He pulled her against him and held her there while she listened to his pounding heart. This was where she belonged, no matter what. He lowered his mouth and kissed her until her soul moved. A lump formed in her throat and she wanted to crawl inside of him.

When his ragged breathing smoothed out, he stared into her eyes. "You slay me." He shook his head and shifted her over. "You're a tough act to follow," he said. "But let me give it a try."

He took something from his pocket, but kept his hand fisted around it. "I wanted us to have a new start this year. So I had these made, because one of the old ones is at the bottom of a river, and the other was put in the safe when we went on the mission a few months ago." He opened his hand, and there, on his palm lay two wedding bands. They were different than their other plain ones. These were wide, with silver and gold woven together in an intricate pattern.

"They're beautiful."

"Platinum and gold, with a new inscription."

He brought a pen light out of his pocket and shone in on the inside for her. There was only one word. "Believe."

"I do." He slid the ring onto her finger and held the other out to her.

"I do." She said, and slid his into place.

She took his left hand, placed hers against it, and they laced their fingers together. "I have no words for how much you move me. 'I love you,' just doesn't seem to be enough, but it's all I have."

"It's all I need. I will love you forever."

"And maybe longer," she finished with a smile.

DEDICATION

This book is dedicated to the horses who changed my life, taught me patience and understanding, showed me what trust and loyalty looked like, challenged me to be the best I could be, and showed me who I was.

From the hundreds, I will name a few of the most special. Twiggy, my first horse and best friend. Mr. Prime Minister, the most troubled horse I ever rubbed, he taught me to look closer. Evergreen State, what a joy he was to train, what a thrill to watch him on the track. Inish Glora, special, from the first moment I put tack on you—luckily, we "got" each other. Killer you were so incredibly loyal. I was your person and you always made me laugh. And Rocky, never uncertain of your place in the universe.

ACKNOWLEDGEMENTS

I've been told it takes a village to raise a child. And as my books are like children, I have a village to thank, so here goes.

Many thanks to: author L. j. Charles for your wonderful critiquing skills and advice; Barb for the sharp-eyed reading and spot-on suggestions; The Formatting Fairies for fabulous formatting and uploading; Judi Fennell of www.formatting4U. com for the awesome editing; The Killion Group Inc. for the incredible cover, blurb, and PR; Cherry Adair for her no-nonsense encouragement (virtual butt kicking); Sandy James for encouraging me to keep rockin' the words; My RWA Kiss of Death Chapter sisters for the endless support; Prince Charming for loving and looking after us all while this story made its way onto the page; Wolfe and Bear for the purring and good company while we were locked in the writing cave with the tunes cranked up; my family, for their love and support throughout this convoluted adventure. You are the constants in my journey. You've egged me on and believed in me always. I love you.

ABOUT THE AUTHOR

Award winning author Kathryn Jane writes about the kind of women she'd like to hang out with—smart, self-reliant, think on their feet ladies who are just as happy eating a loaded hot dog at a ballgame as they are sipping champagne in the back of a limo.

Her heroines laugh as hard as they cry, appreciate good sweaty sex, and know how to keep a secret.

Her heroes are hot, tough, and inherently kind. But often baffled by the women they dare to love.

Kathryn is living her own happily-ever-after in a cottage on the west coast of Canada. Among her favorite things are the smell of the ocean, crisp sunny days, the warm breath of a horse, cats with a sense of humor, dogs that love to please, music, and kind people. She collects beach glass and rocks, has a single string of tiny Christmas lights that she turns on all year round. Besides reading and writing, her favorite pastime is hanging out at the beach with the people she loves.

For more information about Kathryn and her other books, check out her website or join her on Facebook and Twitter.

http://kathrynjane.com/
www.facebook.com/kathryn.jane.921
https://www.facebook.com/authorKathrynJane
https://twitter.com/@Author_Kat_Jane

DEAR READER,

I sincerely hope you enjoyed Quinn and Rachel's story as much as I did!

Now, however, I have both Angie and Trent nagging to have their stories told, so I'm not certain which book will be out next. Probably Angie's because we know she's up to something, but no guarantees because her man is still refusing to show his face.

Have you ever wondered about the writing process? What it's like to spend hours and hours living in a fantasy world with make-believe friends?

It's a dream come true.

The only drawback is the lack of contact with my readers. I love hearing from you, so here's my email address authorkatt@ gmail.com just in case you'd like to say hello, or have a question.

The other awesome thing you could do is log back on to Amazon and leave a review for Voices. But relax, because honestly? A review isn't a book report like we had to do in school. A simple, "great story" or "good read" or "interesting characters" would be fabulous.

Why? A couple of reasons. One, it helps other people find my book. And two? Even a one line review makes me happy-dance around the writing cave, and my writing partners, Wolfe and Bear, appreciate the entertainment.

And if by chance you didn't enjoy Voices, your comments are welcome as well, and kudos for reading to the end anyways, I hope your next reading experience is happier.

Cheers!

Kathryn.

Made in the USA
Charleston, SC
26 December 2014